# CARPATHIA

"Hell comes to the high seas as James Cameron's *Titanic* crashes full-force into the iceberg that is Bram Stoker's *Dracula*. Forbeck sinks his fangs into one helluva horror story, robbing from real history to set up an epic showdown between man and vampire (and between vampire and vampire) on the *RMS Carpathia*."

*Chuck Wendig, author of* Double Dead *and* Blackbirds

"Forbeck effortlessly blends history and horror, the *Titanic* and vampires, along with adventure and romance, in a fast-paced, chilling novel that moves like a bat out of hell."

*Aaron Rosenberg, author of the bestselling* No Small Bills

"What happens when Bram Stoker hits James Cameron with an iceberg? *Carpathia* tears a bloody hole in the side of the *Titanic* legend. It plunges you into the icy waters of horror and holds you under. Chilling!"

*Ken Hite, author of* Cthulhu 101

"In *Carpathia*, Matt Forbeck has taken a why-didn't-I-think-of-that concept and woven it into horror gold! If you like your vampires scary, your plots compelling, and your prose solid, you've got to pick up this book."

*Jeffrey J Mariotte, author of* Dark Vengeance *and* Cold Black Hearts

King of the Night meets 'King of the World' and it's no contest – *Carpathia* takes vampires back from the sparkly boyfriends and turns them into fascinating, terrifying monsters again. Forbeck spins a thrilling yarn against the backdrop of one of the 20th Century's greatest disasters and makes the iceberg that sunk the *Titanic* the least scary night."

y Rain

D1465023

# MATT FORBECK

# CARPATHIA

ANGRY
ROBOT

**ANGRY ROBOT**
A member of the Osprey Group

Lace Market House,
54-56 High Pavement,
Nottingham,
NG1 1HW, UK

www.angryrobotbooks.com
Icy dead people

An Angry Robot paperback original 2012
1

A catalogue record for this book is available
from the British Library.

ISBN: 978-0-85766-201-9
EBook ISBN: 978-0-85766-203-3

Cover design by Nick Castle.
Original 1912 painting by Willy Stower courtesy Corbis Images.

Set in Meridien by THL Design.

Printed an bound by CPI Group (UK) Ltd, Croydon, CR0 4YY.

*Dedicated to my wife, Ann, and our children:*
*Marty, Pat, Nick, Ken, and Helen.*
*They make all the voyages in my life*
*so much better.*

# CHAPTER ONE

"What in hell was that?" Quin Harker said as the ship rumbled beneath him. The words had escaped his lips without him meaning to release them. He blamed the whisky and cigars with which his friend Abe Holmwood had been plying him.

Abe grinned at him with a wide, easy smile. Tall, blond, and broad of shoulders and chin, the young man never seemed at a loss for words. The world suited him in a way that Quin could never hope for, as if he'd been born into it with his purpose etched on the palm of his hand, along with the silver spoon in his mouth.

"It's nothing, I'm sure." Abe clapped Quin on the back, and Quin choked on the whisky that had been swirling around his tongue. "We're in the middle of the ocean, dear boy. What could it be?"

"Lots of things, I suppose," Quin said with a shrug. "German torpedoes? Atlantis rising?"

Abe spread his arms wide, carelessly spilling some of the drink in his hand and taking in the entirety of the first class smoking room, which stood empty but for a single steward and a few other stalwart passengers. Like Quin and Abe, the other men lounged in their now-rumpled dinner wear as the hour slid toward midnight. The mahogany paneled walls still smelled of fresh varnish, and the brass on the fixtures gleamed in the soft glow of the electric lights.

"The problem with you, my friend, is that you don't know how to enjoy what you have." Abe brought his drink back to his lips and squinted at Quin. "You're not still feeling guilty about leaving Lucy behind, are you? What else could we do? They closed down the lounge, and despite our little suffragette's protests, women aren't allowed in here."

Quin squirmed in the chair's plush green upholstery. "Perhaps we should have followed her to bed."

Abe winked at Quin. "Hey, there. That's my girl you're talking about, you know."

Quin looked out of the window behind Abe and blushed. "I know that all too–"

His jaw dropped as he spotted a white wall emerging from the darkness. It loomed so large that he couldn't think of what it might be. For an instant, he wondered if the moon had somehow landed in the middle of the North Atlantic and meant to crush the ship beneath its silvery bulk.

Abe cocked his head at the way Quin's mouth hung open, then turned around in his seat, which, like most of the furniture on the ship, sat bolted to the floor. "Of all the…" he said, as he spied what had torn Quin's attention away from their conversation. "I do believe that's an iceberg."

Quin pushed himself to his feet and wove his way through the smoking room until he reached one of the bay windows that lined the room's starboard side and overlooked the wood-floored promenade that encircled the entire deck. Abe padded along behind him on the pristine carpeting.

"How do you know?" Quin stared up at the massive tower of ice. It stretched up and down and left and right as far as he could see, filling the entire vista. "Have you ever seen one before?"

Closer now, Quin noticed that the ice was moving past them. No, he corrected himself. It was standing still. The ship was moving past it.

"Certainly," Abe craned his neck around, trying to get a better view of the iceberg as it slipped past. The far edge of it appeared to the left and sailed by, leaving nothing but the inky black of the moonless, night-shrouded sea behind. "Unlike yourself, this is hardly my first time across the Big Pond."

"Are they always like this?" Quin watched the white slab recede until it moved too far into the darkness to be seen.

Abe pursed his lips. "Usually they're not quite so close. Do you think we hit it?"

"That would explain that rumbling from before." Quin strove to keep any note of concern from his voice. "How bad would that be?"

Abe clapped Quin on the back. "Another day, on another ship, that might be trouble, but not here and now," he said with a smile. "The ship we're on is unsinkable, after all."

Quin suppressed a shiver by heading for the forward exit. He didn't put much faith in this "unsinkable" label the press had slapped on the *Titanic*. The arrogance of it bothered him.

As he walked, Quin downed the last of his whisky and handed the glass to the steward, resplendent in his stiff white uniform, who held the door open for the two young men. Abe held on to his, raising his glass to the steward as if offering a toast. They emerged next to the aft Grand Staircase, and Quin felt the pull of their stateroom just two decks below. He hesitated there for a moment.

"You're not heading for bed?" Abe gestured toward the wide stairs sweeping downward into the ship. "I'm impressed. Finally learning to put that job of yours behind long enough to enjoy the journey of your lifetime?"

Quin shrugged off Abe's ribbing. It had been a long day filled with food, drink, and far more sunshine than Quin was used to seeing as a solicitor with his father's firm. "I'd like to see what happened." He abandoned the stairs and walked out onto the promenade instead.

The icy winds cut into him the moment he shoved open the door, and if Abe hadn't been right behind him, Quin might have turned back at that point and headed for his warm, safe bed. Instead, he tugged his thin dinner jacket closer around him and stuffed his hands in his pockets, heading for the ship's bow.

"You sure you don't want another little something to ward off the cold?" Abe swirled his whisky in his glass as he caught up with Quin. "I have a little left in my flask still."

Quin shook his head. "I just want to see what happened," he said.

Abe smirked. "That's right," he said. "Find new experiences. Squeeze everything you can out of life. I like this new side of you. A new Quin for the New World."

Quin snorted at the image. "I don't have an idle life ahead of me when I reach New York. Unlike you, I still have to work for a living."

Abe grimaced. "Yes, and that's a damn shame, that is. 'International law.' Sounds like the sort of thing that shouldn't be discussed in polite society."

"Fortunately, there's only you here," Quin said.

"Not so true." Abe pointed up the deck at a group of people standing alongside the forward railing and peering down at the side of the mighty ship. "But I don't think they'll mind."

Quin and Abe joined the rubberneckers and stared down at the ship below. Spotlights illuminated the lower decks all the way out to the gigantic vessel's prow. Quin spotted chunks of ice scattered across the forecastle, and a handful of passengers from steerage had picked them up to launch an impromptu snowball fight with each other.

"What happened?" Abe asked one of the men leaning over the railing, a middle-aged chap dressed in an overcoat flung over his nightclothes.

"You had to have seen the iceberg go past," the man said. "We hit it, best I can tell. Doesn't seem to have done the ship a smidgeon of harm though." He pointed over the railing at the side. "Not a scratch on her."

"Not that we can see," said Quin. "There's a lot of this ship that rides below the waterline."

Abe nudged Quin in the shoulder. "Do you hear sirens going off? Do you feel the ship listing to the side?" He gestured in the direction of the bridge. A pair of officers stood there chatting. "Do those seasoned professionals look panicked?"

Quin sighed. Trained as an attorney, he could argue each and every one of Abe's points, but he knew it wouldn't be worth the bother. Nothing he could say would change his friend's belief that the ship was invulnerable to harm, and to press the issue would only cause Abe to taunt him for being such a worrier.

"Shall we repair to the lounge?" Abe polished off the last of the whisky in his glass and held it up to the light. The cut crystal looked like a chunk of clear ice.

Quin shook his head. "To bed, I think."

Abe smirked. "Got someplace to be? We're trapped on this ship for the next few days at least."

"I hear the captain's lit all the boilers to try to capture the Blue Riband. Word is we might make it to New York by Tuesday night."

Abe scoffed. "I put ten pounds down with old Astor that it won't happen. *Titanic*'s a magnificent ship, but it's hard to imagine something so large moving so fast."

"Either way, that doesn't give us much time on board." Quin bowed his head. The trip across the Pond had been a slice of fantasy so far, a chance to live the wealthy life, but it would only last until they reached land. Then Abe and Lucy would be off on their cross-continental excursion, and he'd be starting his new and far more austere life in Manhattan.

Abe put a hand on Quin's shoulder. "Chin up, my friend. Life's too short. Enjoy the moments you have while you can." As he spoke, he pulled a silver flask out of his jacket's inner pocket. He unscrewed it and handed it to Quin.

Quin hefted the flask in his hand for a moment, then took a stiff belt from it. Abe laughed as his companion handed the flask back to him. "That's the spirit!"

# CHAPTER TWO

"Hell!" Radioman Harold Cottam stared at the message he'd just taken down over the *Carpathia*'s wireless set. He stared at the Marconi-branded form in his hand and double-checked the Morse code to make sure he'd read it right.

*"Come at once. We have struck a berg. It's a CQD OM. Position 41.46 N. 50.14 W."*

"What's that then?" Brody Murtagh said to Harold in his harsh Irish brogue as he peered over the man's shoulder at the distress call.

Brody had been standing there all night, ever since the sun went down, bored enough to practice mumblety-peg with his pocketknife over and over, not much caring if he cut his fingers open or not. He resented being assigned such a dull duty, no matter how important it might be, but he had just tossed that onto the pile of resentment he already bore the man who'd given it to him. He'd decided to grit his teeth and bear it for now, at least until he spied a chance to register his complaint in the violent manner he preferred best. And this was the first bit of excitement that he'd seen the whole trip.

"It's the *Titanic*, sir," Harold said. "It's struck an iceberg and is going down. CQD OM, that means *'Come Quick, Danger Old Man.'* They won't have long."

Brody rubbed his chin as he took the paper from the radioman's hand and considered what he should do. It would be simple enough to crumple up the note and force Harold to forget it had ever been sent. That would be the easy thing to do.

Harold spun about on his worn brown leather chair and tapped out a response to the *Titanic*, speaking the words aloud as he transformed them into code. *"Shall I tell my captain? Do you require assistance?"*

Brody already knew what the response would be. No one mentioned that they'd hit an iceberg simply to start up a conversation. For sure, it was the sort of news that could start a panic.

Harold narrowed his eyes as he listened for the *tap-tap-dash-dash* of the Morse code answer to come back to him. He copied down the letters as they came in and then read the result out loud again. "She says, *'Yes, come quick'*, sir."

Brody grunted at the man. He still hadn't made up his mind about what to do. They weren't on the kind of voyage that should be interrupted. Dushko wouldn't be happy about this at all.

That thought made Brody smile.

He handed the original message back to the radioman. "Go rouse your Captain Rostron," he said. "He'll know what to do."

Harold snatched the note away from Brody as if the man's hands were on fire. Then he bolted from his chair and charged toward the captain's private quarters.

Brody stared down at the empty chair sitting in front of the Marconi wireless set. More than once he'd been tempted to destroy the thing, knowing that it would leave him with nothing to monitor, no duty left to perform. He knew that Dushko would just find something new to hassle him with though. It wouldn't end there.

It never did with that one. Not only was he the eldest of the group but the strongest. If Brody tried to challenge him directly, Dushko would tear off his head. That alone kept him in line.

Brody considered not going to inform Dushko about what had just happened. After all, what did it matter? It wasn't like he'd allow Brody or any of the other passengers who'd come along with them to get involved with the *Titanic*, no matter how much fun it might be.

At the moment, though, Brody needed a bit of fun more than anything. Once Dushko had them back in the Old World, back in his own little backwater homeland, there would be damned little fun to find, not like the kind that offered itself up in New York City, at least.

Brody missed Manhattan already. It had been his home for more years than he cared to count. They'd all blended into each other anyhow.

New York was the most alive city that Brody had ever been in. The place had a pulse, and it always seemed to be beating faster and faster, drumming out a wild dancer's beat that he couldn't help but respond to. His old home in Ireland was a rustic idyll by comparison, a ramshackle hut in the hills, alone and isolated from the rest of the world.

Brody had never been to Serbia before, but from Dushko's manner, he suspected it would be just as warm and inviting as an abandoned outhouse in the mountain snows.

Brody didn't just deserve some final bit of fun. He needed it. Without it, he was sure the wilds of Serbia – or wherever the hell Dushko really planned to drag him and the others – would drive him mad.

If he were to be honest, he had to admit to himself that it would happen sooner or later there anyhow. He'd step out of line, and Dushko would come down on him hard, perhaps in a fatal and final way. Better to go out now, then, and with as much of a bang as he could muster.

Brody chuckled to himself and licked his pale lips as he sauntered off to gather a few of the others, the sort of tortured souls he knew needed a spot of fun as much as he did. He grinned, his white teeth wide in a vicious smile.

# CHAPTER THREE

"Quincey Harker. Tell me, where has your mind wandered off to?"

Lucy Seward's warm laugh brought Quin back to the conversation he'd been half listening to between her and Abe as they whiled away the moments past midnight in the Reading Room. Since women weren't allowed in the Smoke Room and the First Class Lounge had closed for the night, they'd holed up here for one last nightcap before bed.

He gave her a wan smile. "I don't mean to be rude, Luce," he said, "but, perhaps it's time we took this iceberg thing a bit more seriously."

Abe rolled his eyes, and Lucy laughed again, although this time with a hint of nerves in her voice. "I don't think we ever need to take anything particularly seriously," Abe said, gesturing to himself and Lucy. "After all, that's what we have you here for."

"Is that why you ran off with him rather than me this evening?" Lucy asked Abe.

Abe chuckled while Quin blushed. "I couldn't rightly run off with you, now could I?" Abe said with a wicked smile. "There's already enough scandalized whispers around the ship about you traveling with two young scalawags without a proper escort to protect you from us."

Lucy gasped in mock outrage, holding a gloved hand to her pretty mouth. "I can manage to protect myself just fine without a chaperone," she said, "especially from dogs like the two of you. All bark and no bite, doesn't make for much of a threat."

"I prefer to think of us as a pair of seeing-eye dogs," Abe said.

"So I'm blind now, am I?" Lucy arched an eyebrow at the young man.

"Only to the possibilities that lay before us, but don't you worry about that. I'll show you the time of your life during our travels."

Lucy pursed her lips together. "I don't have too long before my studies at Radcliffe begin in the fall," she said.

"We'll just have to make the most of it until then." Abe patted her on her forearm.

"I'm sure you will," Quin said, permitting himself a pang of jealousy. "You'll be whooping it across all forty-eight states while I'm stuck in an oak-lined closet somewhere in Manhattan, I'm sure."

"If you're lucky!" said Abe. "Come on, old man. There's still time to change your mind."

"Yes, Quin," Lucy said, her eyes shining with something like mischief. "Do come with us."

Quin sucked at his teeth. "Would that I was born as independent and wealthy as our friend Abe here. I don't have a future as a lord looming over me or my pocketbook, I'm afraid."

"Oh, this again?" Abe scowled. "It's not my fault I was born to nobility, is it? And that's not stopping Lucy from accompanying me. Why should it stop you?"

"My father's not a wealthy doctor like Lucy's, complete with his own sanitarium. I'm so very fortunate he was able to pay for my education, much less send me off on a trip around the Colonies."

"Growing up surrounded by crazy people wasn't nearly as romantic as it sounds," Lucy suppressed a false shiver.

"It was for me," Abe said, "but then that's life among the lords, isn't it?"

"Look." Quin had left this unsaid for long enough. He turned to Abe. "It's not that I'm ungrateful that you allowed me to join you in your cabin."

"There's a 'but' there," Abe said. "I can hear it."

"But I would have been happy to pay my own way across through steerage."

Abe rolled his eyes. "And what would have been the point of that? I'd have spent every moment dragging you back up into first class then – or, worse yet, slumming with you down in the lower decks. It's so much easier for us all this way, don't you see?"

"I'm here, aren't I?" Quin said.

"And don't think we don't appreciate it," said Lucy. "Just imagine how dreadfully boring it would be if I'd had to spend the entire trip with only Abe around for conversation. I would have had to strike up a friendship with some of the other young ladies here, and you know that would only lead to conversations with them that would irritate their parents to the point at which Captain Smith would have to consider tossing me in the brig or throwing me overboard if only to put an end to the constant dissent."

"Do they even have a brig on this boat?" Abe said. "Seems like they should have a proper prison instead, considering how large it is."

"The point is," Quinn said, pressing on, "I just don't have the resources that the pair of you do, and I'd appreciate not being constantly reminded about it."

The other two, who had been giggling at each other, fell silent at this. Abe glared at Quin, while Lucy lowered her dark eyes, embarrassed.

"So, we're back to this again," Abe said when he managed to open his mouth. "It's always about class with you. How passé."

"Of course it would be to you," Lucy said. "Those standing on the top of the mountain rarely have reason to curse the darkness below."

"Is that really how you think of me? I wonder what I ever did to deserve such a fiancée?"

Lucy held her gloved hand out in front of her, as if peering at her ring finger. "Are we engaged? How did no one inform me of this?"

Quin grunted at this running joke between his two best friends. Lucy and Abe had always seemed to be destined to be married. Both sets of their parents approved of the match, which was one reason they'd allowed the couple to go off on this mad junket around the States. Not that Lucy would have waited for that blessing either way.

Quin knew it was only a matter of time before Abe pulled a ring out of his pocket and proposed to Lucy. She'd put him off so far by insisting that she be allowed to concentrate on her education, but Abe was used to getting what he wanted. Quin didn't think Abe could force himself to wait until Lucy had graduated. In fact, he'd been surprised that Abe hadn't proposed to her during their first night aboard the ship.

He was just glad that it hadn't happened yet. He wanted to be happy for his two friends, but he didn't know if he could manage to muster a smile for them if forced to bear witness to their engagement. It had been hard enough for him to agree to come along with them on this portion of the trip. If his parents hadn't insisted on them all traveling together, he would have been happy to leave England a week later and not put himself through the torture of watching his best friend woo the girl he loved.

"That's not the sort of ice you should be worried about," a man said as he sauntered into the room. A wide and thoughtful American wearing small, wire-rimmed glasses, he fixed them with a serious look that chilled Quin's blood.

"I hope you're not referring to the iceberg, Mr Futrelle," Abe said. "You're letting that novelist's imagination of yours run away with you if you think a little dent is going to bring down the *Titanic*. What would your Thinking Machine say about that?"

The writer raised his eyebrows at Abe. "I don't have to bother my imagination about this one at all. Can't you feel the ship listing toward the starboard bow?"

His voice sounded so calm and even in contrast to the words he spoke that Quin wondered if the man might be pulling their legs. He looked over at Abe's refilled whisky glass, though, and saw that the man had not exaggerated in the slightest.

"What does it mean, Mr Futrelle?" Lucy's voice filled with concern as she turned to face the man fully.

"Call me Jacques, Miss Lucy," he said. "After all, if we're all going to die together, it's best that we do so amongst friends."

# CHAPTER FOUR

"You're sure about this?" Captain Arthur Rostron said as he stared at the scrap of paper Harold Cottam had handed him, running one hand back through his thinning hair.

"Aye, captain," Harold said. "I confirmed it with them. *Titanic* is going down."

The captain pressed his lips together so hard that they turned white. "Damn it." He rubbed his eyes. It had already been a long day for him and his crew, but that paled against the troubles of the people trapped aboard the *Titanic*.

"Right," he said with a sharp nod. "Take this to the bridge. Tell them to head out, full speed ahead. I'll be there presently."

Harold spun on his heel and left, shutting the door to the captain's cabin behind him. Rostron pushed himself to his feet and climbed back into his uniform. He'd been asleep when the radioman had knocked on the door of his cramped cabin, but he was as wide awake now as if he'd fallen overboard into the frigid waters of the North Atlantic.

As he readied himself, he did some quick calculations in his head. At the moment, they had just under seven hundred and fifty passengers on board, but the *Carpathia* could hold over twenty-five hundred, more than three times that. They often had plenty of passengers when hauling emigrants from Europe to New York, but few people came back the other way, mostly American tourists looking to explore the Old World.

The *Titanic* wasn't a Cunard ship like the *Carpathia*. It belonged to the rival White Star line, which meant that the captain didn't know as much about it as he might otherwise. Still, it had been impossible to avoid news about the gigantic ship and its maiden voyage over the past few weeks. He'd absorbed a few facts about the *Titanic* just by the fact that his ship sailed the same lanes.

From what he remembered, the *Titanic* could hold as many as thirty-five hundred souls. He doubted they'd been packed to capacity though, given the premium prices the White Star offices had been charging for travel aboard its new flagship. He didn't know where they'd find the space for so many people on the *Carpathia* if it came to that, but he'd be damned if he wasn't going to try and save as many poor souls as he could either way. They'd double up bunks and have people sleep on the open decks if they had to. Anything would be a far sight better than a watery grave.

By the time the captain reached the bridge, his first officer had already gotten the *Carpathia* moving in the right direction. "Report, Mr Brooks," Captain Rostron said.

"We're underway and already up to fourteen knots, sir."

Rostron frowned. "And how far out from the *Titanic* are we?"

"Less than sixty miles, sir."

Rostron did the math in his head. "We need more speed. At that rate, we won't reach them for five hours."

"Can't *Titanic* hold on for that long, sir?" Brooks said. "She's supposed to be unsinkable."

"I'm afraid the only things unsinkable around here are the icebergs, Mr Brooks. If *Titanic* is as wounded as her radioman claims, they won't last five hours for sure. Tell the engine room to cut the steam to everything but the engines."

"Including the heat in the rooms, sir? Won't the passengers complain?"

"They'll still be warmer than any of the blessed souls who wind up out there in the drink tonight. Tell the chief engineer: divert all available power to the engines. Squeeze every damn bit of speed out that our fine lady here can spare."

"Aye, captain." Brooks ran off to execute Rostron's orders.

"Mr Crooker and Mr Blum," Rostron said to his second and third officers. "We're about to take on more visitors than our ship should rightly hold. We need to make the best use of the next few hours to get *Carpathia* in shape to greet them."

"Aye, captain," the two men said in unison.

"Mr Crooker: get our own lifeboats out on their davits, ready to put to sea. There's no telling how many people we might have to fish out of the water, and it'll give us more room on our decks at the very least. While you're at it, open all the gangway doors so we can take in our guests no matter from which angle they arrive.

"Ready the rope ladders for each of those doors. Get some cargo netting secured too. Some of the older passengers might not be able to make the climb on their own."

"What about any children, sir?" Crooker said. "They'd slip right through the ropes."

"Good point. Gather some empty mail sacks for them. Dump out the mail if you have to. We can secure them with ropes and bring the little ones up that way if need be."

He turned to Blum. "Gather the pursers and stewards and fill them in on our situation. Have them get every room on the ship ready. We may have to double or triple up to fit everyone in."

Blum's eyes widened as he absorbed the enormity of what they were facing. "Can we get beds ready in the middle of the night for several thousand people in just five hours, sir?"

"I certainly hope so, Mr Blum. If our engineer does his job, we might be there in less than four. I also want blankets and hot soup and drinks ready, so alert the kitchens. Get Doctor Griffiths to set up a sickbay in the first class dining room."

"He should know if we have any other physicians on board, I'd think," Blum said. "If so, maybe they can help."

"Excellent point. If that's the case, set them up in the second and third class dining rooms as well. Also, be sure to have the stewards get the names of our guests as they assign them to rooms. We should keep them apart from our current passengers as much as we can. We don't want to lose anyone we bring on board, and having to shuffle through everyone to make sure they're taken care of will only slow things down."

"Yes, sir." Blum swallowed hard at the list of monumental tasks the captain had entrusted him with.

"Don't look so shocked. Grab anyone else you can to lend a hand. Wake everyone up. We need all hands for this. Now get to it!"

"Aye, captain." Blum sprinted off toward the head steward's cabin to set to work.

Rostron glanced over at his third officer, who had the wheel. "Steady as she goes, Mr Shubert," he said.

"Aye, sir." The bearded man had a look of grim determination in his eyes, as if he could make the ship go faster by concentrating on it as hard as he could.

"Mr McPherson?"

The fourth officer, a tall Canadian with a gentle accent, stepped forward. "Aye, sir."

"Gather as many binoculars as you can find – ask the men to haul out their own if they have them – and set watches all around the ship. Turn on every damn light you can find too. We want to see those people out there, and we want them to see us coming too.

"Tell the men to keep an eye out for bergs and to not be shy about reporting them in right away. The ice has already taken down one great ship tonight, and in a few moments we'll be moving faster than this ship was ever designed to go. Let's not be so foolhardy as to believe it might not be able to mortally wound us as well."

"Very wise, captain," McPherson said. With that, he trotted out of the room, leaving Rostron alone with Shubert at the wheel.

Rostron strode toward the front of the bridge and held onto the rail that ran under the windows as he stared out into the inky darkness beyond the nimbus of light that surrounded the ship. No moon sailed across the cloudless sky tonight, just a sparkling scattering of stars that provided too little illumination.

Rostron had gone to sea at the age of sixteen, and at the age of forty-two, he'd spent more time on the ocean than he cared to think about. But he'd spent precious little time *in* it. He thought about being caught out there in the dark, floating in the icy black ocean with nothing more than a lifejacket to keep himself afloat, waiting for help to arrive while the freezing waters leeched every bit of warmth out of him with each passing second.

"Hold on out there, young lady," he whispered to the *Titanic*. "Just hold on as long as you can."

# CHAPTER FIVE

"I'm not going," Lucy said. "Not without the two of you." She stuck out her chin in a way that Quin knew meant she'd made up her mind and wasn't about to let anyone or anything change it.

The band, which had set up in the reopened First Class Lounge, played a lively ragtime tune as people milled about in the chilly air on Deck A, some of them ducking in and out of the lounge to keep warm while they waited for news of the *Titanic*'s fate and what part they might play in it. Many of them hadn't taken the time to dress properly and wore little more than a coat tossed on over their nightclothes. Others, like Lucy and the boys, were still in their dinner clothes, never having resigned themselves to preparing for a solid night's sleep. Nobody seemed particularly concerned by events. It was more like a pleasant diversion had been arranged, an added event to the evening's programme.

While the ship had been moving, there had always been some kind of breeze on the promenade, but with the ship stalled in the freezing waters, Quin realized that the air wasn't moving at all. If it had, he was sure it would have bit into him like a polar bear, raw, fast, and savage. Instead, it seemed to nibble at him like an illness, eating away at the warmth he'd brought out into the world with him. He had no doubt which side would eventually win that battle. Without respite, the chill would consume them all.

"Lucy, dear," Abe said. "When the captain says, 'Women and children first,' I'm afraid he's serious. Despite what you might think of us in your darker moments, Quin and I don't qualify."

"No one else is leaving the ship." Lucy gestured to a lifeboat being rowed away from the *Titanic* on the glassy water, the few people on board pulling at three sets of oars in unison to a beat a sailor in the prow called out. It looked so tiny compared to the great ship, but it had to be large enough to hold dozens of desperate souls. "Only a bunch of worried old ladies and women with babies still on their hips." She put her hands on her hips for emphasis and squared off against her friends. "I'm certain you're not implying I'm such a person who cannot fend for herself."

"You wouldn't go on the first lifeboat," Quin said. "You said you'd wait for the next one." He gestured to Lifeboat 6 as it hung alongside the railing from its davit on the ship's port side. "That's the third one there, and there's plenty of room on it. What's keeping you?"

Lucy threw up her hands and let out an exasperated sigh. The fog of her breath hung around her like a halo, glowing in the lights. "I'd rather not freeze my boots off out there while we wait for the captain to give the all-clear signal and send us back to our cabins. This is a useless exercise, and I don't want to take any part in it."

"Come now," Abe said. "Just think of the story you'll have when we reach New York. You'll be the toast of Manhattan society, the woman who braved the icy waters of the Atlantic while the rest of us cowards huddled here on the ship's deck, too fearful to join you in your grand adventure."

Lucy squinted an eye at Abe. "Abraham Holmwood, don't you think I don't know exactly what you're trying to do here. I'm insulted that you'd think I'd fall for such a transparent appeal to my independent spirit."

Strains of "In the Shadows" streamed out from the nearby lounge as a group of women emerged from the bustle of activity and strode toward the lifeboat. Quin recognized the person in the lead, a lady with whom Lucy had chatted during dinner the night before.

"Mrs Brown," Quin said to the vibrant, middle-aged woman as she strode forward, bundled in her massive furs against the cold, "could you do me a singular favor?"

The woman gave him a hesitant smile. "You know, Quin, there's nothing I wouldn't normally like to do for a handsome young fellow like yourself, but as you can see I have someplace I have to be at the moment, which doesn't give me much time."

"Mrs Brown." Abe stepped between the woman and the boat. Over his shoulder, Quin could see Lucy screwing up her lips in either determination or dismay or some odd combination of both. She knew what they were up to already, but there was little she could do to stop it."

"Maggie," the woman said, placing a hand on Abe's arm. "Told you kids last night, it's always Maggie to my friends."

"Forgive me. Maggie," Quin began again, "we hoped that you might be able to talk some sense into our lovely Lucy here. She's decided to disobey the captain's own orders so she can stay here and go down with the rest of us."

"No one's going to die here tonight." Mrs Brown blushed with embarrassment as she spoke. "And even if the ship does go down, does it hardly seem right for me to take advantage of the way men treat women in modern society when I've been railing against it for so long?"

Quin turned to Maggie. "I don't know, Mrs... Maggie. You're a suffragette yourself, aren't you?"

"Well, of course, I am!" Maggie gave Quin the kind of proud glare that dared him to call her a liar. "I even ran for the US Senate a few years back. I figure we ladies have to go out and grab our rights if no one's going to give them to us."

Quin flashed her an agreeable smile. "That's one of the reasons our Lucy here holds you in such high regard. And yet, despite your dedication toward equality for women, you're heading for this lifeboat, aren't you?"

Maggie's tongue caught in her mouth when she realized where Quin had led her. She closed her lips and narrowed her eyes at the young man. "There's a time and place for everything, my friend, and even the rats know you can't argue with the water on a sinking ship."

Lucy stepped around Abe to take Maggie by the hands. "But if we're not willing to make a stand when it's important, why should anyone be willing to listen to us at any other time?"

Maggie reached out and chuckled at Lucy as she patted her on the cheek. "You make an excellent point," she said. "I look forward to the day women are treated as equals to men as much as anyone, but I don't see the point in taking a fatal stand. Nobody listens to the voices that quit speaking, and I for one would like to survive long enough to take advantage of all our hard work as suffragettes."

"Ladies!" One of the ship's officers called to Maggie and the women who'd accompanied her from the lounge. "You must board the lifeboat now! We have no time to waste."

The other women behind Maggie moved around her, their husbands escorting them to the wooden boat beyond Abe. They ranged in age from a young woman saying goodbye to her fiancée to a gray-haired woman who could have been Quin's grandmother. A few of them, like Maggie, were alone.

Others traveled with their maids. One and all, men and women, every one of them carried fear in their eyes, and in many cases this emotion had brimmed over into tears.

"It's only for a little while, darling," one of the men said to the youngest woman. She clung to his coat as if she knew she would never see him again. He held her close and whispered soft nothings into her ear until the officer called out to them.

"I'm lowering this lifeboat down now," he said. "If you want to be on it, you must board immediately."

"That's our cue, honey," Maggie said to Lucy. She turned to gaze up at the great ship's four massive funnels stretching toward the sky. While the ship had come to a halt, its engines still thrummed. "Come with us, gal. You never know when you'll get another chance to ride on a tiny boat in the middle of the Atlantic. We'll be like Vikings."

Lucy allowed herself a thin smile at that, but then she turned to Abe and Quin. "But what about you two?"

Quin knew what she really meant by that: "What about Abe?" While she may have stolen both boys' hearts, she'd only shown any love for him, and that fact made his heart feel like it was sinking faster than the ship.

Quin had long held out hope that Abe would tire of Lucy someday, the way he had done with all of the other girls he'd dated. Then Quin could step in and finally let her know how he felt about her. He'd already kicked himself a thousand times for not having ginned up the guts to do so before Abe began his pursuit of her, but once his best friend had gone after her, he hadn't seen a way to stand between them – at least not any way that jibed with his sensibilities as a gentleman.

"We'll be fine." Quin mustered up what he hoped would seem like a confident smile. "Once they get all the women and children away, we'll catch the very next boat."

Lucy frowned, and he knew that she'd seen straight through

his bravado. He'd never been able to fool her about his fears –
only about the content of his heart.

Quin opened his mouth. He knew that if he didn't tell her
how he felt right then and there he might never have another
chance. But should he burden her with such things at such a
horrible time? Could she bear it? Did he really have a choice?

Abe stepped forward then and took Lucy in his arms. He
brushed his lips against hers in a tender kiss, and she buried
her face in his shoulder.

"It's now or never, little Lucy." Maggie took Lucy by the
elbow and guided her away from Abe and toward the lifeboat.

Lucy looked back at Quin, a terrible desperation in her eyes.
Instead of speaking to her, though, and confessing his secret
love, he closed his mouth and instead put up a reluctant hand
to wave good-bye.

# CHAPTER SIX

"Where is that little, Irish bastard?" Dushko Dragovich smashed his fist into the great steel bulkhead that separated this part of the *Carpathia*'s cargo hold from the thrumming engines in the room beyond. "And don't tell me none of you know."

The menace in Dushko's voice was enough to set most of the people huddled in the hold on edge. They stood shivering together among the low wooden crates scattered about the chamber, right where they'd been chatting in small groups to pass the time until he'd burst in, bringing both fresh air and the night's chill with him. They stared at him as one with their pale, bloodshot eyes, some of them unaware of what he was talking about, others unwilling to be the first to respond.

None of them wanted to be the one to bear the full brunt of his attention.

Despite that, one of them cracked under the horrible tension that had swept over the room with Dushko's arrival, and he let out a helpless little sound as he cowered in a distant corner. Dushko's red-rimmed eyes zeroed in on that man, and he stalked toward him like a hungry wolf, weaving through the crates and the others as if they weren't there.

Dushko reached down, snatched the little man by the collar

of his jacket, and hauled him up into the air until his shoes dangled beneath him, small clods of dirt spilling from his clothes as he trembled in them. Dushko wasn't a tall man himself, but he had the chest and shoulders of a boxer, and he held his small victim out at arm's length without any apparent effort.

"What is it, Piotr?" Dushko's voice hissed out between his teeth at the man, carrying with it the stench of the grave. "What do you know?"

A thin, rat-faced man with a chin that receded so far that Dushko couldn't tell if he actually had one, Piotr refused to meet Dushko's glare. "I told them," he said. "I told them all."

Dushko slammed Piotr into the steel-plated hull behind him. No one else gasped at the violence of the act. Nor did they move even an inch to put a stop to Dushko's treatment of the man. "What did you tell them?" Dushko asked, each word striking the scrawny man like a bullet.

Piotr cringed and whimpered at Dushko. The man might have cried, Duskho thought, if only he and every other one of the occupants of the hold hadn't given up on shedding tears long ago. "Not to leave the ship."

"But they did anyway," said a slender woman with her steely hair bound up under a babushka. "There was nothing that would stop them."

Dushko snorted at that and released Piotr, who dropped to the hold's cold, steel floor and lay there moaning. "Did you even try, Elisabetta? Did you even say a word?"

The woman shook her head at Dushko as if he were a slow child. "And what good would that have done? Would it have stopped him and his friends for an instant? It's more amazing that we didn't all go with them."

Dushko glared at Elisabetta as he moved closer to her, ignoring everyone else in the room. Despite her startling and natural beauty, her looks had faded more than a bit already on the journey, and they'd only been aboard the ship for two days. She noticed him looking at the wear showing on her face, and she snarled at him. "You can't keep us down here for the entire trip," she said. "We're already starving down here. It's not going to get better."

"You know how this works," Dushko said, looming over the woman with an intimacy reserved for old lovers. He spoke in a quiet voice, as if the words were only for her, even though they both knew that everyone in the hold could hear them.

"It's been a long time since we took that ship to the New World together," she said. "And we'd laid in better preparations that time around."

"We need to keep a low profile," Dushko said. "We are as vulnerable out here on the ocean as anyone else. Maybe more so. Should we be discovered out here, to where would we be able to flee?"

Elisabetta turned her violet-blue eyes away from him. She knew he was right, much as it might rankle her and everyone else in the hold. They'd made the decision to head back to the Old Country as a group because it had no longer been safe in Manhattan for the exact same reason.

They'd blown their cover there, and it had taken every bit of Dushko and Elisabetta's wealth and influence – plus a few applications of a judicious amount of force – to repair the damage done. The writing had been on the wall after that though the mistakes that had been made once could – and would – be made again. If they'd stayed around, they would have been destroyed for sure.

"It is the same old conflict as always." Elisabetta hooded her eyes as she gazed at Dushko. "Between our natural urges to feed and to live. But if we do not feed, then what sort of life can we expect to have?"

"I am not advocating starvation on the part of anyone,"

Dushko said. "Every one of us had our fill before we left America, and that hot repast should have been enough to see us all through to our destination. But that was not good enough for Murtagh and his friends." He glanced at the people pretending to be ignoring them. "I should have killed him when I had the chance. It would have made everything so much simpler."

"And to young Brody, his solution is the simpler one. He hungers, he feeds." She ran her tongue along the edge of her sharp, pointed teeth. "What could be simpler than that? Even an animal could understand it."

"That's the exact problem I'm talking about," said Dushko. "As long as we act like human beings, we have a chance. The moment we behave like animals, we can expect to be hunted down and killed like mad dogs."

"But we're not human beings, my dear Dragomir." A sly and seductive smile curled the edge of Elisabetta's full, red lips as she ran a finger down Dushko's chest. "We haven't been for a long time."

Dushko grabbed her hand in his and squeezed it hard enough that his grip would have broken the fingers of a lesser woman. "You think we're better than them, do you?"

"Aren't we?" Elisabetta rolled her eyes at him. "They're the animals. It is we who feed on them."

Dushko shoved her away from him, disgusted by her lack of concern. How had she survived for so long? "You might have ruled over them in your youth, my dear countess, but those people out there are no longer sheep for us to cull. They have science on their side: cars, planes, machine-guns."

Elisabetta snorted. "And you think that sharpening the sheep's teeth has transformed them into wolves? They're still sheep under that clothing. They have no instinct for the hunt, no scent for the blood."

"Yet their teeth are sharper than ever, and if we corner them

– if we force them to employ those incisors – their bites will cut just as deep."

"Ha! The only thing you're in danger of murdering, my dear Dushko, is that metaphor." Elisabetta strolled away from him, toward the darkest corner of the hold, the place where Dushko knew their crates of livestock sat, their terrified contents shivering in the blackness. "It's been too long since you've fed, hasn't it?" she said over her shoulder. "I can tell from the gray in your hair."

"Should I have stopped to feed while I protected the rest of us from the spotlight? Should I have let the rest of us be slaughtered just so that I could slake my thirst?"

Elisabetta gestured toward one of the others in the room, a tall thin man with a large nose. Understanding her intent, he opened the lid on one of the crates. He reached in with his long arm and snatched up something with a single, sharp move.

The man raised his arm and brought up a young woman along with it. She dangled there from her long, dark hair, pale and sickly, too weak to scream. She reached up with her arms to shield herself from the man as he drew her toward him, but he pinned her feeble limbs to her side by wrapping an arm all the way around her battered form. With his other arm, the man grabbed the woman's head and pulled it back toward him, exposing her naked throat.

"No!" Dushko commanded. "We need those to last us until we reach Fiume. There are barely enough of them to go around as it is."

Elisabetta slid over to the woman, who struggled without a hint of success in the man's arms. She traced the captive's jawline with a long nail, then brought her fingers down to caress a pair of puncture wounds that marred the deathly pale skin there. "Better we feast now, therefore," Elisabetta said, "rather than starve the entire way."

# CHAPTER SEVEN

"You know, I thought she'd never leave," Abe said as he lit the fat cigar he'd produced from somewhere inside his dinner jacket.

Quin recognized that the words had been meant as a joke, but he couldn't bring himself to laugh. For one, he'd shared that exact fear right up until the moment when Lucy had climbed into the lifeboat. They'd watched her go the entire way down to the water and then stood there at the railing with the other men, waving at them as they helped the quartermaster in charge of their boat row away.

Afterward, they had made their way toward the ship's stern, working along the deck as it tipped further and further toward the bow. Every one of the lifeboats had either already been deployed or was being stuffed with nervous women, children, and the occasional man, whom Quin hoped had a decent excuse. None of them seemed like they had a seat to spare for the two young men, much less for the rest of the desperate souls thronged around them.

As Quin and Abe strolled from boat to boat, an unreal sense of doom seemed to have settled over them, accompanied by a resignation to their fate. They'd cut through the Smoke Room when they'd reached near to the stern, if only for a short respite from the shouting and screams and tears that filled the air. The opulent room had stood almost empty at that moment, with the exception of a few men and a pair of stewards who'd given up any hope of finding a rescue for themselves and had decided to content themselves with a final drink.

After chatting for a moment, they'd gone through to the other side of the ship and made their way back through the agitated, shuffling crowds as far as the bow, still hoping to find some way off the ship. They'd had no luck there either and had wound up in the same spot at which they'd left Lucy, which now stood empty.

"Do they have to go so far?" Quin leaned over, his elbows on the railing, and tried to pick Lucy's lifeboat out of the blackness. The lights of the *Titanic* still burned bright, but they only extended so far into the moonless night.

"Afraid so, chum," Abe said. "When a ship the size of *Titanic* goes down, it sucks everything nearby down with it. What's the point of climbing into a lifeboat and then going down with the ship anyhow?"

"How do you know that? There's never been a ship the size of *Titanic*."

"There's the *Olympic*, her sister ship. It's not quite as nice but just about the same size, I hear."

"But it's still afloat."

"The last I heard." Abe drew another cigar from his pocket and held it up for Quin. With deft, practiced moves, he clipped both ends of the cigar and then lit it before passing it over to his friend.

Quin eyed the cigar for a moment before taking a tentative puff on it. "These are Cuban," he said. "Where did you get your hands on them?"

"When we passed through the Smoke Room while we were scouting out the other lifeboats."

"Weren't the stewards too busy with the drinks to stop to sell you a smoke?"

Abe shrugged and eyed his cigar with a mischievous glint. "I didn't want to bother anyone about them." He waved the cigar around with a casual air. "And I didn't think anyone would miss them."

A laugh leaped out of Quin's chest. "You light-fingered swine," he said. "I never figured you for a thief."

"Let's just say I like to squeeze as much as I can out of life."

That cut Quin's laughing short. He gazed out at the void beyond and the abyss below, and he wondered then about all the things he was doomed to miss in his life. He'd miss his parents for sure, but since he was moving to America, he'd already resigned himself to that. He knew then that the thing he would miss the most was Lucy.

He'd allowed himself to be talked into coming along on this trip for one reason, and one alone. Not so that he could be forced to accept his friend's generosity for sharing his first class cabin with him. Not so that he could get to New York City to look for a job in the spring, with all the promise of what a new world might hold. But so that he could be nearer to Lucy, both during the trip and when she registered at Radcliffe in the fall.

Perhaps it would be easier this way. At least now he wouldn't have to face the shame of having fallen in love with his best friend's girl. He wouldn't have to wrestle with the fact he couldn't tell her how he felt about her – but he couldn't keep it inside any longer either. That decision, that chalice, had been taken from him. All it had cost him was the remainder of his life.

Abe saw the miserable look on his friend's face and clapped him on the shoulder. "Lighten up," he said to Quin, unaware of his friend's deepest thoughts. "It could be worse."

Quin stared at Abe. "How?" he said, swinging his arms wide

enough to encompass the entire doomed ship. The fore had tipped forward far enough now that tiny waves lapped at the rails on the bow. It would only be minutes before the water spilled over the tops of the lower decks.

Abe puffed on his cigar before holding it up in front of him, the tip of it glowing like a hot coal. "We're still smoking, aren't we?"

Quin couldn't help but smile at that. "We might as well enjoy them while we can."

The two friends smoked their cigars from the fore railing on the Promenade Deck as the *Titanic* sank further not only into the sea but chaos. The ship began to list to the starboard as the hole the iceberg had torn in there swallowed more and more of the ocean. Shouting sailors lowered lifeboats into the chill waters, some of them packed to bursting with terrified passengers while others left the *Titanic*'s side with seats still empty.

"We should have gone with Lucy," Abe said calmly as his cigar burned down to a stub. "They had plenty of room in that boat of theirs."

"They should have put on more of the women and children," Quin said.

"For sure," Abe said, "but I didn't see them lining up then. We could have gone with her. At least then we could have been with her, all passed on together."

The thought that Lucy might perish out there on the water threatened to crush Quin's heart. "She'll make it," he said, rallying his confidence. "They have a wireless radio on board. They must have put out the distress call. Help is on the way."

"Here's hoping it gets here in time for her, because it doesn't look like it'll reach us." Abe flicked the remnants of his cigar toward the Well Deck below. It hissed when it hit the water, and then it was gone. Quin dropped his on the deck instead and ground it under his heel.

An orange flare went off overhead. They'd been fired into the air every five minutes or so, but to no obvious effect. They reminded Quin of the fireworks he'd enjoyed back home on Guy Fawke's Night, beautiful but transient. They burned so bright that it almost hurt to look at them, and then they were gone like they'd never been there.

"You fellows!" a broad, red-haired man in an officer's uniform shouted from the boat deck above them. "What the blazes are you doing lazing about down there? Come on up and give us a hand here!"

Quin glanced at Abe, who gave him a shrug and said, "What do we have to lose?"

Quin raced Abe to a nearby stairwell on the port side of the ship, just around the corner from where they stood. He took the stairs two at a time and emerged onto the Boat Deck. Quin stopped there so fast that Abe bumped into him and almost knocked him over.

A group of men stood on top of the roof of the officer's quarters, just around the corner from the bridge. They had something in their hands that looked like the bottom of a boat but without any sides.

"Are we going to have to build our own lifeboat?" Abe asked.

"At this point, I'd be willing to whittle myself one if we had enough time," said Quin.

"Sir," Quin called up to the officer, "how can we get up there to help you?"

"Don't you worry about that now, lad. We've enough hands up here to free this damned thing, but I need someone down there to catch it as we lower it down. Just stay right there with the rest of the men, and we'll have it right down to you."

The men on the roof of the ship worked as fast as they could to free the boat from the ropes that had lashed it down. As they lifted it from its spot, a handful of bats flew out from under the barely curved hull and flapped off into the night.

Abe laughed at the creatures as they disappeared into the distance. "Sure hope those little buggers can survive on snow and ice," he said, "or they're as dead as us."

# CHAPTER EIGHT

Dale Chase had had enough of the damn *Titanic*. As the only black man aboard the ship – at least, the only one he'd seen from his position as a stoker in the belly of the behemoth – he'd taken more than his fair share of shit from his bosses. They'd worked him longer hours than any of the others and given him the hardest and most dangerous jobs.

They'd done their best to break him, calling him names, spitting on him, and giving him endless hell, but they'd failed. He'd taken every bit of it without complaint. He didn't give a damn about any of them, and he wasn't about to let them get to him, no matter how hard they tried. He just wanted to get back to Brooklyn, back to his home, and if the only way he could afford that was to work his way across the ocean in the bowels of the biggest ship on the seas, then that's what he was going to do.

From the start, though, the whole trip hadn't gone to plan. He'd gone over to England as a piano player in a band, thanking God Almighty for Irving Berlin and "Alexander's Ragtime Band" finally bringing his favorite sound to the masses. It had seemed like that music had opened the entire world to him like a flower, and all he had to do was reach out and pluck it.

Hadn't he played with Scott Joplin – *the* Scott Joplin – back in New York? Hadn't they played the "Maple Time Rag" together on the same stage? And after that transcendent moment, hadn't Scott encouraged Dale and the others to leave the States and find their fortune overseas?

It had seemed like a fine idea at the time. Leave all their troubles behind and find a new way in the Old World, a place where they could capitalize on their differences, where they'd seem exotic and rare, just like Cole and Johnson. But it hadn't worked out so well for them.

There had been problems almost from the start. Albert Pulliam – the purported band leader and manager – hadn't actually had the seed money he'd promised the rest of them. The investors had gotten shy at the last moment, he'd said, and only given him enough money to get to England and get started. It would have to be up to them to play well enough to make it on their own from there.

But then the concerts that Albert had supposedly set up for them vanished too, and they'd been reduced to playing in bars and even on street corners. It had made for many long, cold, and hungry nights that winter, and the tensions over money soon started to rip the band apart. To top it off, that Rose Wilson had started making eyes at Dale, even though she'd been Albert's girl.

Dale couldn't blame her for looking for greener pastures. Hell, he'd been thinking about ditching Albert himself. Despite that, he'd made a point of not laying a finger on Rose, no matter how clear she made it that she'd prefer he put his hands all over her. Albert might have been a rotten businessman, but even as mad as Dale might be at him, he knew better than to mess with a friend's woman.

That hadn't stopped Albert from suspecting something though. He'd come in drunk one night, having blown what little money they'd made, and he'd thrown the first punch. After beating the man until he didn't want to fight any more, Dale packed up the few things he had and left.

Desperate to get back to Brooklyn but unable to afford a ticket, Dale had started working at the shipyards, doing the dirtiest work they had, hoping to find some way to get back home. He'd caught the eye of the White Star Line, and the managers there had signed him up as one of the stokers for the *Titanic*, despite the objections of Dale's new bosses.

He'd put up with the abuse he'd sustained every day since then. If this was his only chance to get back home, he was damned if he'd let someone push him too far and ruin it.

In the few minutes he had off, he'd stolen away to sneak around the ship, knowing that if they caught him they might toss him overboard. He'd never seen such opulence in his entire life. To him, the *Titanic* looked a lot like how he imagined Buckingham Palace would seem if you gave the building a watertight hull and tossed it into the sea.

He kept well out of sight, though, only moving about late at night, after most of the people on the ship were asleep. On the first evening on the open sea, he'd heard music wafting from somewhere on the ship, and he'd skulked as close as he could toward it. Although he hadn't dared to approach the band and offer to join in, he'd played along, drumming his fingers on his legs as if they held all eighty-eight keys.

At that moment, Dale had thought that despite all his troubles everything was going to be all right. He'd even started to compose a song about it, something he planned to debut as soon as he arrived back home and had a piano to play. He could see the end of this horrible movement of his life from here, and he couldn't wait to turn the page to see what notes he would get to play next.

And then they'd hit that damned iceberg.

Dale had been down working the double-enders in boiler room 6, shoveling endless loads of coal into the gigantic boiler that stood almost three times his height. It had been hard, back-breaking work in infernal heat, made even worse by a slow fire that had started in the aft coal bunker on the starboard side. It had reached deep into the dry coal at the bottom of the bin, and no matter what he and the other stokers had tried, they hadn't been able to put the fire fully out.

But the sea took care of that for them. After the iceberg knocked a hole in the hull, right next to where Dale had been standing, the icy waters beyond had come jetting in. The salt-water drenched Dale and sent up a cloud of steam that he'd had to flail through to find the doorway, doing his best not to lay a hand on the searing boilers on every side of the way out.

He'd reached the door just in time, as someone had decided to lower it to seal the bulkhead. Dale understood why – they had to try to save the ship, after all, and the life of one man didn't measure up much against all the rest, no matter his race or wealth – but he was damned if he'd be caught behind it. He saw it coming down fast and had to dive forward to slip under it beforehand.

His boot had gotten caught on the raised lip of the hatchway, and he'd almost lost his leg to the door. Only quick thinking had gotten him to slide his foot out of his boot rather than mess with the laces. That left him short a shoe, but it beat an amputation any day.

As he'd gotten to his feet, though, his boss had started yelling at him for not staying at his post. It was then that Dale decided, middle of the Atlantic or no, he was going to quit.

He threw down his gloves and stormed right past the boss. The man had put out a muscular arm to stop him, but the withering look of fury Dale focused on him made him put it right back and then move on to doing his job rather than shouting at someone who no longer worked for him.

Dale wasted no time in racing for the upper decks. By the time he'd gotten there, the people above had known something was wrong, but they still hadn't launched a single lifeboat. Knowing there wouldn't be any room for him on any of the boats anyhow, he hunted around for a lifebuoy and found one affixed to the side of one of the walls in the forward well deck.

Dale took the ring-shaped buoy from its steel bracket and brought it over to the port side of the ship, away from the hole the iceberg had torn into the *Titanic*'s hull. Throwing the ring over one shoulder, he reached up and hoisted himself up over the high bulwark there and looked down into the waters below.

It was a long drop, and he knew that it would be cold enough to kill him if help didn't come soon. He sat there for a long time, his back to the people who came streaming out from Steerage onto the well deck. Staring down at the water, he listened to them slide from idle curiosity into horrified panic.

None of them paid him much attention, and if anyone spotted him and thought it was odd to see a soot-covered stoker perched atop a bulwark, they were too busy with worrying about their own lives to say much about it. He sat there in the night air, letting the frigid North Atlantic weather bleed off the heat he'd built up in his skin during his days in the depths of the ship. It wasn't until the ship developed a serious list that he began to shiver.

Dale knew then that this would be his last day on God's own earth. The icy ocean below would be the death of him. He didn't know if it would force the air from his lungs and drown him or leech every last bit of warmth from his bones, but he was sure that the *Titanic* wasn't long for this world and that there were no places for him on any of the lifeboats.

He'd have taken it personally, but Dale could tell from the horrified calls of the throngs of people on the decks and promenades behind him that he would be far from the only one to die tonight.

When the ship pitched toward the starboard, Dale knew exactly what had caused it. The bulkhead between boiler rooms 6 and 5 had finally given way. The heat from that fire they'd never been able to put out would have weakened the metal there, and it had only been a matter of time before it gave way under the tremendous pressure the water would put upon it.

As the waters rose up toward the well deck, Dale decided that his time to consider when he should leap off the boat had run out. He tossed the ring buoy out onto the waters below, and after a moment's hesitation in which he regretted the grief this would cause his mother, should she ever hear of it, he kicked off from the bulwark and dove into the ebony water below.

Dale didn't even feel the impact with the water. The icy temperature drove all other sensations from him, along with the air in his lungs. He wanted to scream in terror and pain, but the water had already closed over his head, and the cold had paralyzed him so that he couldn't have managed it, even if he'd had the air to pull it off.

As the lights of the ship receded above him, Dale realized that he needed to swim for the surface or he would just keep sinking straight to the ocean floor. Despite the cold forcing every muscle in his body to contract at once, he struggled against his own flesh and brought his arms up to reach for the surface. At first, Dale feared that he may have waited too long to start swimming, as the lights above him didn't seem to be getting any closer. Soon, though, he saw the lights growing brighter, and hope rose in him as he clawed his way to the surface.

Before he could break into the clean, cold, precious air though, something snagged his ankle again, much like the bulkhead door had done before. He reached down to see what it was and to pull his sole remaining shoe free from it if he could, but he saw that the question wasn't what had caught him but who.

At first Dale thought that the man who had grabbed him must have been drowning too. He couldn't think of any other reason for anyone to be in the water. As much as it hurt, the only way anyone would be in the near-freezing sea would be because the alternative seemed worse.

Despite identifying with the man holding onto his leg, Dale struggled to kick free. He could tell from the burning in his lungs that he couldn't last much longer, and if the man didn't let go they'd both drown for sure. Try as he might, though, the man's iron grip never slackened for an instant.

Dale bent over then and tried to pry the man's hand off his leg with his fingers. As he reached down, he got his first decent look at his attacker. He was a thin man, young, with ruddy hair and the flat nose of an Irish boxer, and rather than panicking he did the last thing that Dale expected. He looked up at him and smiled.

Dale stared at the man, then noticed something about his attacker's teeth that transformed his shock into sheer terror. The man's incisors were as long as fangs, and he wasn't smiling any longer. He was baring them.

# CHAPTER NINE

"If we don't make it through this," Quin said, "there's something I need to tell you."

"Oh, for Lord's sake," Abe said, as he held up his arms to help catch the lifeboat the sailors and a few other passengers on top of the roof were struggling to free. "Let's not ruin the moment, shall we?"

"What?"

Abe gave him a sidelong look. "I know just how this will go. You'll confess something horrible, and I'll want to tear your head from your shoulders, and it's only bound to distract us while we should really be concentrating on other, more important things."

With each of his last words, Abe jerked his head toward the boat above him. One of the officers was sawing at the ropes lashing down the boat with his knife. He had made some progress, but it was slow work. Even once he severed that rope, though, there would be more to go.

"If I don't say it now, then I might never get the chance," Quin said. "Once the ship goes down, there's no telling what might happen to any of us."

Abe let loose an exasperated sigh, never taking his eyes off the boat looming over their heads. Quin kept at least half an eye on it himself. If the lines holding the boat snapped and it fell at them, it might well knock them straight into the sea.

"Fine," Abe said. "But be quick about it then, like a razor to my throat. Just tell me. How long have you been sleeping with her?"

"What?" Quin's jaw dropped. He forgot about the boat and turned toward his friend. "What are you talking about?"

"You're surely speaking about the lovely Lucy. How long have you been inducing her to cheat on me?"

Quin stood aghast. "I've done no such thing. There is nothing – I repeat, *nothing* – I mean, *no way* that I would ever betray your friendship."

Abe frowned. "Really? I could have sworn… there were all the signs."

"Of course not!" Quin did a double-take. "Wait. What signs?"

"The long hours you two spend together. The easy way you have with each other. The secret smiles she gives you when you're not looking."

"There's absolutely nothing going… she smiles at me?" Quin couldn't help but find himself smiling in response.

Abe clapped him on the back of his neck. "Well, old man, if you say there's nothing going on between you, then I suppose I have to believe you. Have to admit, though, that I didn't think there could really be any other explanation – unless of course the two of you were talking about me the whole time instead."

Abe removed his hand from Quin's neck and sidled a step away. "I mean, that's not it, is it?" He rubbed his own neck now, blushing.

Confused, Quin narrowed his eyes at Abe. "What is it you think you're getting at there?"

Abe grimaced. "Not the love that dare not speak its name?"

"The love that–? Oh, dear God, no! That's not it at all."

Abe's shoulders slumped in relief. "Well, I can't tell you how glad it makes me to hear that. I mean, after all, that would have made our last moments on this planet more than a hair uncomfortable, I think, don't you? I mean, it's not that you're unattractive, but I don't really–"

Quin put up a hand to cut his friend off. "Abe?" he said. "Shut up."

Abe nodded. "Capital idea. I think you're absolutely right about that."

The ship began to pitch forward at an even steeper angle. Abe grabbed Quin by the arm and pointed toward the stern. "Dear God," he said. "Would you look at that?"

Quin couldn't help doing just that. He stared aft along the ship and watched as the back rose farther and farther into the air, like lost Atlantis rising out of the ocean. It wasn't until he started to lose his balance that he remembered that he was standing on the other end of that same ship.

Quin threw himself back against the railing and caught onto it with both arms. An instant later, Abe landed there right next to him. "In my wildest dreams," Abe said, "in my worst nightmares, I never thought it would end like this."

The rear end of the ship continued to tilt up, steeper and steeper, until it struck Quin that they were no longer standing on a ship but clinging to the side of a skyscraper. He'd read that the *Titanic* stretched longer than the Empire State Building stood tall, and staring up the length of it, he wondered how anyone could ever have been arrogant enough to conceive of something so large. Both Quin and Abe clung to the railing as the planet shifted under them and the railing transformed from a barrier between them and the sea into a scaffolding that ran up the length of the ship until it disappeared, too small at the vanishing point to see.

Quin couldn't muster up as many words as Abe. All he could say was, "Duck!"

He grabbed Abe's shoulder and hauled him down tight against the railing. A moustachioed man wearing nothing more than his nightclothes and a lifejacket came tumbling toward them, spinning and somersaulting down the steep-canted decking. He smacked into an exposed bit of pipe as he went, leaving a splash of blood behind on the *Titanic*'s white wall.

Quin braced himself for impact, but the man only brushed by him, not saying a word or uttering a complaint. He left only a rush of wind to mark his passing, and then a splash close behind him.

"Jump!" Abe shouted as he grabbed Quin by the shoulder of his jacket.

Quin glanced down past his feet, which stood on one of the railing's posts, and saw the sea rushing up toward them. He had just enough time to grab a deep breath and crouch for a leap when the water smashed into him and knocked him from the ship.

To Quin, it felt like the entire ocean had hit him. It washed him and Abe clear of the ship, which continued to founder behind them.

Freezing blackness enveloped Quin, and he knew at that moment that he would die. A sense of terror seized him as he realized that Abe had lost his grip on his coat and been spun away, leaving Quin alone in the icy, inky depths, countless miles from the nearest land. For that instant, he resigned himself to his impending death.

Quin tried to pray, to beg God for forgiveness for his sins and to watch over his family and his friends, to console them over his loss. But he couldn't find the words. He couldn't bring himself to do it.

Horror overwhelmed him then as he came to understand something he'd struggled with for years but always in the end denied, even to himself. When it came down to it, even in the direst moment of his life, at which he felt sure he would die, he didn't believe in God. He would drown here in the North Atlantic, and that would be the end of him.

The thought that no Heaven waited for him threatened to send him spiraling into despair, but he consoled himself with the knowledge that there was then no Hell to take him either. And then the need to breathe caught fire, and his brain refused to spare him the effort to worry over such philosophical fears. Instead, it forced him to swim as hard and as fast as he could to climb and claw his way toward the unseen surface.

In his mind, Quin had already given up hope. He knew he had no chance. His will to live, though, shouldered his higher thoughts aside and forced his arms to move and his legs to kick up, up, up, until he either broke through to the atmosphere again or died in the effort.

*Why not?* he thought. If he only had this one life to live, he had to do everything he could to keep it. God might not care if he lived or died – if there was a God in any case – but *he* damn well did.

Quin swam toward the surface of the sea with renewed vigor, not knowing how close he might be. He shoved aside any fears that the lack of air would force him to open his mouth and breathe in lungfuls of seawater instead. He had no control over that. The only thing he could do was keep swimming until he gave out, so that's what he did.

# CHAPTER TEN

Air leaked from Quin's lips as he swam, and it encouraged him to see it rising in the same direction as he was moving. The fact he could see it at all spurred him on again, as he knew that he must be getting closer to the surface. The moon hadn't been shining that night, only the stars, but the lights of the *Titanic* still burned when he and Abe had been washed off the ship. He had to be getting closer to them.

The last bits of used-up air escaped from Quin's lungs, which now burned to breathe in something – anything – to sustain his effort to live. His arms felt as heavy as lead, but he kept moving them, using every last iota of energy he had left to him. Then the lights that had been growing before him began to dim. Blackness ate at the edges of his vision, and he felt like he was falling back down a long tunnel even though his arms and legs continued to propel him forward.

Quin broke through the ocean's surface, his arms still reaching upward and his legs still kicking below. He gasped for air as he flailed about, and his body didn't quit trying to swim up into the open sky above until his vision slid back down through the tunnel that had encroached on its edges and he snapped back to the horrible reality around him.

Quin hadn't truly felt the cold until then. The lack of oxygen and the resultant surge of adrenaline through his body had pushed aside such concerns, but now it bit like a tornado of thousands of razors spinning around him. He hollered out loud in both shock and relief.

Quin saw that he had his back to the ship, so he spun about in the water to see what had happened. He got just a glimpse of the massive ship towering over him, people still losing their grip and slipping and toppling from it. The sheer size of it made him feel as insignificant as a bug in a pond, but compared to the ocean itself, *Titanic* seemed like little more than a stick floating next to him.

Much of the fore part of the ship was submerged now as it sunk into the water at a snail's pace, a single row of portholes slipping under the waves at a time. Quin thought about swimming for the ship. It might be going down, but it had taken hours to get into this position. It might remain afloat for a while longer, he suspected, and at the least he figured being aboard the ship might be better than freezing to death in the ocean.

"Abe!" Quin hadn't seen a sign of his friend underwater, and now that he'd managed to find some air for himself, he hoped to find him. He spotted a deck chair floating in the water and headed for it, calling out as he went. "Abe?"

It was then that the lights on the *Titanic* went out.

A collective gasp went up from every living soul on the ship and in the water around it. To Quin, it seemed like he had just seen the ship die from its mortal wound. The lights had gone out in its eyes. All that was left now was for the ship to bury itself at sea.

The lights flickered on for one more instant, as if the ship were fighting to survive as hard as the people stranded with it. Then they went out again, plunging the entire area into utter darkness.

Screams of horror filled the night, hundreds of people terrified for their lives. Having been caught in the blackness
underwater just moments ago, Quin's eyes were quick to adjust to the lack of light, and he soon could see the outline of
the ship towering over him, a mountainous hulk of blackness
against the brilliant stars filling the cloudless night sky.

"Quin!" someone shouted off to the right. He knew it could
only be one person.

"Abe!" Quin shoved his deck chair in front of him and
kicked toward Abe's voice. The chair made for a lousy raft, unable to support much of his weight without sinking, but it
proved to be better than nothing. Holding onto it gave him
some strange comfort, as if it confirmed that he wasn't alone
out here in the freezing waters with nothing at all to help him.

"Dear God, Quin," Abe said. "After that wave hit us, I
thought I'd lost you for sure."

"I thought we were both dead."

Quin could see Abe grinning bleakly back at him. The
starlight surrounded them, coming not only from the sky but
also reflecting off the water all around them. In it, he could
see the whites of his friend's teeth and eyes.

"That too," Abe said. "It's a miracle we survived."

Quin grunted as he pushed the deckchair toward Abe, who
grabbed on to the other end of it. This made it even more useless as a flotation device, but Quin felt the trade-off was worth
it. "For now," he said.

"You're always such a pessimist," Abe said.

Quin barked a short laugh. "You must admit this is a situation that might call for it."

"Hey, we may be in the water, but the *Titanic*'s still afloat,
isn't she? That's something."

As the words left Abe's lips, a series of loud cracks and bangs
erupted from the direction of the ship. Although Quin hadn't

much experience with firearms, the flat, lethal noises sounded like gunshots to him. He supposed that Abe, who'd often gone fox hunting with his father Lord Godalming, would recognize if that were so.

"Are they shooting people?" Quin asked aloud.

Abe shook his head.

"Are you saying they're not?"

"I'm saying I don't know. I've never heard anything like that."

A board zipped by Quin's head and landed with a splash behind him. Abe gave up his grip on the deck chair and swam for it. Quin kicked along after him for a moment, peering back over his shoulder at the ship as he went.

Then Quin spotted what was making the noise. He stabbed a frozen finger up at the *Titanic*'s towering bulk. "It's not the people," he said. "It's the ship!"

Just above where the ship had entered the water, the whole thing snapped in half. It broke, not clean and sharp like a dry matchstick but instead crumbled, sheared, and tore away with a mighty, extended screech that sounded like the protestations of a choir of angry demons.

As Quin and Abe watched, the top half of the ship – no longer held in place by its lower half, like a knife stabbed into a steak – toppled back into the water, landing on its keel. As it fell, Abe pointed toward the waters behind the ship. Scores of people floundered about in the shadow of the gigantic ship as it came rushing down at them like a great tower chopped off at its base.

Quin could do nothing but watch the massacre in helpless horror. He couldn't have reached any of the people under the falling ship in time, and even if he had, what could he have done, other than be crushed with them? Some part of him hoped that the water would cushion the ship's fall some. Perhaps the wave it caused as it fell would shove some of the people out of the way like beachside swimmers riding the surf.

In his heart, though, Quin knew each of those poor souls – every last one of them – was doomed.

"Dear God." Abe's voice sounded hushed, almost reverent. The words formed not a prayer but a profession of awe at the horrible spectacle playing out before them.

The ship fell over like a gigantic tree felled by an impossible blow. It was so tall that it seemed to take minutes to topple into the water, and when it hit it threw up a wave large enough to swamp any smaller boat that might have been nearby.

"Lucy–" Quin heard himself say.

"She's all right," Abe said quietly. "She had plenty of time to get far enough away. Didn't she?"

Quin nodded, although to reassure himself or Abe, he wasn't sure. "Right."

And then the wave that rushed out from the side of the ship nearest them came straight for them.

Quin had been to the beach at Whitby and had swum in the sea many times. He'd watched the waves there roll in through the worst storms of his life, ones that had ripped the roofs off buildings and even knocked a rickety old building or two down flat. This wave from the *Titanic*'s crash back into the sea dwarfed every one of them.

"Hold on!" Abe shouted.

Quin did the best he could to maintain his grip on the deckchair. He took the deepest breath he could grab and then wrapped his entire body around it. He clutched it to him with all the strength left in his worn and cold-numbed arms.

Rather than crashing into him, the wave rolled right over him as if he wasn't even there. He rode up the face of it for an instant, then pierced straight through its surface, and it enveloped him.

In his shock at the fall of the *Titanic*, Quin had forgotten about the frigid temperatures of the water in which he was swimming. When the wave tumbled over the top of him, knocking him back into the blackness, he felt like an icy hand had grabbed him and was trying to shove him back down into the water because it just wasn't done with him yet.

This time, though, Quin was expecting the wave, and he fought back against it as hard as he could. He let go of the deckchair when he realized it wasn't holding him up but help-ing pull him down, and he punched through the water with his hands, scrambling for the surface.

As he went, Quin spotted a woman rolling through the water below him, being pulled farther into the darkness with every instant. He reached out for her, but she was yanked past him before he could even bring his arm toward her. From her pale color, he wondered if she might already be dead, and then he realized that he would be if he didn't keep fighting the mighty pressure from that massive wave.

A moment later, Quin returned to the surface. After his last dunking, this had seemed almost too easy to endure, and when he spotted Abe's head emerge only an arm's length away, he allowed himself the ghost of a smile.

Then he spied the *Titanic*, and he stared at it aghast. The bow had disappeared beneath the waves, but the stern was rising into the night sky once again. Would it keep breaking and slamming back into the water like a breaching whale slapping its tail? How long would it be until the horror came to a once and final end?

"Over there!"

Abe tapped Quin on the shoulder, and Quin spun about in the water to see that Abe was pointing with his other hand at something large and white floating in the water. It took Quin a moment to recognize it as one of the collapsible lifeboats, perhaps the one he and Abe had been standing ready to help deploy when they'd been on the ship. The water had washed it off the *Titanic*'s roof and sent it floating away, capsized but still floating on the surface.

Several people had already clambered on top of the white-bottomed boat, lying there like beached seals warming themselves on a sun-scorched rock. The waves that had rushed from the sinking ship had shoved the tiny craft farther and farther away, and it would be a long swim to reach it. Still, there seemed like no other recourse, not if Quin and Abe wanted to live.

"That's our chance," Quin said, already crawling through the freezing waters separating him from the overturned boat. "Come on!"

# CHAPTER ELEVEN

Brody Murtagh backhanded Trevor McPherson across the jaw so hard that it would have shattered the bones of a living man. The man only cried out in surprise rather than pain though and glared back at the Irishman as they trod water next to each other in the wake of the sinking *Titanic*.

Just about everyone else unfortunate enough to find themselves in the water was shivering against the near zero temperature, but the two men and their companions didn't feel it at all. The grave had long since robbed them of any fear of the cold.

"What the bloody hell was that for?" Trevor rubbed his jaw.

"For not listening to me," Brody said. "'Stay away from the ship,' I said. 'Give the thing a wide berth,' I said. And what good did that do poor Brigid now, can you tell me? Just tell me that."

Trevor stared at Brody, refusing to utter a word.

"It's not a rhetorical question, laddie," Brody said at last. He turned to the two others with them. "What do you think's happened to our blessed Brigid now?"

"I couldn't rightly say." Fergus Kielty moved away from Brody as he spoke, eyeing the man's hands as he went. "But if she was dumb enough to ignore you, then maybe she got what she had coming."

"Aye," Siobhan Kelly said. "But then it wasn't her bloody idea to drag us out here into the middle of the North Atlantic all by our lonesomes now, was it?"

Brody glared at Siobhan, but as he did he spotted a man swimming toward them from behind her. A grin played across his lips. "Now, you're the one who spent the whole trip so far whining about how damned hungry you were, and you're going to complain to me because I brought you out to the greatest buffet you've ever seen?" Brigid had all of her immortal life ahead of her, barring an unfortunate incident, and what does she do? She gets careless. She goes wandering off after a quick kill, something too shiny for that little bird to ignore, and what happens to her?"

"Just what you said would happen." Trevor gave Brody a sullen glare. "She gets too close to the wreck, and a wave sucks her down."

"Right," said Brody. "Knocks the wind right out of her. In case you hadn't noticed, my friends, we don't carry too much air in our lungs in the first place."

"Well, we don't rightly need it now, do we?" said Fergus.

"That's my point." Brody began to swim around Siobhan with long, languorous strokes. "It means we're not so buoyant as the breathing folks, and it doesn't take much to sink us."

Siobhan let out a little gasp, then breathed in deep and rose just a bit in the water. "Do you think Brigid is dead? Well and truly, I mean?"

"For her sake, let's hope so," Brody said. "Otherwise, she's going to spend the rest of her days trying to walk across the bottom of the Atlantic."

"Help!" the man behind Siobhan said as Brody approached him in the water. "I say. You wouldn't happen to have seen a lifeboat going by, would you? My wife is in number five. Her name is Amiee Achilli."

Siobhan turned around and cackled at the man. "You think if we'd seen a lifeboat we'd still be soaking out here in this frozen stew with you?"

"I– I meant no harm by asking," the man said. "I just hoped to see her and my little girl again."

"Don't you worry yourself, mate," Brody said as he came up next to the slim, bald-headed man. "I'm sure you'll meet each other again soon enough, whether in this life or the next."

The man's voice trembled as he shivered from the cold. "That's all well and good, but I'm afraid I'm not quite ready to give up on this life quite yet. Even if I can't get into that lifeboat, I'd like to know that they're going to make it – that they'll be all right."

"There are no guarantees in life." Trevor, who had dived under the sea's black surface, emerged from the water behind the man. "Who can do more than hope for the best to happen?"

"Right," said Fergus. "We've already lost one of our own tonight. I'd thought her invulnerable."

"You mean the ship?" the man said, turning back to where the *Titanic* had disappeared beneath the waves. "I think we were all guilty of that to some extent. It's hard to believe she's gone, isn't it? And that she took so many souls with her."

"What's your name, my friend?" Brody asked.

"Justin," the man said with a faint smile. "Justin Achilli of Atlanta at your service. I'd offer to shake your hand, but I'm not sure I can feel mine any longer."

"Fair enough," Fergus said. "I've had that same problem for years."

The others laughed at this, all but Fergus, who only scowled at them.

"Is there anything around here I could cling to?" Justin asked. "I'd hoped that the four of you might have discovered something stable and laid claim to it."

One by one, the others shook their heads at him. "We just came out here for a swim on this beautiful Sunday night." Brody smiled, but took care not to show his teeth. His fangs had extended, but he didn't want Justin to see them and spoil all the fun.

How often, after all, did any of them get to play with their food like this before feasting? If they wished to feed back in the States, they always had to strike fast and take great pains to make it look like an accident. The failure to do that properly was one of the reasons that Dushko had herded them all on to the *Carpathia*, after all.

Brody hadn't seen the harm in it. Who cared if people knew who he was or what he was? He'd been a killer before he'd died, and he was a killer now. He could handle the heat from such revelations. All you had to do was pick up and leave.

Not all of them had done so well though. Siobhan, for instance, had been discovered feeding on a child and had to kill off an entire family once they started screaming about it. Brody snickered to himself as he thought about it. That was the first time he'd ever actually heard someone scream "Bloody murder!"

But once it had happened, Siobhan had refused to leave her home behind. "I've been here since before I died," she said, "and nothing's ever going to make me leave."

She'd been wrong about that, of course. When the police started poking around, even Siobhan had realized that it would only be a matter of time before she was found out. She'd killed the first patrolman to become suspicious of her, but that had only brought more attention to the murders.

The cops didn't always care if a family of immigrants turned up dead, after all, but when it was one of their own they went out of their way to figure out what happened and put a stop to it. A certain sense of self-preservation motivated them. A killer who was mad enough to murder a policeman might be mad enough to do it again.

"Very funny," Justin said to Brody. "I'm glad you're doing well enough here to be able to find the humor in this horrible tragedy. Did you have no one on board that ship that you cared about, sir? Did you think it such a pleasure to be dumped into the freezing drink that you couldn't be bothered to find safe passage for your young lady there?"

"Now," Trevor said, coming closer to the man. "There's no need to be nasty about it."

"It's a nasty situation," Justin said. "We're all going to die nasty deaths. Us lot here, we're all going to freeze to death, but all things considered we might be better off than the women and children shoved into those lifeboats. How long do you think they'll be able to make it out there without food and water."

"Perhaps they'll be forced to turn to cannibalism." Fergus chortled at the thought.

"That's exactly what I'm talking about," Justin said. "At least we'll be spared the horrors of that prospect. It's one hell of a day when you have to count freezing to death or drowning among your blessings."

"That it is, friend," Brody said, moving straight toward the man now. "That it is. But perhaps we can help you with that problem."

Justin barked a short, bitter laugh. "How? Do you happen to have a submarine under there that you're standing on."

"You misunderstand me," Brody said. "I can't offer you salvation."

"Of course not," Justin said. "That is in no man's power."

"No, you're right." Brody reached for Justin and held his face between his ice-cold hands. Despite having been in the frigid water for so many minutes, the man's skin still burned with life, and Brody could feel that fading heat leeching into him through his long-dead skin.

Justin's eyes grew wide as a sharp terror sliced through him. He brought his hands up to try to pry Brody's fingers from his head, but he found them to be as strong and unforgiving as steel bands. "No," he said softly, his voice trembling from far more than the cold.

"But," Brody stretched open his jaw, exposing his long, white predator's fangs, "I can allow you the blessing of an even quicker release."

# CHAPTER TWELVE

"The ship is gone!" Lucy shouted at the sailor in charge of their boat. "We have plenty of room aboard our boat! We must go back!"

Her fellow passengers murmured at her outburst, some of them agreeing with her and others clinging to their fears. With one exception, though, none of them proved willing to stand with her against the sailor that had been placed in charge of the boat. He'd refused whatsoever to return to the ship, even when Captain Smith himself had shouted an order through a blowhorn for the man to do so.

"Mr Hichens," Lucy said. "We only have twenty-four people on board, and this boat can hold three times that without issue. It is a crime against our fellow passengers and against humanity itself that we were put out to sea when so many were still aboard the *Titanic*, and you compound that error every minute that you refuse to return to the scene of that crime."

Hichens leaned back against the lifeboat's prow and glared down at Lucy. She had been complaining to him for over an hour, and the bald-headed sailor had ignored her pleas as if they were little more than the wailings of a small child. As the grand ship finally disappeared beneath the waves, frustration got the better of him, and he shouted back at the woman.

"How many times do I have to spell it out for you idiots?" he said. "If we return there, it's death for every last one of us!"

Lucy turned to look back at the other sailor in the boat, a Mr Fleet, who sat in the aft with his hand on the tiller. He hadn't said much all night. He just continued to nod his head in glum agreement with Hichens.

"But the ship is down now," Lucy said. "The so-called suction you warned us about hasn't formed a gigantic whirlpool there waiting to pull us to the bottom of the sea." She stabbed a finger toward where the *Titanic* had been until just moments ago. "There are people out there! They're swimming about in that freezing water while you insist we do nothing at all but sit back and listen to them die!"

Lucy wouldn't admit it to Hichens or any of the other passengers, but she knew exactly who she meant when she said "people." It tore at her heart to think that Abe and Quin might be out there somewhere, still alive and floundering about in the wake of the *Titanic*'s absence. She knew they might already be dead, that it was not just possible but even likely, but she hadn't yet been able to give up hope.

Lucy hadn't explored the depth of her feelings for her two friends. There had always seemed like there would be plenty of time. They were young and heading to America, and she was going off to college, far away from her parents and her home, so that she could learn about the wider world and how it worked. Despite pressures from her parents and her female friends, she hadn't time for things like romance or marriage.

She supposed that was the reason she'd accepted Abe's request to court her. She had already been spending plenty of time with him and Quin, and it put the endless badgering about her romantic plans to rest, at least for a while. She had hesitated at first, unsure if it was fair to lead Abe on in that

way, but he'd been so insistent and so sweet that she had decided to go through with it.

While she had allowed outside pressures to force her into
producing a suitor, she had sworn to herself that she would
not allow that to build into the kind of inertia that would
transform her into a young bride. She had no designs on Abe's
wealth or his title. The notion of someday becoming the next
Lady Godalming held no allure for her.

Even the idea of the nobility – that one person was inher-
ently superior to another by nature of his birth – rankled her.
That sort of notion was cut from the same cloth as the idea
that women were second class citizens, the kind who could
work and pay taxes and contribute to society in a myriad of
ways but were unable to vote. She'd become an outspoken
suffragette to fight against such injustices, and she had zero
desire to become part of a similar problem.

And then there was the way that Quin looked at her, with
the sort of burning intensity that the callow Abe had never
been able to muster. She had long wondered if he'd had feelings for her, but he'd never once given voice to such longings.
So she'd settled for Abe, who seemed content to give her as
much space and time as she required, which suited her well.

Now she'd let the boys put her on a lifeboat and send her
off to live without them while the two of them suffered a
noble death. It galled her that she'd permitted them to get
away with that, and now that the *Titanic* had slipped beneath
the waves, she felt a terrible guilt squeezing her heart. She already worried that it might never go away.

That fact had prodded her to protest Hichens's behavior, and
she had vowed to herself that she would not stop until either
he gave in or the point had been rendered moot. As far as she
could tell, they were still a long way off from that moment.
People still splashed about and screamed and bellowed and

called and begged for help out there in the darkness. There had to be not just scores of them but hundreds.

"There isn't enough room!" Hichens said. "Not for all of them. If we go anywhere near that mob, they'll pull us under. They'll swamp and sink us for sure."

"Then we go back and save the ones we can," Maggie Brown cut in. She had been arguing for Lucy's points the entire time, and that fact had given Lucy the resolve to carry on, even in the face of the fear-ridden apathy evinced by the rest of the boat's passengers.

"Right," said Lucy. "If we save even one more person, isn't that worth it? Don't you think he'll be grateful? That his family will be thrilled to see him delivered safely from this disaster?"

Lucy turned to the rest of the passengers, appealing to them. Perhaps if she could get enough support, they could override the cowardly Hichens. "Think of that," she said. "Every person we save is one less family left bereft."

"She's right," said Maggie. "We're almost all women here in this boat. Where are your men? Your husbands? Your boys? Are you going to just let them all die?"

"By the time we'd get to them, they'd already be dead," Hichens said. "The water's filled with nothing but stiffs, and there's nothing you can say or do to make me row through that God-damned graveyard out there!"

Lucy stood straight up in the boat now and glowered at the repulsive man. "If you're not going to help, then get the hell out of the way," she said. "We can pull those oars as well as anyone!"

"You touch those oars, and I'll toss you overboard with my bare hands!" Hichens said, the veins on his neck popping out as he bellowed his threat.

Maggie stood up next to Lucy now and put a hand on her shoulder. She scowled straight into Hichens's hateful eyes, and in a voice filled with quiet menace said, "I'd just like to see you try that."

Hichens tensed up, and Lucy braced herself for the man's attack. Would no one, she wondered, come to her aid?

There were two men on the boat besides the sailors: a yachtsman named Major Peuchen and an older Arabian gentleman, named Mr Leeni, who seemed to have sneaked on board. Would they stand by and watch Hichens murder two women? Would the other women scream in horror and cower from the man's actions as much as they had from his threats?

Lucy was about to find out.

Hichens stood halfway up and then sat back down again, curling up against the bow on his other side. "Fine," he said, shaking his head. "Do whatever the hell you like. It's a fool's errand. It's too damned late for any of them anyhow."

# CHAPTER THIRTEEN

"There's no room here," one of the bedraggled crewmen already on top of the overturned lifeboat said. "Go find your own bit of flotsam."

Quin glanced around and saw that there were precious few things to find this far out from where the *Titanic* had sunk. Most of the people must have been too exhausted after escaping the wreck to swim the distance required to reach the lifeboat, but Quin and Abe – who'd had a head start on most of them – had managed it. Now they'd found that their effort might have been made in vain.

"But there's plenty of space on top of there." Abe pointed to the other end of the boat, on which Quin could see a few open stretches of whitewashed wood. "Be a good chap and give us a hand up."

Exhausted men lay stretched out across the rest of the overturned vessel. Many of them wore the uniforms of the *Titanic*, while others were dressed in cheaper, unadorned clothes, the kind that indicated they'd either been working below decks or traveling in steerage. No matter their class, though, Quin hoped they were trying to catch their breath and weren't in fact already dead.

The man who'd accosted them shook his head and brandished an oar at both Abe and Quin. "I can't make any exceptions. Stay back. Don't force me to use this."

"No one's forcing you to do anything," Abe said, anger rising in his voice. "Least of all, trying to kill us. You swing that thing at me, and I'll make you eat it!"

"Forget it." Quin tugged at Abe's shoulder. "There's nothing we can do about it."

Quin tried to keep his voice resigned, but his mind had already started working on an alternate plan. He just needed Abe to play along with him for it to work.

"Are you insane?" Abe spun about in the water and slapped Quin's hand away. "There's nothing else out here. Either we get on top of this lifeboat, or we're done for. We can't make it back there," he said, pointing at the raucous thrashing about of the hundreds of people who'd gotten free from the wreck. "Even if we did, all the decent bits to grab on to are sure to be taken. We have to make our stand here!"

Quin had seen this same look in Abe's eyes before. The man's sense of honor and righteousness had been insulted, and he wasn't about to back down from that without a fight. In the past, Abe had called it his *noblesse oblige*. Quin recognized it as Abe being bullheaded.

When faced with an insurmountable wall, Quin backed down, reassessed the situation, and found a way around it. Abe, on the other hand, beat his forehead against it until either the wall or his skull cracked. This obstinacy had landed Abe in police custody on more than one occasion, but his father's money and influence had extricated him from those situations without any further ill effects. Once Abe explained to his father why he'd refused to back down, Lord Godalming always gave his son a proud slap on the back and then sent him back out into the world to sin in exactly the same way over and over again.

In the past, Quin had contented himself with watching Abe go through this noble pantomime of his, often to the point that he'd been willing to be arrested alongside him. In each case, Lord Godalming had extended his pull to helping Quin out of the resulting troubles too. Quin's parents, however, had not been nearly so understanding of their son's behavior.

This time, though, Quin knew that Abe's refusal to try another way might get them both killed, and he had to do something to stop it.

"You *will* let us on this boat!" Abe shouted.

"Or what?" the crewman said. "You'll report me to the captain?"

Abe launched himself toward the boat, and the crewman brought the oar down at him hard. Abe saw it coming and tried to catch it, but the flat of it smashed into his arm instead and drove him back.

"You unbelievable bastard!" Abe said.

"Bugger off!" The crewman raised the oar again, this time turning it so he could strike with the edge of the paddle instead.

One of the other crewmen atop the boat leaned over to his side. "What's this then, Amos?" the man said.

"Our little lordship here thinks he deserves a seat next to us." Amos held the oar in front of him, never taking his eyes off Abe.

"Sorry, gents," the second man said. True regret tinged his voice. "We're full up here. Off with you then, and best of luck to you."

"Luck?" Abe growled and splashed armfuls of freezing water at the men. "We need help, not luck!"

Amos drew back the oar to attack Abe once more.

"Forget it," Quin said, grabbing Abe by the arm. He pulled his friend back, out of range of Amos's length of polished wood.

"Forget it?" Abe threw up his arms as he struggled to get free. "You can't be serious."

"Abe." Quin pitched his voice low and serious, but soft enough that he hoped the men on the boat couldn't hear. "I have a plan."

Abe snarled. Quin couldn't tell at who, but he held his friend's arm fast, even when Abe tried to pull away.

"Trust me," Quin said. "You have to trust me."

Abe hesitated. Quin could tell he wanted nothing more than to leap straight out of the water and thrash the men on top of the lifeboat within inches of their lives – and then knock them another yard past that. Abe glared at him with naked hatred for getting between himself and the objects of his fury, but Quin refused to flinch or turn away.

"Fine." Abe shrugged out of Quin's grasp. He stared up at the boat with sullen, heavy-lidded eyes, but he spoke to Quin. "Let's try it your way – for once."

Quin swam away from the boat, back in the direction of the mass of people struggling to survive in the churning froth of water where the *Titanic* had gone down. Abe followed after him, but as he went, he called back to the boat. "I hope you realize I'll be forced to write a sternly worded letter to the president of the White Star line!"

No one – not even Abe – laughed.

Once they were twenty yards away, Quin hauled up short and waited for Abe to catch up with him. "All right," Abe said. "Spotlight's on you, my friend. What's your plan?"

Quin pointed back at the boat. "There's space on the other side, and no one there guarding it. We just need to get there."

"And how do you propose we do that?" Abe said. "They're watching us. Hell, they're watching all around. There's no way to get around them."

"True," Quin said, jerking his head toward the boat. "But we can still get under them."

Abe nodded as he considered the plan. "Under normal

circumstances, it might work, but – well, I don't know about you, but I'm knackered. I might be able to make it to the other side of the boat, but I'll come up gasping so hard, they'll be on us in an instant."

"Right," Quin said. "But we don't have to make it all the way to the other side of the boat. We can stop for a break along the way."

"You happen to have a diving bell and an airline down there? You've been holding out on me."

"Not necessary," Quin said. "What do you think is holding up that boat those men are guarding so well?"

An impressed grin split Abe's face wide. Quin basked in it for a moment, knowing full well how hard it was to get such a response from his sometimes jaded friend. He tried to avoid wondering if it might be the last time he ever saw it again.

"Exactly," Abe said. "So, we dive down and swim for the underside of the boat. Then we wait there in the air pocket for a moment and gather our strength."

"From there, it should be simple enough to slip around to the other side of the boat and from there onto the dry side of it."

"Here's hoping." Abe grabbed him around the back of the neck. "You ready?"

"I don't think it's going to get any easier if we wait," Quin said. As he did, he noticed that the screams and cries for help from the people drowning behind them had already started to fade.

# CHAPTER FOURTEEN

Brody smiled to himself as he swam through the icy waters, unaffected by their temperatures in the slightest. Although he no longer required the oxygen, he had enough air in his lungs to lend his body the perfect level of buoyancy. It kept him just beneath the ocean's surface without causing him to sink like a stone to the abyssal depths below.

The waters around where the *Titanic* sank had stabilized now, and he no longer feared that he or any of the others would be sucked down after the ship as had happened with Brigid. The sea still foamed from the thrashing limbs of those who'd survived the sinking of the great ship – at least for now. Those poor souls beat at the waters incessantly, struggling to keep themselves afloat in waters so cold that Brody had no doubt every one of them would freeze before help from the *Carpathia* or any other ship might be able to arrive.

That only gave Brody and his compatriots a short window of time in which they could grab themselves a fresh, hot meal though. He'd told the rest of them to leave the lifeboats alone, which only left the people who'd fallen into the drink available to them for their repast. They'd fed on a number of these people, and it had been as simple as crossing the street.

All they'd had to do was yank someone underwater before they could send up a cry for help. And even if someone did start to scream for aid, what difference would it make? In the heart of this incredible disaster, that just made for one more voice added to the hellish choir.

The four of them had gorged themselves on blood, blood, and more blood, each bit of it tainted with the sweet tang of adrenaline shot through the victims' systems by the many horrors visited upon them that night. They would each have been covered with it, but for the fact that the ocean diluted whatever they didn't manage to consume.

Brody had rarely felt so vibrant, so young, not since he'd died in that back alley in Dublin so many years ago. The flood of fresh blood in his belly sang through him, causing him to tingle from his head to his toes. Although it still passed for a pale excuse for the sensations of the living, it sent thrill after thrill through him as he dispatched one victim after another.

At one point in the feast, Brody had wound up floating on his back in the middle of the chaos, content as a swimmer soaking up the rays near a sunny beach. He'd just laid there for many long minutes, digesting the blood in his belly and enjoying the terror reigning around him. He only stopped when a woman swam up to him and grabbed onto him, thinking him to be something she could use to help her stay afloat.

She'd been disappointed – and delicious.

Later, Brody met up with Siobhan, whose skin glowed with stolen life. "Now that we're fat and happy," she said to him, "what do you say about having some fun?"

"I dare you to tell me of a time at which you've had more fun." She just giggled at him and swam away, daring him to try to keep up with her.

He managed to do that when she hauled up short only a few yards away from a capsized lifeboat. A group of men clustered on top of the overturned craft, some of them half dead, others all the way there.

Siobhan pointed to them. "You said to keep away from the people in the lifeboats," she said. "Does that one qualify?"

Brody rubbed his chin. "Well, it is a lifeboat," he said, "no matter what condition it might be in. I believe that prudence would tell us to leave it alone."

"Prudence?" Siobhan laughed. "Is that your pet name for Dushko these days?"

"He is *not* my master." Brody spoke without a trace of amusement in his voice. "If he were, do you think we'd be out here right now, doing this?"

"But you still follow his orders?"

"His suggestions don't lack all merit, do they?" Brody said. "Believe what you like, not everything the man believes is as ridiculous as he is."

Siobhan snickered. "Those people are as good as dead anyhow, right? Hell, some of them already are, from the look of them. They won't last the night, none of them."

Brody cracked a smile, then winked at the lass. "Fair enough," he said, "but let's not be so crass about it. In fact, let's make a game of it."

"There's my sport." Siobhan reached out and caressed Brody's cheek. Her skin burned hot from the fresh blood coursing through it, and the sensation sent a thrill through his entire body. She smiled at him, baring her beautiful fangs.

Brody motioned for Siobhan to follow him, then grabbed a breath for buoyancy and slipped back under the water's surface. Moving deep enough that he was concealed from view, he made for the boat with long, lazy strokes. He had no reason to hurry. His belly was full, and their dessert wouldn't be going anywhere soon.

And they had hours until the dawn.

Brody glanced back to see Siobhan close behind him. She gave him a little wave, and he turned back to the project at hand. He came up under the boat and spotted two pairs of legs dangling underneath it.

These legs still moved with vigor, and Brody considered taking each of the men attached to them down one at a time. No one would miss them, he knew. But no one would hear them scream either, and where was the fun in that?

Brody had taken enough of the easy prey. He craved something with a bit more challenge to it – something that would ratchet up the survivors' terror to an even higher level. He pointed at Siobhan and motioned for her to stay over on the near side of the overturned lifeboat, still deep enough to be out of sight of the men above. She nodded her understanding to him.

From there, Brody moved around the boat and came up toward the surface on the other side. He gave himself a bit of room to move and build up some speed, then swam toward the boat's gunwale as hard as he could. He struck the edge of the boat and bumped it hard, right along the edge farthest from where the *Titanic* had disappeared.

Shouts of dismay came from above, and then Brody received the reward he'd expected for his actions, or at least hoped for: a heavy splash. One of the men who'd been staring back at the *Titanic* and waving an oar at anyone foolhardy enough to approach had fallen into the drink.

Brody dove deep then, avoiding the men hiding under the boat for whatever odd reason they might have had. By the time he came up on the other side, Siobhan already had a hold of the man's leg. She had torn off the leg of his pants, and as Brody watched she drove her fangs deep into his calf.

As Brody had hoped, Siobhan had allowed the man's head to remain just above the water. When she bit into him, he screamed in agony and terror, and the men still on top of the overturned lifeboat answered him with their own cries of dismay.

Siobhan didn't drink deep from her victim's leg. Instead, she tore his flesh away with a wrench of her powerful jaws. He screamed again, and blood poured from the gaping wound she'd left behind, clouding the water around them with fresh, hot blood.

The precious fluid emerged from the man like a black cloud illuminated by what faint, silvery starlight could penetrate this deep into the water. Like a squid's ink, it billowed out fast and served to conceal the actions of those hiding inside it. Brody and Siobhan, though, had no plans to flee. Not yet.

Brody yanked on the man's leg and pulled him under the water. The man's screams turned to horrified gurgles as he tried to draw another breath to voice his protest and sucked in water rather than air. Brody gave Siobhan a gentle push away then, and they both released the man.

Despite his ugly wound and the suffocating water in his lungs, the man had a lot of fight in him yet. He kicked his way back to the surface and let out a horrible bellow sure to shake the soul of anyone who heard it. "Help me!" he shouted. "Shark! Shark!"

Brody's little game had gone as well as he could have hoped, but he wasn't done with the man yet. He reached up and grabbed the man by his belt. He gave him just an instant to snatch a final breath and then pulled his victim under.

The man came back down into the water clouded with his own still-gushing blood, and Brody let him see his face. The man's eyes bulged in uncomprehending shock. He'd expected to find a shark chewing him to pieces, after all, and here he'd found a youthful Irishman instead.

Brody wondered if the man might think he was there to

save him. To sink that hope deeper than the *Titanic* itself, he opened his mouth and bared his long, sharp fangs.

The man struggled as hard as he could, but he could not break Brody's grip on his belt. He thrust out his fists, trying to punch Brody's face, but the water between the two rendered his blows useless. Brody allowed himself a short laugh as he held the desperate man there and waited for him to die.

Siobhan wasn't willing to be so patient though. She came up behind the man and wrapped her arms around him like a long-lost love. Then she sank her fangs straight into his naked throat.

Brody allowed Siobhan to enjoy herself as she drank her fill from the man's severed arteries. When she was done – which did not take long, as she'd already gorged herself on several others – she let the man go and gave him a gentle push toward Brody.

Brody got under the man's belly and gave him a shove toward the surface. He came up out of the water just enough to let loose a wet and horrible death rattle. Brody held him there long enough for the men atop the lifeboat to see the ruin that Siobhan had made of his neck.

Then he yanked him back under the water again.

# CHAPTER FIFTEEN

Quin dove as deep as he could and swam straight for the collapsible lifeboat. He could still see the starlight filtering through the water overhead, and the lifeboat floated up there on the surface like a black cloud blotting out part of the sky. As cold as he was, Quin found it harder to hold his breath as long as he would have liked, and he struggled to reach the lifeboat before he ran out of oxygen.

When he emerged underneath the boat, gasping for air, the first thing that popped into his head was that as hard as getting under the boat had been, it had been like strolling along the Promenade Deck when compared with being dumped into the sea from the Boat Deck. Abe broke the surface next to him a moment later. It was too dark under the boat for either of them to see each other, but he recognized his friend's voice when he spoke.

"I don't know how much more of this... I can take."

Quin shushed him and whispered. "If they figure out we're down here, they'll be looking for us when we come up."

"All right," Abe said, his voice much softer. "Just let me catch my breath."

They remained there for several minutes in the pitch dark,

the icy water slapping against them. Quin reached up and grabbed onto the overturned seats above his head and hung there, grateful to not have to tread water any longer. He heard Abe do the same.

"Could you hear her?" Abe said after a while.

"Hear who?" Quin's first thought was of Lucy, but he realized that Abe couldn't have possibly meant her.

"*Titanic*. I couldn't tell for sure. I thought I might have heard her still going down."

"Sound travels funny underwater. What did you hear?"

"Shouts. Screams."

Quin knew the sounds. He'd heard them too. They'd not been from the boat but from the people it had left behind, he felt sure. He couldn't bear to mention it.

"Do you think she's hit the bottom yet?"

Quin shrugged, then realized that Abe couldn't see him. "I doubt it. It's a long way down to the bottom of the ocean, isn't it?"

"Let's hope we don't have to find out."

Something bumped into the side of the boat just then, hard. It startled Quin enough that one of his hands lost its grip.

"What the bloody hell was that?" Abe said.

"No idea."

Quin heard movement on the boat above him, and he grew more frightened. Until now, everyone atop the overturned boat had remained still, not making a sound. He'd assumed they were watching the waters before them, making sure that no one else tried to join them in the relative safety of their rare, dry perch. Now, though, they scrambled about the wooden surface, shuffling back and forth like dancers on an open deck.

"We need to get up there," Abe said.

"Let it play out," said Quin.

"Something's happening up there. We can't just wait for it to pass us by!"

Quin sighed. Of course they couldn't. "Just wait a moment," he said. "Just until we can make sure we won't come up right in front of them."

"We can't just hang here forever."

Quin shushed him once again, and Abe shut his mouth. "Follow me."

Quin hauled himself hand over hand along the bottom of the boat until he reached the point at which he estimated himself to be as far away as possible from the crewmen who had kept them from the boat. He listened hard, and he heard shouts from above, and then a huge splash coming from somewhere on the other side of the boat.

"Now," Quin said.

Without another word, he slipped under the water again and began hauling himself down and then back up around the lifeboat's collapsible canvas edges, which had never been deployed before the ship wound up in the water. The moment his head entered the water, he heard screaming once more. He'd braced himself for it, hoping it might have diminished a bit while he and Abe had been waiting under the boat.

Instead, the scream proved to be much louder. The best Quin could guess, the sound came from just about where he'd heard the heavy splash a moment ago. He did his best to ignore it and tried instead to take it as a blessing that something had happened that he could be sure would distract the people on top of the boat.

As his head broke the water on the far side of the boat, Quin heard shouting even louder than screaming, and this time from many voices raised at once. One word they kept saying rang out over the rest: "Shark!"

The word triggered something primal in the back of Quin's

brain. He scrambled up on top of the boat as fast as he could, not giving a damn if anyone heard or saw him. He found Abe there at his side, clambering up right next to him.

As they went, Quin pulled on the legs of a man lying on top of the boat. The man slid off and into the icy waters below with not a word of protest. Quin didn't know for sure if the man was dead, but he assuaged his conscience with the knowledge that if the man hadn't yet stopped breathing he would no doubt have done so soon, with or without Quin's accidental help.

"Hey!" a man standing nearby said as he spun around. He was a hard-faced, middle-aged man with a severe, wide mustache from which hung frost that was mutating into icicles. He wore a long Norfolk jacket, which marked him as a passenger rather than one of the crew. "Where did you two come from?"

Abe sprang to his feet and helped Quin to his. "We're not going back into that water," Abe said. "You can't make us."

"Fair enough, dear boy," he said, sticking out his hand. "Colonel Gracie. Call me Archie."

Quin shook hands with the man, wary for any tricks, and gave him his name. Once Quin had finished the ritual with Archie without being thrown into the water, Abe followed suit.

"It's one hell of a spot to find ourselves in, men," Archie said. "The world's largest ship sunk from underneath us, my pal Clinch gone missing, and now sharks circling around us. I don't mind telling you I've had better days."

"I think we can all report the same without fear of contradiction, sir," Abe said.

# CHAPTER SIXTEEN

Dushko stood on the edge of the iceberg and peered out at the ocean around him through his telescope. He had not yet found anything he'd come searching for. Not Brody nor any of his compatriots. Not even the *Titanic*.

Off to the west, hundreds of frozen corpses bobbed up and down in the icy waters, but not a single person stirred among them. A couple of lifeboats partially filled with survivors roamed about that floating graveyard, hunting for those in need of aid, but even from here Dushko could tell that they were wasting their time. Anyone who had spent the last couple hours in the water would be beyond their assistance.

That didn't stop them from trying, though, and Dushko had to at least admire their persistence. The living often fought on long past the point they had any hope of success. That was what made them so damned dangerous.

As Dushko surveyed the flotsam from the wreck, a lone bat flapped overhead, then spiraled down to join him on the iceberg. Dushko had no doubt that anyone who might see the bat would wonder how such a creature could find itself here, so far away from wherever any of its kind might call home. He knew better, of course.

A moment later, Trevor spoke from behind him. "You missed one hell of a party, boss."

Dushko collapsed his telescope and put it in his pocket. He did not bother to turn around to see Trevor as he spoke. "Did you enjoy yourself?"

Trevor snickered. "You know I did. Has it been so long since you've indulged yourself? Have you forgotten what it's like?"

Dushko ran his tongue across his fangs, feeling their sharp tips. "Have you forgotten why we had to leave the United States of America?"

"Come on now," Trevor said. "Are you here to give me a spanking and send me back to my coffin? I thought we were all grown-ups here."

Dushko gritted his teeth. "Adults do not run off on some insane hunt and put the rest of us all at risk."

"This wasn't a risk," Trevor said. "It was a massacre. These people never stood a chance in the first place. It seemed like a shame to let all that food go to waste. Didn't your momma teach you better than that?"

Dushko smirked. "My mother has been dead for a very long time," he said. "And I do not think it is me who is in need of a lesson."

Before Trevor could respond, Dushko turned on him and backhanded him so hard that the blow embedded the man into the wall of snow and ice behind him. Trevor tried to stand up, to shove himself out of the hole he found himself in, but Dushko was on him before he could manage it.

"Do you realize what you have done?" Dushko loomed over the injured vampire. "Do you even understand why it is we had to leave the States behind and escape back to my homeland?"

"Because you got scared," Trevor said. "Because you've been dead so long you've forgotten what it's like to live."

"Very prettily worded," Dushko said. "It still does not change the fact that we would certainly have been discovered there if we had remained much longer. As a group, we'd started taking too many chances. We had grown too bold."

"And so what if we did?" Trevor trembled, and not from the cold. "What's so wrong with that? Should we worry that the sheep might know that wolves live among them?"

Dushko scowled down at Trevor. "You underestimate your prey. These are not sheep. They have weapons, and they have science, and they grow stronger with them every day. And we are not so many that they might not be able to wipe us out once they learned of our presence."

Trevor extracted himself from the iceberg and staggered to his feet. "Let them try," he said. "They're cowards, every one of them. A few public feedings, and they'll be too frightened to do anything more than hide in their burrows and make messes in their pants."

"So now," Dushko said, "are they rabbits or sheep? Or do you have some other metaphors you would like to stir into that terrible stew of an argument you are concocting?"

"The hell with you," Trevor said. "You think because you're older than the rest of us – because you got yourself some schooling – you're better than anyone among us. Just remember this. We're not sheep either! Or rabbits, or metaphors or whatever the hell you're nattering on about."

"No," Duskho said. "No you are not such gentle or harmless things. You are like mad dogs. Vile, rabid things that wreak havoc and put the rest of us in danger."

"So you say." Trevor sniffed at Dushko. "Brody begs to differ with you. He says we're wild animals, and you're trying to keep us tamed and chained. There's only one solution for a wild animal that makes sense. You got to break free."

Dushko grimaced. "I can see why you feel that way. The restrictions of modern life chafe at me too. But it is better to live within your borders than to die outside of them. Those that refuse to do so are a danger to us all. That is why we had to leave New York for the old country."

"And if we refuse to go?"

Dushko looked Trevor up and down. The man had gorged himself on blood, and he looked younger and healthier than Dushko had ever seen him. With that rejuvenation, though, had come a willfulness the man had never displayed before either, and Dushko knew that he had to root this out – for the good of them all.

"Then I will do for you as I would for any other rabid monster that threatens the pack." Dushko held his hand before him as if he could use it to weigh the responsibilities burdening him at that moment. "I will put you down."

Trevor tried to meet Dushko's steely stare but failed. He turned to flee, transforming into a bat as he went.

Dushko charged at him, morphing into a magnificent wolf in mid-leap. He reached out lightning fast, and his jaws closed on Trevor's wings.

Trevor screamed in pain and fear as he took the form of a man once again. Dushko refused to let go of him, and his teeth tore raw red furrows across Trevor's arms and chests as they reformed between his jaws.

Trevor started to say something then, possibly to surrender or to simply beg for mercy, but Dushko didn't let him finish. Instead, he let go of Trevor's arm and tore out his throat.

Trevor's hands flew to his neck as he tried to staunch the jets of stolen blood from leaving his body. Meanwhile, Dushko ripped open Trevor's chest with his claws and stuffed his snout into the hole he'd created there. He rooted around inside the chest cavity until he found what he was searching for: Trevor's heart.

The dead muscle beat once more, pounding the blood of the man's victims through his veins. With a single bite, Dushko put an end to that, severing it from its veins and arteries. A wrench of his neck yanked the organ from its home, and an instant later, Dushko had devoured it whole.

Dushko wanted to return to his human form then. There were others he needed to deal with: Fergus, Siobhan, Brigid, and most importantly Brody.

But for all Dushko's talk of restraint, the taste of all that blood running down his gullet proved too much for him to resist. He wouldn't be done with Trevor for a long time.

# CHAPTER SEVENTEEN

"They're dead." Lucy leaned over the edge of the boat again and pulled another person from the water by the edge of his lifejacket. "They're all dead."

"Of course, they're dead, you idiot," Hichens said. "How long do you think anyone could survive in that?"

He'd not left his post on the lifeboat's bow the entire night. He'd just sat there and hurled one insult after another at Lucy and Maggie and any of the others determined to help them keep searching for any more possible survivors until they'd exhausted every avenue of hope.

"Just shut your mouth," Lucy said angrily. "Leave us to our work in peace, you lazy pig."

"Forget him, sweetie," Maggie said. "He's just like my kids back home: not worth the breath it takes to scold him." She'd given up on arguing with Hichens any longer or even responding to him directly. Instead, she'd gone to take another turn at the oars.

Lucy took heart in the fact that their efforts hadn't been entirely in vain. She and the other passengers who'd finally sided with her and Maggie had pulled three people out of the drink: two women and a child, all of whom had failed to escape steerage until just before the ship went down. The child had died after they'd brought him aboard, and one of the women already on the lifeboat had spent the entire time cradling his body and weeping over him since, even though Lucy was sure that he was not her own.

As the lifeboat nosed its way through the terrible flotsam of human bodies littering the sea, Lucy poked at them with the tip of a boathook someone had found stowed under the seats. It had been a long time since she'd seen any of them stir, and she'd started to believe that perhaps the vile Hichens was right. Perhaps there really wasn't anyone else they could rescue.

Despite that, Lucy kept at her grisly work. To herself alone she admitted that she wasn't only looking for the living but for the faces of her friends among the dead. She knew the chances were that both Quin and Abe had gone down with the ship or perished in the waters afterward, either having drowned or frozen to death. At this point, she'd all but given up hope of finding them alive, but the thought that she might never know their ultimate fate gnawed at her.

How could she report their deaths to their parents? She knew how heavy her heart already weighed with grief, and she suspected that the news would simply crush their families flat. If she could at least tell them that she'd seen the boys one last time, or if she could even make sure their bodies were recovered and given a proper burial, then maybe that could do some slight good in the face of this devastation.

Lucy rested her tired arms for a moment and surveyed the waters around her as she let the long pole in her hands drift alongside the boat. The first hints of dawn were breaking behind her, and the light showed her just how many people the disappearance of the *Titanic* had left in its wake. Hundreds if not thousands of corpses floated on the surface of the sea. Some of them lay there flat, only their backs cresting out of the water. For others, their lifejackets held them upright, their heads slouched over into their chests, making them appear to be sleeping. The lack of any breath wafting from their mouths in the chilly pre-dawn betrayed their true state.

"So many dead," Lucy said to herself. She wanted to weep. "So many gone."

It was then she felt the shaft of the boathook move in her hands.

Lucy looked down into the water and let out a little scream. A man floated there, icicles already formed in his unkempt hair, his skin as pale as the moon. He bore a small gash in the skin over his right eye, but it seemed to have stopped bleeding already. His eyes burned with life, red around the edges, and he had his hand on the far end of her boathook.

"Please, miss." The man's voice was no more than a soft croak. Despite him being soaked to the bone, it sounded hard and dry. "Help."

"We have another!" Lucy reached down with the hook and snared the collar of the man's coat with it, then used it to haul him closer to the boat.

Maggie came to her side in an instant. It would have been easier if one of the sailors would have lent her a hand too, but Hichens still refused to have anything to do with the rescue efforts. The other man had kept his hand on the tiller, helping at least that much, and he was all the way at the far end of the thirty-five foot boat anyhow.

"Grab him by the shoulders, sweetie, then just fall back into the boat," Maggie said. "Just like last time."

While the women might not have been strong enough to haul a waterlogged man up into the boat on their own, Maggie had taught Lucy that they could use the entirety of their weight to manage it. All they had to do was get a good grip on the man first.

Once Lucy had the man close enough, Maggie reached down to grab him by the arms and wedge her hands under one of his shoulders. Lucy put down the boathook and then did the same on his other side. Behind them, another woman grabbed them both by their collars and prepared to add her weight to their cause.

"All together now, ladies!" Maggie said. "One. Two. Three!"

On the last number, they all threw themselves backward. The combined weight and strength of the three women, along with whatever feeble effort the object of their endeavours was able to add, raised the man up and out of the water and dragged him over the gunwale and into the boat.

Hichens snarled at them as they performed this operation, just as he had every other time. "Careful!" he said as he leaned out of the boat in the opposite direction, trying to provide some balance against the new passenger's weight. "You'll tip us all into the drink!"

The women ignored him. As the boat stabilized once more, they dragged the half-frozen fellow into the middle of the boat's floor and swaddled him with as many blankets as they could spare.

Lucy set to rubbing the man's exposed skin with her hands, trying to bring some life to it. It felt as cold as that of a dead fish, but she didn't let that stop her.

"How is he?" Maggie peered down at the man from over Lucy's shoulder. "It's a miracle he's alive. He is alive, isn't he?"

"He spoke to me," Lucy said, working his hands faster. "He grabbed the boathook."

Maggie put a hand on her shoulder. "Oh, sweetie," she said. "He doesn't look good."

Lucy ignored Maggie's fatalistic tone and kept working over the man with her fingers, rubbing his hands and his face until they started to show pink. She couldn't tell if that was from circulation returning to his skin or if she'd just managed to somehow bruise him, but she chose to count it as an improvement either way.

After a moment, Maggie sat down next to Lucy. "You get back to working the prow and looking for others," she said. "I'll take care of our friend here."

Lucy's hands stopped working, and she nodded at Maggie. She didn't want to give up on this man, but she knew Quin and Abe might still be out there. If this man had survived for so long in the freezing water, then perhaps she still had a chance of rescuing them too.

Lucy got up to leave, but the man's hand reached out and grabbed her by the wrist. "No," he said, his voice as thin as smoke. "Don't go."

"There might still be others out there," she said. Hichens snorted behind her in disgust, but she paid him no heed. "I have to keep trying."

"Dear God!" The sailor at the tiller stood up and pointed off toward the east. "A light. It's a ship! We're saved!"

Lucy looked down at the man who still had his hand clamped around her wrist. He was smiling.

"You're going to make it," she said to him. "Just hold on."

"I will if you tell me your name, angel," he said.

"Lucy Seward." She stuck out her hand, and he shook it, his grip strong and tight.

"Brody Murtagh," he said with a soft Irish lilt. "Very pleased to be making your acquaintance, Miss Lucy Seward."

# CHAPTER EIGHTEEN

It took them hours to get out of the ocean and onto the ship that had come to their rescue, the *Carpathia*. It hove within sight fast enough, but then it had to navigate gingerly through a field of icebergs to make sure that it didn't meet the same fate as the vaunted *Titanic*. Even then, a ship of that size couldn't maneuver about all that well, so the lifeboats had to row over to it.

It seemed to take forever, but Lucy didn't mind it at all. She even took a turn at the oars herself to help keep fresh rowers in every seat. In between rounds at that duty, she checked in on the few people they'd been able to save. The two women were chilled to the bone, but they'd become more communicative by the moment.

The man – Brody – on the other hand, had grown even more quiet. He sat there, huddled under his dripping blanket, and watched the *Carpathia* grow closer, but he didn't say a word for the longest time. When he did, it was only to inquire after the time.

"It's nearly half after five now," Lucy said. Although she'd left every bit of her luggage on the ship, her watch had survived all the excitement intact.

Brody glanced off toward the false dawn in the east. "Do you think they'll let us on board before the sun comes up?"

"They certainly do seem to be taking their time," Lucy said, "but I don't think we'll be down here all that much longer."

"That's good," Brody said with a weak smile. "Very good. Thanks, angel."

Lifeboat number five had made it to the *Carpathia* first, and Lucy watched as they hauled the people in it up to the ship. They hadn't, as she had first suspected they might, tried to raise the entire lifeboat into the ship on its davits, people and all. Instead, they'd lowered a rope ladder to the boat and had people climbing up it.

Not everyone was able to use the ladder. Lucy watched one elderly woman get hauled up in a sling chair, and a few children were even brought up by ropes attached to mail sacks. While it seemed unorthodox, Lucy had to admit she would have felt safer riding up to the ship in a canvas bag rather than being forced to brave the fragile-looking ladder.

When it came their turn to leave their lifeboat behind, though, Lucy stood up and grabbed onto the rope ladder's wooden planks, already slippery from the fine spray whipped up as the winds increased with the coming dawn. Taking it one step at a time, she hauled herself up to the gangway door the crew there had opened for them, and when she got there, a pair of strong sailors pulled her over the threshold and onto the *Carpathia*'s main deck.

A pair of stewards dressed in Cunard Line uniforms approached her then, one with a dry blanket and the other with a mug of steaming hot tea. They took down her name and found her a place to sit in the first class dining room. A tall, well-dressed man came by to look her over.

"I'm Doctor David Griffiths," he said. "I just want to check you for frostbite and the like." He had her show him her fingers and, after offering some polite apologies, he helped remove her boots so he could check upon her toes. She passed his inspection without a single hitch.

"How do you feel?" he asked.

Lucy hesitated before she answered. "Numb."

"In your extremities?"

Lucy shook her head and tapped at her heart, suddenly overwhelmed.

The doctor sighed. "That's to be expected, I'm afraid. There's nothing I can give you for that. The best remedy is time. You just need to establish a little perspective, chronologically speaking."

"I don't think a hundred years would give me enough room for that," she said.

The doctor gave her an understanding chuckle, then moved on to the next patient.

A moment afterward, Maggie entered the dining room between her own pair of guides, and she sat down next to Lucy and patted her on the knee.

"That was one hell of a night," Maggie said, her voice soft and reverent.

Lucy stared down at the tea clutched between her hands and let the mug warm them. "I don't know what to do with myself," she said. "I can hardly believe that we survived. That it's over."

"Oh, darling," Maggie said. "It's only over for all those poor people who aren't going to make it onto this ship. For us, it's just getting started. When we get back home, there's going to be such a ruckus. Just you wait and see."

Lucy frowned. She understood why that might be. The unsinkable *Titanic*, the largest and greatest ship in the world, foundered on her maiden voyage? It would be too juicy a story for anyone to ignore. It would shock the world.

"And wait until the congressional hearings begin. You think it's bad watching your Members of Parliament squabble over things? You haven't seen anything until you've borne witness to the organized insanity of the US Government, sweetie."

Lucy shuddered, and not from the cold. "I don't care about any of that," she said. "They can… I just want to know what happened."

"To your friends?" Maggie gave Lucy a knowing look. "Those two strapping young men who brought you to the lifeboat?"

Lucy lowered her eyes and nodded. "Do you think there's any chance they're all right?"

"Well," Maggie said. "I'll be honest. I wouldn't lay a lot of money on it. Of course, before today I'd have given you long odds on anything horrible happening between England and New York City, so you obviously can't trust my judgment."

Lucy forced herself to laugh at that. Otherwise, she was sure she would break down and cry.

Maggie kept her company until another steward came back to find them and reported that he'd been able to assign them cabins. "Fortunately, we were heading back to Europe, and we don't normally have too many passengers going that way this time of year. Immigrants fill the ships coming over to the States, but not so many want to work their way back."

"You think you'll have enough room for us each to have our own cabin?" Maggie said. "If you need to match me up with a roommate, do me a favor and stick me with little Lucy here."

"I don't think that's going to be a worry, ma'am," the steward said, his face both grim and sympathetic.

Lucy frowned at that. "No," she said, "I suppose it won't."

Maggie patted her on the back of her hand. "Chin up, sweetie." She stood and helped Lucy to her feet. "Whatever happened to your chivalrous young heroes today, we don't have any control over any more. Maybe we never did. The best thing you can do is go take care of yourself now. You know that's what they'd want."

"You speak as if they're already dead."

"I couldn't say one way or the other about that, I'm afraid. All I know is those friends of yours put you on that boat – and they stayed off it themselves so that you and the rest of us on it could live. For that, I'll always be grateful, no matter what happened to them."

The steward showed Maggie to her cabin and then came back to escort Lucy to hers. As she left, she scanned the dining room, hoping to see some hint of either Quin or Abe in the crowd of people assembled there, but she had no such luck. She spotted a few people from the lifeboat, but Brody Murtagh and the two women they pulled out of the drink were nowhere to be seen. Lucy wondered what might have kept them, and then she realized that they might well be in the second or even third class areas of the *Carpathia*.

There hadn't been any lines marking out the classes on the lifeboat. The only thing that had mattered there was that you were human and needed help. Lucy missed that sort of honesty already.

She stood in the drab cabin assigned to her and stared out the porthole, watching the people on the last few lifeboats get collected onto the *Carpathia*. She couldn't tell who any of them were, and after a while she became so tired she gave up trying. She sat on the bed and stared at the cabin's closed door, consumed with terrible thoughts.

# CHAPTER NINETEEN

Lucy hadn't realized that she'd tipped over onto her pillow and gone to sleep. She awakened to a knock on the door, still in her clothes, lying atop the bedspread. The full light of day streamed in through the room's porthole.

The knock came again, and she tried to ignore it. She was so worn, so tired, so overwhelmed she thought she might never rise from the bed again.

"Miss Seward?" a voice said.

"What is it?" She sat up on the bed now, struggling to not be irritated with one of the fine people on this liner that had rescued her from the wreck.

"I'm sorry to trouble you, miss."

"No." Lucy rose and went to the door. "It's no trouble. You've been so kind to me."

She opened the door, and the steward who had escorted her to the room stood there, a look of contrition on his face. "My apologies, Miss Seward, but these two gentlemen insisted—"

Before the man could finish, Lucy shoved past him to find Abe standing in the hallway just beyond. She threw herself into his arms and held him as if he might somehow try to slip away. He kissed her on top of her head and wrapped his arms around her and held her just as tight.

"It's all right," Abe said. "We're safe now. We made it."

"We?" Lucy pushed back so she could look up into Abe's face. "Do you mean you and me, or–?" She stumbled over her words, her voice thick with emotion.

Abe held her by her shoulders and craned his neck down toward her. "What is it?" he said.

"Quin." Lucy wiped her eyes, removing tears she hadn't realized were there. "What happened to Quin?"

Abe grimaced, and Lucy felt her heart shrivel up and fall out of her chest. "What happened to him?" She couldn't force her voice above a whisper. "You were with him."

"Oh," Abe said, surprised, "he's fine. He made it to the ship with me." He shrugged to explain. "Well, not exactly fine. He picked up a bit of frostbite. Doctor Griffiths, I think it was, wanted to get a better look at him."

The tears flooded Lucy's eyes this time, blurring her sight. She broke down against Abe's chest, and he held her in his arms again, keeping her on her feet.

"He's going to live, Lucy," Abe said. "The doc just wants to make sure he keeps all his toes. Do you want me to take you to him?"

Lucy's throat had closed up, and she found she couldn't speak. She just nodded up at Abe, and he escorted her up through the decks to the first class dining room once again. The room was crowded and noisy with huddled and shivering survivors. They finally reached Quin sitting in a far corner of the room, wrapped in a thick blanket, his feet soaking in a tub of steaming water.

When Quin spotted Lucy, he shot to his feet and staggered toward her, leaving a trail of small puddles behind him. She dashed forward and grabbed him in her arms, lending him what strength she had so that he might not topple over on whatever ruin the freezing waters had made of his feet. He held her tight and kissed her on her face, his lips still cold against her flushed cheek.

Quin shuddered into her arms with a deep sigh. "Thought I might never see you again, Luce."

"Thank God," she said. "Thank God."

"God had nothing to do with it," Abe said from behind her. "You can chalk up our survival to our man Quincey here."

Lucy gazed up at Quin. "What happened?"

"Well," Quin said with a half smile, "it's a hell of a story."

"Mr Harker!" the doctor called to Quin from across the room. "If you'd care to be able to count to ten on your toes again, I suggest you get your feet back into that tub."

"Yes, sir!" Quin called back. He let Lucy and Abe help him back to the chair he'd been sitting on, and he slipped his feet back into the tub, wincing as they entered the hot water.

"Does it hurt?" Lucy asked.

"Only like I caught it in a bear trap. But it's really just the right foot, after all. I have a spare." Quin tried to reassure her with a smile, but she could see the pain in his eyes. She reached out to hold his hand, and he squeezed it with tender gratitude.

They told each other then what had happened to them since they'd separated. Lucy went first and finished fast. The boys' story was more complicated, and they went on at length, with Lucy gasping in sympathetic horror for them at several points in their tale. When they got to the part at which they'd made it onto the overturned lifeboat, she interrupted them.

"But what happened to Quin?" she said. She couldn't understand how it could have gotten so bad for him. If Abe had made it through the ordeal intact, how was Quin in danger of losing toes – and on just one foot?

"Go ahead and tell her." Abe gestured for Quin to take over the story. "You're the hero, after all."

Quin blushed. "I didn't do anything heroic. I just defended myself."

Lucy's eyes widened. "Against who?"

"More like what," Abe said.

Quin shrugged. "There was a shark. It knocked up against the boat, and one of the men on top of it tumbled into the water. That's how we got from under the boat to on top of it. Everyone up there was too distracted watching the man fall victim to the shark."

Lucy covered her mouth with her hand. She hadn't considered the possibility of sharks. She wondered if it was natural for them to swim in such cold water, but perhaps the presence of so many bodies swimming in the open sea had called them there.

"How horrible," she said.

"Certainly," said Abe, "but we weren't too proud to take advantage of it. We got up on that boat in a heartbeat or less."

"And after the shark had its fill, it went away?"

"Not exactly," said Quin. "We'd thought we'd escaped it, but the boat kept sinking lower and lower as the night wore on. And then the wind picked up as the dawn crept toward us, and that brought waves with it as well. They started lapping over the top of the boat."

Lucy gasped. She knew that Quin and Abe had survived, of course, but she felt the echo of the terror they'd endured.

"That wasn't the worst of it. Mr Lightoller, the *Titanic*'s second officer, was atop the boat with us, and he knew how to handle that trouble. He showed us how to move back and forth on the boat to adjust for the waves as they came. I can't tell you how long we spent going to and fro like that, each time worrying that this might be the wave that finally capsized us for good."

"How did you have room to do that?" Lucy looked at both Quin and Abe. "I thought you said the boat was almost too crowded for you to get on it."

"That had been true at the time," Quin said. "But some of the men there succumbed to the cold. They collapsed right there on the boat, and nothing we did could revive them. When the waves came, many of them slipped overboard before anyone had a chance to grab them, and they disappeared into the sea."

Abe rubbed the stubble on his chin. "Maybe that's what brought the shark back. Or maybe it was a different shark. I couldn't say for sure. We never saw it."

"Then how do you know it came back?" Lucy felt afraid to ask, but she had to know.

"It bumped the boat again, just when we were moving about it to avoid an incoming wave. It hit hard. Hard enough to knock me off the boat."

Lucy stared at him and then at Quin. "But you're fine, while Quin here's the one who's hurt."

Quin demurred. "It's only a touch of frostbite, the doctor says."

She narrowed her eyes at him. "The point stands, I think."

Abe gestured toward Quin. "He went in after me."

Quin busied himself with inspecting his thawing foot. Lucy squeezed his hand in gratitude and pride.

"You'd have done the same," Quin said. "I saw you go in, I went to help you back up."

"And that's when the shark attacked," said Abe. "It grabbed Quin by the foot and pulled him under."

Lucy stared down at Quin's foot. Other than a bit of paleness to the skin, it seemed unharmed.

"It's still there," Quin said. "The beast had a good grip on my sole, but I kicked out at him and pushed as hard as I could to get free. I got my wish when my foot slipped out of my boot."

"And you managed to scramble back onto the boat?"

Quin inclined his head toward Abe. "He was there to help me up."

"And the shark never came back?"

Abe shook his head. "Old Quin here must have kicked some sense into the beast. I'd say thank God for that, too, but we all thanked Quin instead."

"I just got lucky," Quin said. He squeezed Lucy's hand once more. "We all did. We're every one of us fortunate to be alive."

Lucy leaned over and kissed Quin on the cheek, which felt warmer now. "I'm just glad those troubles are finally over – at least for us."

# CHAPTER TWENTY

Quin slept most of the day. He awoke to find the sun slanting in through the porthole of the cramped but very welcome cabin the stewards had assigned to him and Abe, and for a moment he could pretend to himself that they were still aboard the *Titanic*. The *Carpathia* wasn't nearly as well appointed a ship, but if he kept his eyes on the ceiling and the porthole, he could almost manage to convince himself it was real.

"Almost seems like it could all have been nothing more than a nightmare, doesn't it?" Abe said.

Quin looked over to see his friend getting dressed in a suit with a distinctly American cut to it, nothing like what he'd been wearing the day before. "Where did you get the fresh clothes?" Quin lay under his sheets in nothing but his underwear, and he felt the lack of his own clothes sharply.

"Some of the passengers and crew pitched in their spares," Abe said. "Damn kind of them, don't you think?"

Although he'd paid it no notice at the time, Quin's clothes had been torn and ruined last night, as had Abe's. When the steward had taken their garments to dry them out, Quin had assumed he would have to wear them for the remainder of the voyage and be grateful for it. He'd never expected anything else.

"Very," said Quin. He slipped out of his bed and found another set of clean clothes waiting for him, hanging in the wardrobe. He took them out and held them up to his shoulders.

"They're even my size."

"The steward checked the labels in the clothes we gave him." Abe tapped his temple. "Sharp folks, these."

Quin glanced around and spotted a clock. It showed the time to be a quarter to five. "It's time for dinner already?"

"That's what happens when you sleep away the bulk of the day."

Quin started to object to the implication that he was lazy, but Abe put up a hand to stop him. "It was the longest night of our lives. You more than earned it. I'd have been happy to let you sleep all the way until tomorrow morning."

Quin began getting dressed. After having spent so long in icy rags, it felt wonderful to slip into clean and dry clothes. "Can I join you for dinner?"

Abe laughed at Quin's formality. "Could I stop you?"

"Not if Lucy's going to be there."

Abe arched an eyebrow at that. "Do you have plans for our young lady tonight?"

Quin faltered. He'd been about to talk to Abe about his feelings for Lucy back on the *Titanic*, but somehow he'd never gotten around to it. They'd been far too busy trying to stay alive instead.

"Abe," Quin said. "I tried to tell you this back on the Promenade Deck, but I…" His voice trailed off. How could he do this to his friend? To the fellow with whom he'd been through so much?

"It's all right, Quin." Abe spoke in a gentle voice. "I know you love Lucy."

Quin froze with one leg in his borrowed pants. "How?"

"Anyone who sees the way you look at her knows, my friend. There's no way to miss it."

Quin winced and then resumed dressing. "Do you think she knows?"

Abe shook his head. "She's probably the only one who doesn't, I'd think. She's as sharp a girl as I've ever met, but like most of us she has a blind spot when it comes to herself."

Quin regarded his friend. "I'd like to tell her. About how I feel, I mean."

"Of course you would."

"Will you object?"

Abe put his hands in his pockets. "Would it stop you if I did?"

"I don't think so. No."

Abe rocked on his heels for a moment, letting Quin stew. "Then what would be the point in me trying to stop it?" he finally said.

"I don't want to do it without your blessing."

"She's my girl, Quin. If you're going to confess your love to her, I can't give you my approval."

Quin's face fell. "I have to do this. I don't want to lose your friendship, Abe, but I–" He stopped and reset himself.

"When we were out there on that lifeboat, when that shark came after us, hell, throughout that whole night, we had so many times when I thought we might die. When I was sure of it. And do you know what went through my head every damn time?"

"Get me out of this bally water?"

Quin shook his head without a hint of a laugh. "I thought about Lucy every damn time. And I cursed myself for being such a coward about baring my heart to her."

He pointed out of the room's porthole. "While we were out there on that overturned lifeboat, I made myself a promise. I said that if I got through that – if I survived – then I'd find Lucy and let her know what's in my heart. I'd let her know and let her decide what to do about that."

Abe grimaced as he nodded at Quin. "I know. I understand why you have to do this. I just can't give my blessing for it. I love her too, Quin."

"All right. That's what I expected to hear."

"And that doesn't change your mind at all."

"Should it?"

Abe waited in silence as Quin finished getting dressed. Quin felt good about the conversation. He'd finally spoken about his love for Lucy out loud. To her boyfriend no less. He'd half-expected it to culminate in a fist fight.

"No matter what happens between Lucy and me, I don't want this to end our friendship," Quin said as he buttoned his borrowed jacket.

"It won't. I might not be able to give you my blessing over this, but can I offer you something else?" Abe stuck out his hand.

Quin stood tall and shook it. "What's that?"

"My best wishes. No matter what."

# CHAPTER TWENTY-ONE

When Quin and Abe reached the first class dining room, it had already been returned to its original purpose after having served as a makeshift hospital for most of the day. The place had not half the luxuriance of the *Titanic*'s dining room, but it was warm and dry, and – most importantly – not sitting on the bottom of the ocean. The service was enthusiastic, and the food came hot and in large helpings.

Lucy looked angelic in a borrowed dress that fit her like a tailored glove. The deep blue of it brought out the color in her eyes, and Quin had to think hard to find a time he remembered her appearing so lovely. This had the unfortunate effect of tying his tongue as he took the seat next to her while Abe took the one at her other side.

"I can't tell you how happy I am to be able to sit down to a meal with you two again." Lucy spoke with a sparkle in her eye as she reached out and patted both of the young men on the hands closest to her.

Abe grinned at this. "I don't think I'd be wrong to say that we both looked forward to this as much as you." He gave Quin a meaningful glance, but when Lucy turned toward him, the other man discovered that his lips didn't seem to want to work for him.

"You're not usually so silent, Quin." Lucy flashed a smile that dazzled him. "Don't tell me the doctor forgot to check your tongue for frostbite too."

Quin offered up a weak smile. "Doctor Griffiths has pronounced me in good health, all the way from my head down to my maltreated toes."

"Wonderful!" Lucy grinned, showing her perfect teeth.

"Yes," said Abe, "he'll be out there tripping around Manhattan in no time at all, and without a cane, no less." He turned to Quin. "Now that you've regained the use of your tongue, what plans do you have for it?"

Quin blushed. Having made the decision to confess his love to Lucy, he wanted nothing more than to do so and throw his heart at her mercy, but he hadn't planned to do so over dinner. "I'm sure I'll find something worthy of it," he said. "In the right place and at the right time."

Abe threw his hands wide. "But what better place than here? What better time than now? You're safe and sound and among friends once more. Why wait?"

Quin nodded. He seemed to have annoyed his friend more than Abe cared to admit straight out. Quin would have preferred to chat with Lucy in private rather than risk making a scene in front of the entire dining room, but if Abe wanted to press the issue, then Quin wasn't about to back down.

He turned to Lucy and took her hand in his. "Abe is a wise man."

"I think you mean 'wise guy'," Lucy said with a smile.

"Forgive me, lady and sirs." A steward walked up to their table and gave a little bow. "Because of our recent influx of passengers, we're a bit tighter for space than we normally are. I wonder if you might be willing to make room here for some of our other passengers?"

The steward stepped aside to reveal a handsome older man and his gorgeous young companion. He was dressed in a black tuxedo in a classic cut, while she wore a dress of shimmering red that Quin thought might have been more appropriate for a nightclub than dinner aboard a trans-Atlantic liner. They each wore a thin smile that showed none of their teeth.

"Only if they're willing to forgive us for causing them so much trouble," Abe said. "After all, we didn't pay for our passage aboard the *Carpathia*."

"You have to admit, though," Lucy said, "they do treat their stowaways awfully well."

"Please." Quin had given up on talking with Lucy for now. He gestured to the open chairs across the table from them. "Join us. We would be most delighted."

"You have our gratitude," the man said, as he pulled one of the chairs out for the woman. Once she was seated, he introduced them both. "My name is Dushko Dragomir, and my lovely companion here is Miss Elisabetta Ecsed."

"Charmed." Elisabetta spoke in a forced tone that made Quin wonder just how much of an imposition she and the rest of the passengers on the ship must see the survivors of the *Titanic*. Her accent matched that of Dushko, which Quin placed as being influenced by some Slavic tongue.

"I am Abe Holmwood, and my friends here are Lucy Seward and Quin Harker." As Abe spoke, a wine steward supplied each of them with a glass of merlot.

"We really must apologize to you," Lucy said. "I'm sure this disaster has disrupted your travel plans dreadfully."

"Not nearly as much as yours, I am sure," said Dushko. "And our lives have not been in peril for the entire voyage so far."

"I understand the *Carpathia* made such good time to reach us that it might not delay you too much in the end," Quin said.

"That would be true, I'm sure," said Elisabetta, "had the captain not ordered the boat turned around and headed back for New York."

"Seriously?" Quin hadn't heard news of this yet. Looking back, he probably should have realized from the sun's position on the port side of the ship that they were heading west, but he'd been too tired and distracted to make the connection. "I thought they would bring us back to England to start over again rather than complete our trip for us."

"Do not worry yourself about it," Dushko said. "It is a small inconvenience to us compared to the horrible event that has befallen you."

"We were among the fortunate ones on the *Titanic*," Quin said. "It's hard to believe that we deserve any more luck in our lives."

Elisabetta picked up her wine glass and raised it for a toast. "Then here's to the survivors of the *Titanic*," she said. "May they never need any more luck until their dying days."

# CHAPTER TWENTY-TWO

Brody hadn't wanted to get back on board the *Carpathia*, but he didn't see as how he had a choice. Fergus had watched Dushko destroy Trevor, and after he'd reported the event, Brody had realized just how much trouble he was in. If Dushko was willing to administer the true death to someone like Trevor, who'd only become caught up in Brody's plot to gorge himself on the *Titanic*'s victims, how much worse would it be for the man who'd instigated the scheme in the first place?

The alternative, though, would be to hole up on a lonely iceberg somewhere nearby and hope that another ship would pass by close enough that he could reach it. He might have been able to manage it. It would take a lot for him to starve to death, he knew, but he disliked hunger more than risking any threats from Dushko, so he had to get back on the ship.

It was then that he came up with the idea of sneaking back onto the ship by posing as a survivor of the wreck of the *Titanic*. All he had to do was wait for someone to rescue him, and that lifeboat full of women had come along before his joints had frozen too stiff for him to move. There was nothing he enjoyed more than taking advantage of the kindness of strangers.

He'd given the stewards a fake name once he'd gotten on board, and he'd managed to avoid the doctor altogether. The last thing he needed was for some nosy physician in a white coat using a stethoscope to try to find a beat in a heart that hadn't budged for years. Fortunately, the man had been too busy with the real survivors to worry about him.

Brody had spent the rest of the day hiding out in his private cabin. Now that the sun had set, he found himself getting anxious and – worse yet – hungry. He fought his urges for as long as he could, but eventually they became too great for him to ignore.

He slipped out of his cabin and tried to decide which way to go. The only part of the ship he knew well was the cargo hold, where Dushko had tried to keep him and the others cooped up for the entire voyage. If he returned there, though, chances were good that Dushko – or someone loyal to him, which would be just as bad – might spot him and try to take him down.

After the night he'd had, Brody wasn't in the mood for a fight. He rubbed his forehead and felt the edge of the flap of skin that had come off when that desperate young man had kicked him in the face. That wouldn't have put him off most nights, but he'd been so gorged on blood already that he had to let it go rather than slaughtering the man on the spot just to prove a point.

Having ruled out the lower decks, Brody decided to move upward instead. He soon found himself up on the Shelter Deck. He moved to the aftmost part of the ship, where nothing more than a railing separated him from the blackness beyond, and he gazed out at the darkened sea and took the night air deep into his lungs. It didn't do him any physical good any longer, but he liked the way it smelled.

He noticed a pale, long-haired woman standing alone near the railing a bit to the port of where he stood. She wore a thick coat that was too large for her, but she still managed to shiver in the chill breeze that wafted over the back of the ship. As he watched, she wiped her face and sniffled.

Brody edged his way along the railing closer to her. "I don't mean to be too forward, ma'am, but are you all right?"

His voice startled the woman, and for an instant he feared she might bolt back along the length of the ship, screaming for help the entire way. She steeled herself then and responded to him. "No. No, I'm not."

"You were on board the *Titanic*, weren't you?" Brody said. "You lost someone close to you."

The woman nodded. "My husband and my son. They said that Edward was no longer a child. They wouldn't let him get onto the boat with me."

"How old was he?"

"Only fifteen! Tell me, does that sound like an adult to you?"

Brody stifled a snicker. At fifteen, he'd been on his own for a year already, and he'd made his way from Ireland over to the States. He couldn't say he'd been the most mature man back then, but he'd never doubted that he was a man.

"Of course not," he said, hoping he sounded sincere. It was so hard to tell. "When did you last see him?"

"He and his father brought me up to the lifeboats. I didn't want to get into one of them, but they both insisted. They promised me that they'd get onto one of the next ones and meet me later."

Brody reached out and put a hand on one of the woman's icy fingers, right where it rested on the railing. "And you never saw them again?"

"They promised." Tears flowed freely down the woman's face, down her twisted mask of emotional turmoil. "They *promised*!"

She turned toward Brody then, and he took her in his arms and did his best to comfort her, which even he had to admit wasn't much. She was too distraught to notice how half-hearted his attempt at exhibiting sympathy went.

"I don't know how I'm going to make it without them," she said. "How am I going to live without my husband to support me? Without my son, what is there to live for?"

Brody glanced around to confirm that there was no one else hanging around. Just about everyone on the ship must have been at dinner right then. Perhaps some of the survivors had remained in their cabins, too exhausted or ill from their experiences to venture forth that evening. Either way, this poor woman here was the only one who'd come up onto the open deck to stare back in the direction of the disaster they'd left behind earlier that day.

"What is it with this 'women and children first' policy?" the woman asked. "Is it supposed to be humane to make sure that we survive without any means of support? Now here I am without a husband or a child. I have nothing left and no reason to go on."

"Perhaps I can help you with that," Brody said. He looked down at her. He could see her pulse pounding in her neck.

"I don't see how," she said. "It's impossible!"

"Nothing's impossible, ma'am. We live in an amazing world filled with things far more amazing than your imagination allows for."

"Sometimes," the woman said, "sometimes I think they were the lucky ones. The dead have no troubles. Not any more."

Brody smirked at this. "For the most part, sure, but not even the dead are created equal."

She stared up at him then, confused at how little sense he must be making to her. He reached down and held her chin so he could stare into her eyes. Tears flowed down her cheeks like rivers.

"Let me help you," he said. "Let me make everything all right."

"How?" the woman said. "Nothing can ever make me right again."

"Let me show you," he said. With that, he bent his head until he could reach her throat, and he covered her mouth with his hand.

She began to struggle then, realizing that she'd made a horrible mistake in confiding in this stranger, in letting him find her by herself. She tried to pull away from him as he drank the life pouring out of her severed carotid, but it was too little effort to prevail against him, and it had come far too late. Scant moments later, Brody had fulfilled his promise to her by ensuring that she would never have to worry about anything else ever again.

When he was done with her, Brody wiped his mouth clean on her clothes and then dumped her over the *Carpathia*'s rear railing. He watched her corpse splash straight through the ship's wake and disappear. Then he cocked his head to see if he could hear anyone else wandering the ship alone and forlorn and in desperate need of the gift he'd just given that sad woman whose blood was still on his breath.

The night was still young, after all, and they had many miles to go.

# CHAPTER TWENTY-THREE

Quin awoke late the next morning, his head sore and his mouth as dry as a desert. He groaned at the weak sunlight streaming in through the porthole and buried his head beneath his pillow. He found little comfort there, and soon he resolved to leave the bed and from there the room.

When he sat up, his head swam and his muscles protested. Every bit of him ached, and not just from the vast amounts of wine he'd helped his dinner table consume last night. He hadn't been this sore the day before, but it seemed that his adventures in the middle of the sea had finally caught up with him and demanded he pay for all the energy he'd borrowed during the disaster, with compounded interest.

"Good morning, sunshine!" Abe spoke loud and clear enough that the words entered Quin's head like sonic bullets and bounced around inside his skull until they'd tortured him plenty. "That was one hell of a dinner last night, wasn't it?"

"It was?" Quin thought back to it, but it was all a blur of food and conversation and wine. He remembered feeling relieved that his life seemed to have turned back to normal so quickly, even after such a horrible night – and then it had fallen apart.

A woman sitting at the table next to theirs had started to weep in the middle of her soup, and that had set off the rest of the people with her. Soon the somber mood had infected the rest of the room, and within minutes there were children openly sobbing in their seats. Their mothers had wiped their noses and tried to stifle them, but a few of them had refused to play along.

That was when Captain Rostron had stood up and spoke. Every eye in the room had turned to watch him, even those that still ran with tears.

"My good people. On behalf of my crew, the entire Cunard Line, and the passengers who set out from New York with us, I wish to welcome our new passengers to the *Carpathia*. We know that you've all been through a horrible experience, one that the rest of us can barely contemplate, and we know that you've only just set your feet on the road to recovering from this terrible disaster.

"Know this, though. You are among friends here. My staff and I will do whatever we can to make your journey to New York as pleasant as possible. If you need something, you have but to ask. Please consider your time aboard the *Carpathia* as your first leg in your convalescence. We will care for you as best we can until we bring you safely to the dock and set you down on solid ground."

The captain's voice softened then, and he spoke to them not as the man in charge of the ship but as a fellow traveler.

"I know many of you feel as if you have lost everything, or close to it, including those dearest to your hearts. There is a time to weep, and no one with a heart would dare begrudge you that. Still, I implore you to dry your tears for at least a little while and join me in a celebration of the fact that we have you here among us.

"While we may have lost the *Titanic* and many of the souls

who were aboard her, we still have you fortunate folks with us. That delights me to no end, and I hope you will not think me too shallow if I choose to focus on the joy that brings me rather than the sadnesses you have all suffered."

He raised his glass in a toast. "To the *Titanic* and all who sailed on her. May their memories outlast us all."

The tears had all dried during the captain's speech, and everyone in the room had joined in the toast. Afterward, Quin had spent the entire evening trying to figure out how he might pry Lucy away from the others, but in that he had failed.

"Do you remember nodding off at the table?" Abe said as he sat down on the bed across from Quin's. "I've never seen wine have that kind of effect on you before."

Quin stood up and groaned from the aches that came with the effort. "I think I may have been pushing myself a bit too hard last night, before I was ready." He remembered excusing himself and stumbling back to his room. He'd had just enough energy left to shed his dinner clothes before collapsing back into the bed. "What happened with Lucy?"

"Wouldn't you like to know?" Abe's eye glinted at Quin for a mischievous instant, but he waved off Quin's concerns. "I brought her to her room straight after dinner. She was nearly as spent as you."

Quin grimaced. "I just couldn't find a chance to talk with her."

"Well," Abe said. "According to Elisabetta, we should be in New York by Thursday evening."

"Forgive me," Quin said, "but what day is this again?"

"Tuesday. You slept most of Monday away."

"Right. That gives me two full days before we land."

Abe gave Quin a smile that never quite reached his eyes. "Can I give you some advice?"

"As long as it's not 'Don't do it.'"

"I think you're past that point. I hope you are at least."

Quin stretched, feeling the soreness in his trunk and limbs. A part of him enjoyed the sensation. As much as it hurt, it meant he was alive – and warm enough to feel things again too. "Then spit it out."

"Don't wait too long for this."

"You think I'm going to play the coward when I look into Lucy's eyes?"

Abe winced. "You've been holding this one deep inside you for a long time, Quin. It's become a habit."

Quin peered down at his old friend. "Why are you, of all people, pushing me to do this?"

Abe laughed. "I've been wondering for months when this moment might come. I thought I might go one day to call on Lucy and find the two of you had run off together. Now that the time's finally here for it to all come out, I'd like to get it over and done with so we can all move on."

"And if we had disappeared, Lucy and I, what would you have done then?"

Abe grunted. "Assuming I couldn't somehow find you? I suppose I'd have spent a lot of time deciding which one of you I would miss the most."

Quin's heart sank. "Abe," he said. "I– I wish I had some kind of control over this, over how I feel about her."

"So do I," Abe said. "None of us get to have that, though. The emotions come to us no matter what. We only get to decide what we do with them."

# CHAPTER TWENTY-FOUR

Quin didn't see Lucy until dinner that night. Having slept late, he'd missed breakfast entirely, as had Abe. They managed to make luncheon, but she was nowhere to be found. Quin left Abe to lounge on the Bridge Deck while he went to look for her, but he never managed to connect.

He hesitated to call on her in her cabin. The topic at hand required a certain amount of privacy, of course, but Quin didn't want to harm Lucy's reputation by having her seen entertaining young men in her quarters. He determined to make a full circuit of the ship first.

Quin had never been on an ocean liner before boarding the *Titanic*, and while the *Carpathia* was a fine ship, it suffered some by comparison. The *Titanic* had to be at least half again as large as the *Carpathia*, both in terms of length and width, and it only had four decks with passenger cabins on it, as opposed to the *Titanic*'s seven.

The *Carpathia* had to be older than the just-launched *Titanic*, but it had been maintained well and with a clear amount of pride on the part of the Cunard Line's crew. It could not compare to the *Titanic*'s no-expenses-spared accoutrements, but then neither could any other ship in the world. The fact that it still sailed the seas while the *Titanic* now served as a watery grave for hundreds of innocents put it much in Quin's favor though.

Crowded with grieving survivors though it now was, Quin found he felt far more comfortable on the *Carpathia* than he ever had on the *Titanic*. The bigger ship had reeked of so much money that it had sometimes felt stifling. Quin had often felt like a child dressing up as an adult on board the *Titanic*, but here he felt much more like his own man, even though he wore borrowed clothing.

He wound up on the rear of the Shelter Deck, staring out over the aft railing in the direction from which they'd come, toward where the *Titanic* now lay. So many of the people he'd met or even just brushed against during his short time on the ship were still out there with her. None of them would ever be coming home.

"It's a desperately sad sight, isn't it?"

Quin turned to see Lucy standing right behind him. She tucked a loose strand of hair behind an ear as the wind whipped at her dress. He remembered how blonde it had been when they were children, shining like gold in the sun. It had darkened over the years but grown no less beautiful.

"It's not the things I see out there that make me sad."

Lucy smiled at that and joined Quin at the rail. "You know what I mean," she said. She gazed out at the sea. "Abe said you were looking for me."

"He's right."

He turned to face the ocean with her, and they stood there for a while, wordlessly watching the sunlight sparkle off the surface of the sea. Quin reveled in that moment, never wanting it to end. He wished he could stuff it in Abe's hip flask, seal it, and keep it with him wherever he went, taking little sips from it whenever he needed to remember it.

"I heard a terrible thing happened here last night." Lucy leaned over the railing and stared at the churning wake far below them. "The watch saw a woman fall overboard from this exact spot."

"How horrible." Quin put a hand on Lucy's shoulder, keeping her from leaning over any further. "Did she slip?"

Lucy shrugged. "At breakfast, I heard she'd lost her husband and son to the *Titanic*." She looked into Quin's eyes. "It may not have been an accident."

Quin swallowed hard. He'd been so thrilled that both he and his two friends had survived that he'd not dwelled for long on how such a loss as others had suffered might unhinge him.

"She took her own life?"

"Can you blame her?"

Quin grimaced. "Yes. Yes, I can. If there's one thing my parents taught me over the years it's that where there's life there's hope. That woman may have lost everything that meant anything to her, but she still breathed. I can't imagine that her husband and her son would have wanted her to die."

"Maybe she just wanted to join them."

Quin pushed away from the railing, stretching his arms out against it. "But think of the sacrifice her husband and son made for her. They died knowing that they had at least arranged for her to survive. And despite them giving their lives for her, she throws that away. Better she had stayed on the ship with them. At least then they'd have been together at the end."

Lucy wrinkled her brow at him. "You really can't understand how she felt?"

"Understand? Sure. I just can't muster up any sympathy for her actions. It was a selfish thing for her to do. She had a responsibility to go on."

"And what if you and Abe had gone down with the *Titanic*? Would you dismiss my grief so easily?"

Quin gaped at her. "Lucy, we put you on that lifeboat, fully expecting we'd die."

"That's not what you told me at the time. You lied to me."

"Of course we did. You were being stubborn about it, and it was a far more polite alternative."

Lucy put her back to the railing and crossed her arms over her chest. "To what?"

"We'd have tied you up into a sack and thrown you into the back of that boat if we'd had to."

"So," Lucy said, "no respect for me as an individual. It's 'women and children' first, is it?"

"Yes!" At the horrified gasp from Lucy's lips, Quin spun in the opposite direction. "I mean, no!"

Lucy put her gloved hands on her hips and glared at him. "Well?" she said. "Which is it?"

Quin ran his hands through his hair and tried to collect his thoughts. He'd never been good at that when she was mad at him. "I didn't lie to you to trick you into that lifeboat because you're a woman."

"Really?" she said. "I notice you didn't do the same for Abe."

Quin winced. "True," he said, "but–"

"But he's no gentle flower of a woman, someone who needs to be protected, shielded from the challenges of life. He's a strapping young man who can fend for himself, right?"

Quin shook his head. "No, that's not it. That's not it at all."

"You think about it for a moment, Quin. You think about it and tell me I'm not right."

"I don't have to do that, Luce. I know why I did it!"

"Is that right?" She stepped up into his face now, her eyes blazing at him. "Well then tell me all about it, dammit. And this time no lies! I want nothing from your lips but the honest truth!"

"It wasn't chivalry. I did it because *I love you!*"

Lucy gaped at him and his naked revelation. As the words

left his lips, Quin wished he could snatch them back, but it was too late, and he knew it. Instead, he embraced them and the wild sense of freedom that came rushing at him now that he'd finally given them voice.

"That's right," he said, "I love you. And not in that 'known you since childhood, we'll all be friends forever' way. More in the 'let's get married' way."

Lucy brought her jaw back up and swallowed. "Oh, Quin." She stared at him with glittering eyes. "What about Abe?"

Quin's heart tightened up at his friend's name. "I love him too, but in the 'brothers forever' way." He stepped toward her. "But that's not the real question is it? What about you, Luce? How do you feel?"

"You can't make me do this." Lucy's jaw clenched as she fought back tears. "Not here. Not now. Just yesterday, I thought I'd lost you both."

Quin reached out to put his hand on her shoulder, but Lucy spun away from it. She followed her momentum and kept going then, leaving Quin standing there alone at the back of the ship.

# CHAPTER TWENTY-FIVE

The sun had set, and the last streams of light over the horizon painted the dusk sky vibrant reds, oranges, and purples. Lucy did not take the time to appreciate this as she strode into the first class dining room for dinner. She was already late.

She had thought about missing dinner entirely, but the growling in her stomach had argued forcefully against her. By the time she had given in to its flawless reasoning, she'd hoped to at least skip as much of the small talk during the opening courses as possible. Maybe she'd be lucky and discover that the boys had already eaten and left for the lounge, but she discovered upon entering the room that she'd only been half as fortunate as she'd hoped.

"Where's Quin?" Abe asked as Lucy sat down next to him at a table in the first class dining room. "I haven't seen either one of you all afternoon. I figured you might be enjoying each other's company."

Lucy's hands formed into fists as she settled into one of the empty chairs beside Abe, and she had to struggle with herself to keep from punching him in the arm. If there hadn't been other people at the table with him – including Dushko and Elisabetta, who had joined them last night too – she might have given in to the urge. As it was, she steeled herself for the conversation she'd both wanted to have, and avoid, ever since she'd spoken with Quin.

"He isn't with you?" She unfolded her napkin, refusing to look at him. "I thought you were in charge of his social schedule."

Abe smiled. "Nothing could be further from the truth. Our Quin is an independent young man. He sets his own agenda. I just help him cross off the items on it."

"Is that what you were doing when you sent me to talk to him earlier today?"

Abe raised his eyebrows at her, catching the edge in her voice. "Can I take it that you've had the opportunity to speak with him?"

"You may."

"And might I ask what the results of that conversation were?"

Lucy glared at him. "You may not."

Abe nodded. "Ah."

Elisabetta giggled at them from across the table. She nudged Dushko in the ribs with her elbow, and he squirmed away from her in his chair.

"It is not polite to listen to other people's conversations, my dear," Dushko said to Elisabetta in a quiet voice.

She dismissed him with a curt wave. "Then they shouldn't have them right in front of us." Having confessed to eavesdropping on Lucy and Abe's conversation, she gave up all pretense of doing otherwise and leaned across the table toward Lucy. "Are these two boys fighting over you, dear? How exciting! You must be flattered to have two such handsome suitors pursuing you."

Lucy replied to Elisabetta but never took her eyes off Abe as she spoke. "I don't know if I'd agree with that," she said. "I think I'm seeing something ugly about them both right now."

"Come now, Lucy," Abe said. "What would you have had me do? Poor Quin has been heartsick over you forever. It was time to get it out in the open."

"And you had absolutely no concern over how this might affect our relationship?"

Abe gave her a resigned shrug. "I thought the two of you would work it out and let me know what happened. I figured you'd either run off with him or break his heart."

"And what do you think transpired?" Elisabetta said. Dushko put an arm on her shoulder to restrain her, but she removed it with a sharp shrug.

"Well," said Abe, "she's here with me instead of him, isn't she?"

"I wasn't talking about Quin and me." Lucy felt herself starting to seethe at Abe. "I meant you and me."

"Oh." Abe sat up straighter in his chair. "I thought that an enlightened and modern young lady such as yourself would appreciate the opportunity to make any decisions about your love life with all of the information available."

Lucy reached for the glass of wine that a steward had just filled for her. Abe put his hand on hers before she could throw it at him.

"Wait," Abe said in a contrite tone. "That came out wrong. I just meant–" He glanced over at the others at the table. "I felt I owed it to you both."

Most of them were pretending not to notice. From the way Dushko peered into his wine glass, he seemed to have found something intriguing floating in it. Only Elisabetta stared at them with unabashed glee. Lucy glared at the woman, but she responded to the hostility with a sly wink.

"Quincey is my best friend," Abe said. "He deserves to be able to tell you how he feels about you."

"And what about me?" Lucy said. She didn't understand Abe's motivations at all. He'd pursued her for months before she'd given in to him. The way he'd treated her after that, though, made her think that perhaps he'd enjoyed the chase far more than the prize.

"I thought you deserved it too."

Abe took his hand off Lucy's. She looked at her wine glass and considered tossing it at him and storming out of the room. But she wanted to hear what he had to say, and her stomach growled at her to stay.

Abe turned to her then and spoke in low, private tones. Elisabetta cupped her ears to make sure she got every word. Lucy ignored her and focused on Abe instead.

"I'm not staying in the States, Lucy," Abe said. "Once I drop you off at college, I'm on my way back to Old Blighty. And once that's done, I'm sure you're going to find yourself a handsome young Yank who adores the ground you traverse."

"That's not the plan at all." Lucy frowned at Abe. "You know that."

Abe shrugged. "The plan is to have a wonderful summer wandering about the US with you and then let you go. And I mean that in every way."

Lucy parted her lips to protest, but Abe held up a hand and continued on. "I thought that if you wound up with some Yank, wonderful as he might be, I would never see you again. Sure, we might still write letters to each other, but I doubt I would be moved to cross this blasted ocean again to see you with another man."

"So what does any of this have to do with Quin?"

"Ah." Abe's eyes lost their touch of melancholy and lit up. "That's all part of my wicked Plan B, of course. I figured that if I couldn't be with you, then I'd want someone else I know and trust to be there to treat you right. Who better than our man Quincey?"

"You can't be serious." Lucy raised an eyebrow at Abe. "You're hardly so selfless."

Abe put a hand over his heart. "You wound me, Lucy. I have always… Very well. Sure. There was a part of me that figured that if you wound up with Quin, you and he might eventually move back to England at some juncture."

"And then you would be able to see me again?"

Abe grinned. "And then I'd have my chance to steal you back."

# CHAPTER TWENTY-SIX

"I don't think this is a good idea," Dennis Cherryman said as he and his compatriot stole their way toward the upper decks of the *Carpathia*. They'd come to a railing gate across one of the outer stairwells, and the sign across it read FIRST CLASS PASSENGERS ONLY. It was a simple matter of reaching over the railing to the other side to unlatch the gate, but Dennis came up short against it.

"Come on now," David Ritter said. "Is it our fault we don't have a penny on us to be able to pay for a snifter or two?"

Dennis looked both himself and David over. The staff on the *Carpathia* had provided some clothes for him once he'd made it aboard, but they hadn't been anything fancier than the clobber he'd left England in. David had started his journey in New York, though, and his clothes were even more tattered than Dennis's.

"Everything I had – which wasn't much, I'll grant you – went down with the *Titanic*," Dennis said. "What's your excuse?"

David ran his thumbs through his frayed suspenders. "Lost every bit of it to a card shark. Can you believe they let those sorts of people bother us down in steerage? You'd think he'd have been after bigger game than me."

Dennis nodded slowly. He wasn't convinced that his new friend, with whom he shared a cabin on the Main Deck, all the way in the lowest part of the ship, was truly broke rather than simply larcenous. Desperate times might call for desperate measures – the sinking of the *Titanic* had taught him that – but Dennis wasn't all that sure about how desperate they were.

"Come on now," David said. "They aren't going to give us any drink on credit, and without it we'll have a long, dry voyage home."

"So we have to steal it?"

Dennis winked at David. "Did you see the way that lass with the blonde curls was looking at you, lad? A little drink to loosen her up, and you're in, there."

David blushed. He had seen the girl, and there was nothing he'd have liked more than to share a drink or three with her. The stewards on board the *Carpathia* had been awful kind to him, providing him with everything he needed. They'd been a bit more reluctant with their response to his requests for booze though, and they'd refused to sell him anything on credit.

"I suppose you're right," he said to Dennis as he reached over and undid the latch. "If we're going to do it, though, let's be fast. I'd hate to survive the *Titanic* only to get into trouble over a wee bit of drink." He pulled the gate open and slipped past it, Dennis right on his heels.

The sun had just gone down, and the artificial lights scattered about the *Carpathia* allowed many long shadows along its decks. The two men stuck to them as much as they could and managed to slip all the way up to the Bridge Deck, which put them on the same level as the first class dining room. The lights inside blazed bright, which David knew would make it hard for anyone in the room to see them as they walked past.

Still, they kept their heads down and their noses pointed forward as they strolled along the deck.

"The Smoke Room's at the aft end of the deck," Dennis said. "They have a bar there, and there's a small storeroom that backs on to it. The doorway's straight up there on our right."

"And just how are we supposed to get into this place?" David said. "You don't think they'd keep something like that locked up tight?"

"Of course they do," said Dennis, "but I happen to have a key that will get us right in." He held it up before him, golden and shiny, even in the scattered lights.

"Now where in hell did you get that?" David asked.

"From the same gentleman who told me about the storeroom." Dennis said. "He set it all up, but he can't be caught stealing from the ship if he wants to keep his job. All he wants is a share of whatever we can bring home."

"Seems fair enough," David said, "but they won't throw him in the brig if we get caught, will they?"

"Do they still have brigs? I thought that was something you only read about in pirate tales, right up there with keel-hauling."

"You figure they'll toss us overboard instead?"

Dennis rushed past David as they reached the storeroom door, the key glittering in his hand. "I figure they won't catch us if we move fast and act like we know what we're doing."

He had the door open in a flash, and an instant later he and David slipped into the darkened storeroom. Worried that someone might see them, David shut the door behind them, plunging the room back into blackness.

"Couldn't you have waited until I found the light?" Dennis said.

David heard Dennis stumbling about in the dark, but he remained in one place, his feet rooted to the floor. He fumbled for a switch near the entrance, but didn't find it. Instead, he found the arm of someone leaning up against the wall next to the doorway, and he jerked his hand back right away.

"Is that you, Dennis?"

"Of course it's me, you idiot. Who else did you bring in here with you?"

David's breath caught in his throat, and he could not respond. Dennis's voice hadn't come from next to him where the arm hung but from across the small room instead. David reached out to grab the arm, but it had disappeared.

Someone fell to the floor with a thud then, and David heard a soft but urgent gurgle from Dennis's direction.

"Are you all right?" Fear crept up from David's gut, threatening to close off his throat. He'd had a hard enough week already, and it was only Tuesday. He wasn't in the mood for this. "Quit playing around, Dennis. It's not funny."

David heard someone swallowing, and that set him off. "You little bastard. You had to go for a goddamn drink already? Couldn't you wait until we got back below decks?"

David found the light switch then and flicked it on. He stared in horror at the scene it revealed.

A man with wild, unkempt hair knelt crouched over Dennis's slumped form, cradling him in his arms. The man looked up at David as he lowered Dennis to the ground. He wore a wild look in his eyes, and a trickle of blood ran down from his lips, staining his chin and shirt.

"Sorry about that, lad," the man said with a drunken grin. "I couldn't help myself."

David drew in a breath to scream, but the man stepped up and punched him in the throat before he could unleash it. David crumpled to his knees, clutching at his ruined airway as he gasped with all his might for one last breath. He never found it.

The man stepped around David and reached for the light switch. Just before he put it out, he looked down at David with a satisfied grin and said, "When you get to Hell, my boy, tell the Devil that Brody Murtagh sent you."

# CHAPTER TWENTY-SEVEN

"Quin?" Lucy said. "Quin, where are you?"

Quin could hear her from where he was hiding, but he didn't want to reveal that to her quite yet. After their conversation that afternoon – after he'd finally revealed how he felt about her – he'd wanted to crawl back into his bed to curl up and die. That way, he'd have at least saved Lucy any more agony, and he'd have put himself out of his own misery at the same time.

Abe hadn't let him get away with that though. He'd insisted on Quin joining him at dinner, which was the last thing that Quin wanted to do. He wanted to talk with Lucy again but at the same time feared to hear what she might have to say, but either way he dreaded the idea of having that chat in the middle of the dining room, not only in front of Abe but anyone else who might be within earshot.

When Abe had decided to relieve himself before they went up to dinner, Quin had slipped out of the room without a word. He'd taken the nearest stairs straight up to the Shelter Deck and made his way aft. He'd soon found himself near the back railing, right where Lucy had failed to renounce Abe and fall in love with him on his say-so.

Worried that Abe or – worse yet – Lucy would find him lingering there, Quin decided he had to hide. He couldn't just go back to his cabin, as Abe would check there for sure, and he knew the same would be true if he tried to hole up in the smoking room or any of the ship's lounges. He had to actually conceal himself someplace if he wanted to be sure of avoiding them, or anyone else who might feel like striking up an unwanted conversation with him.

He just wanted to be alone.

As he strolled along the railing, Quin ran his hand along one of the lifeboats from the *Titanic*. The captain of the *Carpathia* had ordered many of them hauled up from the water on davits once the survivors of the disaster had been brought aboard the ship. Now they sat tilted on the *Carpathia*'s decks, covered with canvases and lashed to the rails.

Quin didn't know why they'd bothered to recover the lifeboats, but he was glad that they had. At the very least, he figured that the *Carpathia* would be sure to have more than enough lifeboats should disaster strike it too. He also felt a strong sense of affection for the collapsible to which Abe and he had clung, and the thought that it hadn't been abandoned in the North Atlantic along with the dead made him somehow feel more secure.

Quin had found that lifeboat and knelt down next to it. There was a bit of space where it leaned up against the railing, and he found that if he got on his hands and knees he could wriggle through it. He sat there on the part of the deck the lifeboat sheltered, leaned back against the inside of the hull behind him, and stared out at the ocean as the sun fell into it and disappeared.

By the time Lucy had come looking for him on the Shelter Deck, dinner must have come and gone. The air had grown chilly again, but the lifeboat's hull had offered some protection from the salty breeze at least. Quin's stomach had growled at him, but he'd resolved to ignore it. The ache in his heart trumped anything the rest of his body might have put up against it.

"Dammit, Quin," Lucy said. "Where are you?"

Quin couldn't help but laugh. Lucy often liked to act scandalized when someone would swear in the presence of a lady, but he knew better. When it came to it, she swore as often and as well as anyone he knew. Still, the seriousness of her tone against the coarseness of her language brought a giggle to his lips.

"Quin?" Lucy said. "Is that you? Where are you?"

Quin flashed back to a moment from their childhood when they'd been playing Hide and Seek in the grounds around her family's home back in Whitby. She'd been unable to find him hiding in the bushes under a window until he'd started laughing at her pleas for him to show himself. He'd been unable to stop himself then either, and he had to come to one conclusion about that. He'd always wanted her to find him.

Quin poked his head around the edge of the lifeboat and waved up at Lucy with a smile. She started in surprise when she spotted him, and a laugh escaped from her red lips too. It changed from that into an angry scowl though.

"Do you have any idea how long I've been looking for you?" she said. "I've been over nearly every inch of this ship."

"I can guess. I spent most of the morning doing the same thing, looking for you."

"It's hardly the same." Lucy bent down on one knee to peer around the lifeboat's gunwale. "Is there room under here for two?"

"If we press in." Quin scooted over to give Lucy some room, and she filled it.

"Why, there's plenty of room under here," Lucy said, looking down the length of the boat. "If Abe kicks you out of your cabin, you could stay here quite comfortably, I'd think."

Quin nodded. "It does have the best view on the entire ship. No other quarters feature such panoramic vistas."

Lucy laughed at this, her voice full of warmth and fun, and for a moment Quin could pretend that he'd said nothing at all to her earlier in the day. He wondered if he would want for it to be that way, to be able to take back his confession of his affections for her. Then he looked up into her eyes and realized that he wanted to tell her about it all over again.

"So," he said.

"So." Lucy grimaced, and Quin feared the worst. She would try to let him down easy, of course, but it would make him feel like perhaps it would have been better to go down with the *Titanic*. At least once they got to New York they could say goodbye and he might never have to see her again.

That thought both offered him hope and tortured him. He couldn't bear the idea of life without her, but at the same time he didn't know if he could stand being around her after she'd rejected him. He braced himself for the fact that he would have to find out.

"I'm still working through my feelings for you, Quin."

His heart leaped at these words. He'd been so sure she'd put him down that anything else felt like a victory.

She stared at him. "And that makes you smile?"

"No!" He put his hand on her shoulder to reassure her. "Well, it does, but only because I'd been so afraid that I'd be weeping at this point."

"Quin Harker," she said, "I don't think I've ever seen you cry, not since you were in short trousers."

He gave her a wistful smile and took her hand in his. It felt warm, dry, and wonderful. Her fingers intertwined with his in perfect sync, like the most natural thing in the world. "I don't much, but I'd be willing to make an exception over you."

She lowered her eyes at that, and Quin's heart sank as he

wondered what she might have to say. They stayed quiet like that for a long moment, neither one of them willing to break the silence. Quin hoped they might be able to stay like that forever.

Something landed on the deck behind them, hard. The impact shook the floorboards. A soft grunt accompanied it.

Lucy opened her mouth to speak, but Quin held a finger up to his lips. He didn't want anyone finding them back here. They might ask them to leave, and then Lucy and he would have to find someplace else just as private to have their talk.

Quin moved away from Lucy and peered around his end of the overturned lifeboat. At first he thought the deck to be abandoned, just as he'd hoped. Then he spotted someone – a man dressed in black and heading aft.

He had another man slung over his shoulder.

# CHAPTER TWENTY-EIGHT

"What is it?" Lucy whispered.

Quin waved her off, but her curiosity would not be denied. She got up on her knees and leaned right over the back of him, a sensation that Quin would have reveled in had he not been so astonished by what he'd seen. "Let me see," she said.

He hushed her again, and the two of them watched in silence as the man with the body over his arm strolled toward the ship's aft rail. He carried his load as if it weighed nothing, like a father giving a small child a piggyback ride, yet he swung his eyes about, taking care to make sure that no one was watching him. Quin wondered if the man might be able to see Lucy and him in the shadow of the overturned lifeboat. He hoped they wouldn't have to find out what the man might do if he could spot them.

The man walked straight up to the aft rail and tossed his unconscious burden over it without the slightest bit of ceremony.

The shock of witnessing this terrible act brought the moment into high relief. Quin could feel the engines thrumming through the ship beneath him as he listened for the victim to say something, but not a scream or word passed his lips as he flopped over the railing like a rag doll and disappeared. He must have landed and disappeared in the ship's wake, but Quin couldn't even hear a splash over the ship's ambient noise.

Lucy screamed.

The sound brought Quin back to himself, and he launched himself forward, squeezing out from under the overturned lifeboat. "Hey!" he shouted at the man who still stood at the railing, looking down over the edge at his handiwork. "See here!"

The man spun about and glared at Quin, his eyes glinting with feral rage. They seemed to glow red in the darkness. He came toward Quin and into the ship's lights, and Quin saw that he wore dark, shabby clothing, his white shirt stained and grimy under a fresh splash of bright crimson that ran from his neck down his chest.

Quin had no doubt the man had mayhem on his mind. As a trained attorney, his brain spun, searching for some likely explanations of what he'd just seen. Try as he might to come up with something reasonable, all signs kept pointing to murder.

He spread his arms wide to protect Lucy and keep her behind him, but she would have nothing to do with it. She pressed past him and stared at the oncoming man in horror.

The man hauled up short when he spotted Lucy moving around Quin. She did the same as she got a good, clear look at him. Then she screamed again, louder than before, and Quin heard footsteps pounding along the deck from somewhere behind them.

Quin grabbed Lucy by the arm and pulled himself in front of her, between her and the man. He had never been much of a scrapper, but he wasn't about to let this man threaten Lucy, not even for an instant. "Back off!" he said to the man in the most commanding tone he could muster.

The man snarled at Quin and Lucy, then glanced up behind them to see a handful of sailors stomping their way, coming to see what had given rise to all the screaming. He uttered a curse, then spun on his heel and marched toward the aft rail.

"We saw what you did!" Lucy said. She pressed her way around Quin, but this time she stood next to him rather than shoving past.

"There's nowhere to run," Quin said. He crept forward, Lucy on his arm. "Give yourself up!"

"You got me there, boyo," the man said in an Irish accent. He slung his arms around the railing and leaned there as if he were waiting for a date. "But I'm not quite done yet."

"Brody?" Lucy gasped. "Brody Murtagh?"

Brody's face cracked into a wry grin. "Ah, Miss Seward, is it?" He shook his head. "It's a damned pity we had to meet again like this. I'd hoped for better circumstances."

Quin goggled at Lucy. "You know him?"

Lucy kept staring at Brody. "I hauled him out of the water. He was next to dead."

Brody winked at her. "True enough, lass. You did me a fine service that morning."

"What did you do?" Lucy said.

Brody cocked an ear at her as if he hadn't heard her properly.

"To that man," Lucy said, pointing a thin finger past him, over the railing and toward the open ocean beyond. "What did you do to him?"

Men shouted from behind Quin and Lucy. Quin risked a glance back to see a number of sailors coming their way.

"As a favor to you, I'll spare you the grisly details, Miss Seward." Brody turned and climbed up onto the railing behind him, using it like a ladder until he reached the top rung. He grabbed a vertical pole there to steady himself as he teetered on the slippery metal tube.

"Did you kill him?" Lucy moved forward, and Quin followed her. He could feel her muscles tensing, and he knew she planned to leap forward and grab the mysterious man if she could. He prepared himself to grab onto her. Should she succeed, he didn't want the much larger man to haul her overboard as he fell.

Brody looked down into the *Carpathia*'s wake. "If he wasn't dead before he hit the water, I'm sure he is by now."

"Hold it right there!" a sailor shouted from behind as he came tromping up the deck.

"That's the one thing I'm afraid I can't do." Brody's voice was tinged with regret. "My apologies to you for ruining your evening, Miss Seward. I hope our next meeting will be under kinder circumstances."

With that, he gave Lucy a little salute and then leaped from the railing.

"Wait!" Lucy charged forward and hit the railing at full speed. Her fingers brushed the man's leg, but that was as close as she got to him before he plummeted away.

Quin chased right after Lucy and grabbed her shoulder before her momentum could take her over the railing. He stared down into the darkness beneath the ship's decks with her and saw the white waters of the ship's churning wake spreading out behind them.

"Where did he go?" Lucy gaped at the water below. "We should be able to see him! Where did he go?"

Quin couldn't answer that question. He'd hoped to see the man bobbing along in the water, perhaps to throw him a lifebuoy, but nothing disturbed their pristine wake.

Lucy turned to Quin then and wrapped her arms around him. He responded in kind. As the sailors brought them back into the ship's warm and well-lit interior, he reflected that he'd hoped to wind up in Lucy's arms before the end of the night – but not like this.

# CHAPTER TWENTY-NINE

"What do you mean, sir?" Quin gaped at Captain Rostron and wrapped his arm around Lucy a little tighter. It was warm on the *Carpathia*'s bridge, far more so than it had been out on the Shelter Deck, but Lucy continued to shudder.

"Just what I said, Mr Harker," Rostron said. "I'm afraid this isn't the first such report I've received since we came to the rescue of the *Titanic*."

"Is this normal?" Lucy said. "For survivors of a great shipwreck to hurl themselves to their deaths?"

The captain gave Lucy a grim shrug. "I've been on the sea a long time, miss, but it's passing rare to see a disaster like this. I've never seen anything as bad as what happened to the *Titanic*. It's possible, perhaps, that the minds of the survivors snapped. Or perhaps they simply lost the will to live."

"But to have fought so hard to survive in those icy waters and then to take your own life?" Lucy shook her head. "It just doesn't make any sense at all."

Doctor Griffiths piped up then. He'd come to check on Quin and Lucy and had already declared them to be in respectable health. Quin even seemed to be recovering from his frostbite symptoms well. "Survivor's guilt can be a devastating thing.

The thought that it should have been you who died instead of those who did can eat away at a man's psyche until there's little left to use in your own defense."

"But to go from guilt to suicide?"

Quin held her tighter. He could tell she couldn't believe this explanation, and he wasn't sure how much sense it made to him either. They'd had such a surreal voyage to this point that anything seemed possible.

"The guilt comes from the feeling that your survival was a fluke of fate, some kind of horrible mistake. You believe that good people should have lived instead of you, and it destroys your sense of self-worth. It's not surprising then that those who suffer horrible cases of it might decide to rectify that mistake by finishing the job that fate failed to complete."

"That seems like madness," Quin said.

"And so it is." Doctor Griffiths affirmed this with a nod of his head. "I've had a number of chats with Mr Dragomir about this over the past couple days, and he concurs."

"Dushko?" Lucy said, surprised.

"Yes. He's a bit of an amateur psychologist, or so he claims. I find his arguments to be intriguing."

"Do you have any other explanations?" the captain asked.

The doctor shrugged. "None that come to mind. If the loss of the *Titanic* teaches us anything, it's that we live in a senseless world."

"You're right, in that none of this makes any real sense," said Lucy. "I helped pull Brody Murtagh from the water myself. He was not a man who wanted to die."

"That's another matter we should discuss," the captain said. He waved one of his officers forward, a man with sharp, black glasses and a neatly trimmed beard. "Mr Blum? Were you able to find this Murtagh on the *Titanic*'s manifest?"

"I'm afraid not, sir. There's no record of him."

Lucy leaned forward, concerned. "But that's impossible."

"What does that mean, sir?" Quin asked the captain. "Are you trying to say this man just popped out of nowhere in the middle of the North Atlantic?"

Captain Rostron raised his eyebrows at that. "Of course, not. There are a number of possible explanations for this."

"And they are?"

The captain ticked off the ideas on his fingers as he spoke them. "He could have been a stowaway. He could have given a false name. He could have been a last-second addition to the staff. He could have entered the ship under someone else's name, either using their ticket or assuming their position on the ship's staff."

"Perhaps he was a time traveler who'd decided to bear witness to the sinking of the ship." All eyes turned to focus withering glares at one of the other officers, a broad man with a sharp Van Dyck beard, standing in a corner of the bridge, a tattered book in his hand. He cringed at their attention.

"Mr Shubert, I don't think you're treating this situation with the gravity it deserves," Captain Rostron said. "You need to put away that HG Wells trash I've seen you reading, at least until we reach port. It's coloring your imagination."

"Yes, sir." Shubert stuffed the book onto a nearby shelf, next to several rolled charts, and sealed his lips.

"But what about the gentleman who Mr Murtagh threw over the railing?" Quin said. "Do we have no way to find out who he was?"

The captain shook his head. "That we might be able to do. Mr Shubert over there will put his spare time to better use by overseeing a full headcount of the passengers and crew aboard this ship. By a process of elimination, we'll figure out who's missing. From there, we can hope to have a good chance to learn exactly what happened."

"Thank you, captain." Lucy's shoulders slumped with relief. "It's all just so…"

"Overwhelming?"

Lucy threw up her hands. "Insane! I can barely believe it."

"You've had enough happen in the past few days to last anyone a lifetime," Doctor Griffiths said with a sage nod. "I suggest you get some rest. In the morning, this may all seem like a bad dream."

"Yes." Quin stood up and helped Lucy to her feet. "I think that sounds like an excellent idea."

The captain looked over them both with kind eyes. "Very good, then. With any luck, we'll have some more answers to your questions by breakfast. If you can stop by the bridge afterward, I'll be happy to bring you up to speed."

"You're too kind, sir," said Lucy.

The captain smiled kindly. "Given the circumstances, it's the least I can do."

# CHAPTER THIRTY

Dushko knew the instant Brody entered the hold. He'd been in the Smoke Room in the aft part of the Bridge Deck when some woman had started screaming on the deck below, and he'd been the first man out of the room to go see what had happened. That had procured him a bird's-eye view of the entire incident.

He'd watched as the idiot had talked with the couple who had seen him do something horrible, and he'd wanted to leap down, grab the bloody little bastard, and wring his neck until his head fell off. If need be, he'd have slaughtered the couple as well and tossed all their bodies overboard to hide the evidence. The woman's screams hadn't gone unnoticed by others on the ship though, and he wasn't prepared to kill each and every person who'd stuck their nose out of the warmer parts of the ship to see what in hell was going on.

So Dushko had held back and waited. He knew that Brody would get away. The only real question was if he'd kill the young couple as he left or not.

Then the woman had recognized Brody somehow, and Dushko had buried his face in his hands. This was a disaster beyond any fears he'd had for this journey.

All he'd wanted to do was transport as many of his kind as possible back to the Old Country to keep them from accidentally revealing their presence to the inquisitive people in the New World. Setting up the trip had been a monumental undertaking, but he had plenty of patience. He had pulled it off perfectly, and he had seen nothing but clear skies and easy seas ahead. And then the *Titanic* sank. He wondered if Brody had somehow managed to trigger the disaster himself. He would not have put it past the man. He had proven a total catastrophe from the first day that Dushko met him. If Elisabetta hadn't had a soft spot for him, Dushko would have ended the man long ago.

He almost wanted to see the young couple down there pull out a stake and hammer it through the bastard's cold, dead heart. Instead, he'd gasped along with the woman when Brody had leaped off the back of the ship and disappeared.

Dushko knew what Brody had done. It didn't take a genius to figure out that he'd transformed himself into a bat the instant he'd fallen out of sight. Such a small creature flapping through the night sky would be practically invisible, and he could easily wend his way around the ship until he found a safe place to land.

Of course, with the woman's testimony as to Brody's identity, every staffer on the ship would soon be looking for him. There were only so many places even a man such as Brody could hide. Dushko picked out the most comfortable of those, went to it, and waited.

He did not have to wait long.

The hatch to the part of the deck that included cabins for steerage passengers opened, allowing a crack of light to slice through the darkness in the hold. The shadow of a man cut it off for an instant, and then the door creaked closed behind it again.

Dushko launched himself at the figure that had entered the room and slammed it into the steel bulkhead beyond. The entire room seemed to ring like a gong from the impact. He knew Brody was as tough as they came. To top it off, if the body he had dumped off the ship was any indication, he had fed recently and would be full of life. To counter that, Dushko hit the man hard and fast and kept pummeling him.

He rained blow after blow down on Brody, right up until the moment the man backhanded him across the room. He saw Brody tense up and get ready to deliver the attack, but he could do nothing to stop it. The younger man struck with blinding speed and the strength of a bull elephant. The blow would have killed an ordinary man, leaving him little more than a red paste sliding down the opposite wall.

Dushko, though, hadn't been an ordinary man since long before Brody had been born. He scrambled to his feet just in time as Brody charged at him like a mad bull at a red cape. He then executed a veronica as well as any master matador, using his arm in place of a cape, and Brody smashed into the bulkhead behind him headfirst.

While Brody lay stunned on the hold's steel floor, Dushko hauled him up into the air by his collar with one hand and clasped his other hand around the Irishman's throat. "I have put up with you for long enough, I think," Dushko said as he increased the pressure on Brody's throat. "How dare you risk exposing all of us? *How dare you?*"

Dushko didn't get a response from Brody, nor did he expect one. All he wanted out of the man at that moment was for him to be dead. As he prepared to tear out Brody's throat, though, someone else hit him from behind with the force of a speeding car.

The impact sent Dushko sprawling along the hold. He came to a halt when he smashed into a crate and crushed it, along with the coffin that lay hidden inside it. He lay there for a moment, covered in splinters and dirt, and tried to recover from the blow before whoever had attacked him came after him again.

The attack he braced himself for never came. Instead, Elisabetta appeared above him, snarling like a rabid wolf. "You stay away from him," she said. "He is not yours, but mine!"

Dushko gave her such a fierce stare that she took a step back, and he pushed himself to his feet with deliberate and slow grace. "He is a menace to us all," he said. "He will expose our true nature to the people on this ship, and then we will be in for the fight of our lives."

"And would that be so bad?" She glanced over at Brody, but he was gone, having disappeared into a puff of mist that zipped off toward the hold's still-open door. "It would be the *feast* of our lives too!"

Dushko sneered at her. "I have not grown so tired of life as you. When we return to the Old Country, you can leave us. Wander far away and implement your mad plans. I do not give a damn any more. But we are in a delicate situation on this ship. I will not permit you to destroy us all!"

Elisabetta reached up and patted him on the cheek with a condescending hand. "Oh, my dear Dushko. What makes you think what we do is up to you?"

# CHAPTER THIRTY-ONE

"You're not actually going to bed already, are you?" Abe took another sip of his whisky and slouched into his high-backed overstuffed chair.

The first class lounge was subdued tonight. While the survivors of the *Titanic* might have cause for celebration, none of them could bear acting joyfully knowing so many of their fellow passengers on that ill-fated boat hadn't made it to share the moment with them. Instead, they seemed prepared to drown their sorrows in a series of toasts to lost family and friends, honoring their memories one after another.

It seemed to Quin that they lived in this strange purgatory between what had happened and what would be. When they arrived in New York, their temporary respite would come to an end, and they would be forced to become part of the world again. He wanted to hold on to these horrible, numb moments, to treasure them for the short and fleeting amount of peace they allowed him and the other survivors to absorb the enormity of what had happened, and begin – at least in part – to come to their own terms with it.

In the meantime, though, Lucy and he had stumbled upon some sort of mystery that his brain refused to let be. Tempting as it might be to slip into a drunken haze and forget about everything that had happened for the past few days, he couldn't help but want to determine what had happened with this strange Brody Murtagh whom Lucy had helped haul out of the frigid sea – only to see him voluntarily return himself to it. A quick glance at Lucy told him she was of the same mind.

"Of course not," Lucy said. "How could I possibly sleep after what we witnessed out there?" She waved toward the aft end of the ship and the railing from which Brody had jumped.

"I'm sure if you asked the ship's doctor, he'd be happy to give you something," Abe said. "I've noticed many of the ladies of the *Titanic* looking rather haggard during the daylight hours today, and a good number of them hustled off to their quarters with a dram of something from the good doctor to drag them off to dreamlands, I'm sure."

Looking around, Quin realized that Abe must be right. The vast majority of the people sitting in the lounge with them were men, even despite the fact that this room was open to both genders while the Smoke Room was not. Knowing that many more women and children had escaped the *Titanic* than men, he would have expected the ratio to be reversed.

"You're a pig," Lucy said to Abe.

Quin couldn't stifle the smile that her tone brought to his lips. Abe caught him and arched a mock eyebrow. "See, this is the sort of abuse you open yourself up to as her beau. Are you sure you want to put yourself in the path of such wretched wickedness."

Quin blushed and found that he couldn't come up with a snappy answer that wouldn't embarrass him even further.

"What?" Lucy took trumped-up offense at the remark. "Do you think our Mr Harker here has just met me for the first time?"

"Touché," Abe said, a smile creasing his face. "But your answer to my question brings up another query. If we're not going to bed, then exactly what do you suggest we do to while away these tiresome hours?"

"We need to get to the root of this," Lucy said. "Just because Captain Rostron is happy to sweep this under the rug until we disembark doesn't mean I am. I want to know what happened there. Who was that man that Brody Murtagh was carrying? What happened to him? And how exactly did the fellow get away?"

"Is that what people call suicide these days?" Abe said. "'Getting away.' How quaint."

"He didn't kill himself," Lucy said. "I'm sure of it."

"We saw him, Luce," Quin said. He didn't want her to think he was siding with Abe against her, but he knew what he'd witnessed. "He leaped to his death. Even if he survived the fall into the water, we all know how long he'll survive out there in the freezing waters without any sort of aid at all."

"He never even hit the water," she said. "I'm sure of it. Did you see the glint in his eyes just before he jumped off? That wasn't the look of a suicide. More like a magician about to pull off his greatest trick."

"So you think it was some kind of illusion? That perhaps he wasn't really there?"

"I can't say that for sure," she said. "The only thing I know is that Brody Murtagh knew exactly what he was doing when he leaped off that railing, and his plans didn't involve him taking his final bath in the icy Atlantic."

"You think he's still on this ship." Quin marveled at her. In so many ways, she was a never-ending delight.

Lucy leaned forward in her chair. "I'm sure of it. Where else could he have gone?"

"Go on, Lucy," Abe said. "I'm enjoying this little intellectual exercise of yours. Tell us, where is he now?"

"I don't know." Lucy stood up. "But I plan to find out – with or without the help of you two brave young gentlemen."

# CHAPTER THIRTY-TWO

"What in the devil's damned names are you doing here?" Elisabetta stormed across her first class quarters and stabbed a red-nailed finger straight at Brody's chest. "If Dushko discovers you here, he'll kill us both!"

Brody gave her his best smirk, the one she found irresistible when she was in good spirits. At the moment, it would only infuriate her, he knew, but he didn't mind that. He wanted her as flush with excitement as he was from the fresh blood that flowed through his veins.

"Don't you dare give me that look," she said. "You know all too well what you've done here, don't you? You forced my hand."

Brody slouched down into the thick couch that sat against the room's outer wall. "Nice digs," he said. "A fellow could get used to these sorts of accommodations."

Elisabetta growled at him. "Don't you dare think about getting comfortable here. This is my place, and I don't share well. You're going back down to the hold by dawn."

"If I do that, Dushko will kill me, and you'll have attacked him for nothing. Do you really want that?"

Elisabetta opened her mouth to launch into a tirade against Brody. Her fangs had extended from the rest of her teeth, an involuntary reaction to the fury building in her. Brody braced himself for a tongue lashing – maybe even a full-out attack – but instead of diving at him, Elisabetta closed her mouth, spun about, and fell down onto the couch next to him with a heart-felt sigh.

"Why, Brody?" she said, looking up at him past her thick eye-lashes. "Why do you do this? Why can't you just play nice with Dushko? Just until we get to Fiume?"

Brody snorted, then put a gentle arm around her and let her snuggle up into his shoulder. "For one, we're not headed for Fiume any more. Our next stop is New York City, and you can bet they'll herd us all off the ship while they get everything sorted with all those waterlogged souls from the *Titanic*."

"But we'll be back at sea in no time at all."

"What? In a few days? A week?"

Elisabetta frowned. "When you've lived as long as I have, weeks pass like hours do for the young."

"Either way, it's too long. The plan's finished. Most of the people down in the hold didn't want to get on the ship in the first place. Dushko tricked or blackmailed them into going along with his little 'back to the homeland' plan. Once we get to New York, they'll scatter like cockroaches from a light. He'll never get them all back on the ship again."

Elisabetta's frown deepened. She looked older than Brody had ever seen her. "Dushko thinks we're at a crucial juncture. There are too many of us now. We've been too careless. If we don't leave America soon, we're going to be found out, and then all hell will break loose."

Brody sat up. "If it's going to happen, then let's make it go down on our terms. Why wait for the world to discover us and hunt us down like vermin? Stand up and strike first, I say. Bring the battle to them before they even know they're in a fight. Then we'll see who hunts who."

A hesitant smile warmed Elisabetta's lips. "You always did talk a good game."

"I'll do more than talk," Brody said. "I'll lead the whole bloody revolution."

Elisabetta's smile widened. "Very well," she said, "you can share my resting place tonight. But such largesse comes with a price."

Brody crossed his arms over his chest. "If you're going to charge me with being a good little dog for Dushko, forget it. The price is too high."

She ran a cool hand along his cheek and spoke low and soft into his ear. "Nothing of the sort, my sweet. I was thinking of asking you to surrender something a great deal more entertaining – and intimate."

Brody's head swam, the way it always had since the first time they'd met. A lusty smile curled his lips. "I may have overfed myself," he said, thinking back to the men he'd murdered earlier. "I think I have plenty to share."

"Excellent." Elisabetta grinned as she threw a leg over Brody and straddled his lap. "I've been holding back too long, I'm afraid, trying to keep a low profile the way Dushko demands."

"Doesn't that bother you?" Brody arched his head back, exposing a long, warm section of his neck. He could feel his stolen pulse still pounding there. "That sort of discipline always puts me on edge."

Elisabetta nodded as she lowered her fangs to Brody's jugular. "I'm absolutely starving."

The first time Elisabetta bit him, Brody had screamed in terror and pain. It had taken him a while, but he'd learned to anticipate the thrilling sensation it sent through his body rather than fear it. He gave himself over to her control willingly and wholly.

With both of them so consumed by the feeding, neither of them heard the gentle knock at the door that Elisabetta had left partially open when she'd stormed in. They didn't see the steward who'd been roped into helping out with the ship-wide headcount until he'd stepped into the room and caught them in their horrifying act.

The embarrassed "Whoa, pardon me," that erupted from the steward – who thought he'd interrupted them in the middle of a sexual act – got their attention.

Startled Elisabetta sprang off of Brody's body, blood still streaming down his neck and from her fangs and lips. The steward goggled at her.

"Dear God, miss," he said. "What's happened to you?"

Then he caught a glimpse of the ruin she'd made of Brody's throat. Brody clamped a whitened hand over the wound and tried to stand up, to offer some sort of explanation for what the man had seen. Dizzy from the loss of blood, he swayed and fell back to the couch in what he knew must seem like crumpling to his death.

The steward opened his mouth and screamed. The horrible noise still erupting from his throat, he spun on his heel and sprinted from the room, slamming the door behind him.

Without even a glance backward, Elisabetta raced after the man. Groggy as she was from the feeding, she fumbled with the door for a moment before flinging it open. Then she was gone, leaving the door wide open behind her.

Brody pushed himself to his feet. After steeling himself for an instant, he staggered toward the door and after Elisabetta and the hapless steward. When he reached the corridor though, he couldn't see a trace of either one.

Brody cursed to himself and held his neck tighter, hoping the wound would seal itself fast. He couldn't see a single way that this incident could finish without more bloodshed, but that didn't mean it couldn't end well, at least for him. He hadn't wanted to be discovered – exposed to the world, as it was – in this exact way, but as he'd told Elisabetta just moments before, if they were going to be found out, he was determined to own the moment.

# CHAPTER THIRTY-THREE

"It came from that direction." Quin stabbed a finger up the hallway to where a door stood open near the aft end of the Bridge Deck. Abe and he had failed to talk Lucy out of her mad plan to scour the ship for some sign of the man they'd seen leap overboard, and she had led them all over the ship on her wild goose chase. So far, it had proved fruitless, but perhaps that was about to change.

Abe and he had escorted Lucy down to the second- and third-class lounges, which became wilder and noisier the farther they delved into the ship. After poking through the smoke-filled chambers for many long minutes, Lucy had given up on finding this Brody Murtagh in them. That didn't mean she was ready to call it quits though.

"He could be anywhere on the ship," she had said. "From the captain's quarters to the deepest hold. We need to keep looking until we find him."

"It's late, Lucy," Abe had said. "Can't we go hunting for your mystery man in the morning?"

"And what if he kills again before that?"

"Then at least we'll have had a good night's sleep before we have to do anything about it."

Lucy had spun on her heel and stormed off then, her fists balled up beside her. Quin had followed her, and despite his obvious reservations Abe had too. It was when they were coming up the stairs to the Bridge Deck once more that they all heard that horrible scream.

Lucy had raced up the stairs and then come to a halt as she cast her gaze around, looking for some sign of who could be screaming, but she saw nothing that tipped her off. When Quin joined her, he decided to hazard a guess as to the proper direction from which the scream had come, and off all three of them went. Quin reached the open door first, and he burst inside without so much as a knock. Lucy followed right after him, and Abe brought up the rear.

Inside, they found a couch stained with what looked like fresh blood. Otherwise, though, the room stood empty. It seemed that no one had spent much time here, and Quin wondered if the cabin had been assigned to one of the other survivors of the *Titanic*, someone like them who had come aboard without any belongings to their name.

Quin moved forward to examine the stained couch, and Abe moved over to the left where there stood a closed door. That surprised Quin a bit, as the cabin he shared with Abe was a relatively small affair when compared to the luxuries of the *Titanic*. He'd figured that all of the first class cabins would be similarly made, but if that were the case, someone had taken the liberty of knocking out the wall that separated this cabin from the next one over.

Quin touched the stain on the couch with the tip of his finger, and it came away covered with blood that was still warm. Lucy covered her mouth as she gasped at it. As brave as she was, Quin knew she'd rarely had to face such horrors outside of the occasional novel. None of them had.

Surviving the sinking of the *Titanic* should have been

enough to inure them all to the worst things in life. That hadn't proven true for Quin, and he could see from the look in Lucy's eyes that the experience hadn't armored her against such darkness either. He wiped his finger clean on an unstained part of the couch and then held her hand. She accepted it with quiet gratitude.

"Dear God!" Abe said from the adjoining room. "Quin! Lucy! You're going to want to see this."

Quin was at the doorway in a heartbeat, Lucy peering around his shoulder. Inside, Abe gestured toward a large piece of polished mahogany furniture that sat along the hull wall in the room, right where the bed would normally be. It seemed so out of place there that it took Quin a long moment to identify it.

Lucy made a horrible sound in the back of her throat. "It's a coffin."

"You must be joking." Quin shuddered in revulsion. He'd been to funerals before and seen many coffins. To find one here in place of a bed, though, disturbed him to his core.

"Brody Murtagh is a vampire!" Lucy's tone was hard and sure this time.

Quin's head spun. It made perfect sense, of course it did, but only if you were willing to accept the basic premise that fictional monsters like vampires existed. Nothing in his life had prepared him to believe that such creatures were anything other than the figments of disturbed imaginations.

"This has to be some kind of cruel joke," Abe said.

"Perhaps someone is simply returning a body to be buried in Europe," Quin said. "That would fit."

"Sure," Lucy said, "that's why it's here in a first class cabin rather than tucked down in the hold with the rest of the baggage."

"You don't need to poke holes in everything," Abe said. "Quin's right. That's the simplest explanation."

"Along with the blood-drenched couch out there," said Lucy. "And the scream we heard that brought us here."

Quin stepped into the room, waving off their argument. He'd heard them bicker over things like this before, and he knew that it would not end well for him. They'd both beg him to take their side, and he'd wind up disappointing someone. He had a better idea this time though.

"It's a simple question," Quin said. "Is this a vampire's coffin?"

"Thank you, my good attorney," Abe said. "And just how do you propose to answer this quandary?"

"Easy," Quin said. "We open it."

Abe edged backward and eyed the coffin. "Of course." He gestured toward the coffin. "Be my guest."

Lucy put a hand on Quin's shoulder, but he realized she wasn't holding him back so much as pushing him forward. He crept up to the coffin and looked it over. He didn't see any hinges on his side of the lid, which he hoped meant he just had to reach out and push up to remove it.

He did just that.

The lid gave at the slightest pressure, lifting up an easy inch on well-oiled hinges. Quin smelled something like the scent of rotting flowers emanate from it, and he steeled himself. Then, with a single shove of his arm, he flung the lid open wide.

It lay empty.

# CHAPTER THIRTY-FOUR

"There's nothing in it?" Lucy's voice rose with disbelief as she peered around Quin's shoulder into the coffin.

On closer inspection, Quin saw that this wasn't quite true. While no body lay in repose in the coffin, soil covered every inch of the floor of its satin-lined interior. He reached a hand into the coffin and scooped up a handful of the dirt, then crumbled it between his fingers and let it fall back into the polished wooden box. The dirt was stale and had been packed down hard, although not evenly from one edge to the other.

"Look." Quin pointed at the rough impression of a body in the dirt. "It's not always been empty, has it?"

"Damn," Abe said. "Damn, damn, damn."

Quin nodded. "A vampire."

"It can't be," Lucy said, her face contorting in confusion. "That's not possible."

"She's right," said Abe. "That's just a fairy tale Uncle Bram wrote down to scare stuffy Victorians like our parents."

Quin shrugged. "It's either real or an incredibly elaborate practical joke. I know the Americans take their Halloween seriously, but it's April, not October, right?"

Lucy backed up until she ran into the wall behind her. Its

solidity seemed to give her the strength to process what they faced. "It's not a joke, is it?"

"Of course it is," said Abe. He raised his voice, calling out to someone unseen as he glanced around the room. "And a damned funny one too! Ha ha! You got us good. You can come on out now."

"We came in here because we heard a scream," Quin said. "There's blood on the couch out there, but the door was wide open. It seems to me that someone left here in an awful hurry."

"The vampire?" said Lucy.

"There's no such thing." Abe spoke as if he needed to convince himself more than anyone else.

"Whether it was a vampire or not, it's clear there's something foul going on here, right?" said Quin. "We need to alert the captain."

"Right." Abe took a deep breath to steady himself. "Absolutely right."

"Then let's be off."

Quin took Lucy's hand and guided her toward the door into the adjoining room. Abe beat them there and headed straight for the hallway without a glance at the blood-soaked couch. When he reached the doorway and peered down the hall, though, he stopped cold, then stepped back and slammed shut the door and locked it.

"What are you doing?" Lucy said. "We want to leave, *now*."

"It's her." Abe's voice shook. His face had turned as pale as a full moon. "This must be her room. She's covered in blood."

Lucy gave a sharp gasp. Quin grabbed Abe by the lapel of his jacket and gave him a good shake. "Who is it?" he said. "Who?"

The name seemed to stick on Abe's lips, but he managed to peel it off and spit it out. "Elisabetta," he said.

A knock came at the door, and all three of them jumped.

"Excuse me," came Elisabetta's voice, calm and soothing. "I think you must have wandered into the wrong room."

Abe breathed a sigh of relief. "Maybe we can talk our way out of this," he whispered to the others.

Quin looked back at the couch and the open door to the adjoining room and thought of the open coffin lying there. "There is no way that this ends well," he said. "*She's* the vampire."

"That's insane." Abe rolled his eyes. "There's no such thing."

"Then you talk to her," Lucy whispered. "Quin and I will leave through the other room."

"Hello?" Elisabetta called through the door. The knob rattled. "Could you please let me in? The door seems to be locked."

"My apologies," Abe called. "One moment. Frightfully sorry!"

He waved Quin and Lucy off toward the door to the adjoining room. Lucy beckoned for Abe to come with them, but he gave her a firm shake of his head. Quin took Lucy by the hand and led her out of the room, then closed the adjoining door behind them.

Quin went to the open coffin and closed the lid. As he did, Lucy opened the wardrobe and plucked a wooden clothes hanger from the rod inside of it.

"I don't think this is the time for examining her clothing," Quin said.

Lucy handed the hanger to Quin and then grabbed herself another. "What works against vampires?" she said.

Quin stared at the hanger and realized it was made of polished wood. "You want me to stab someone through the heart with this?"

"Do you have a better idea?"

Quin glanced around the room. He saw no guns, no knives, and certainly no wooden stakes. He shook his head.

Lucy moved toward the door. Quin tried to get there before her, but she shouldered him aside and put her ear against it.

She listened there for a moment, then nodded and stepped back to ease open the door.

Lucy tiptoed out of the room, and Quin followed on her heels, each of them clasping a clothes hanger so tight that their knuckles had turned white. She turned down the corridor, away from Elisabetta's room. Quin stopped her with a hand on her shoulder.

"What about Abe?" Quin asked. "We can't just leave him there."

"I'll find help," Lucy said. "You wait here."

Quin swallowed hard as he considered the wisdom of that plan. His gut told him that they should go in and drag Abe out with them right now, but the memory of that bloody couch persuaded him otherwise. At the very least, sending Lucy for help would put her out of harm's way.

He nodded at her. Lucy swept down the corridor, glancing left and right. Every one of the doors was closed, but she should be able to find a steward soon, Quin thought, or maybe even one of the ship's officers. Meanwhile, he had Abe to worry about.

Quin looked down at the clothes hanger in his hands and grimaced. He brought it up and then snapped it down over his knee. It came apart in a crack and splintered into a number of jagged pieces. He grabbed the longest of them – part of the straight strut that had run between the hanger's shoulders – and hefted it in his hand.

It felt like little more than a toothpick, but he figured that if he stabbed someone with it in the right spot it would hurt. He had no idea if it might be enough to help.

Then he heard Abe shout from inside the room. "Help! Oh, God, *help me!*"

# CHAPTER THIRTY-FIVE

Quin grabbed the doorknob and turned it, but the door was locked. He threw his shoulder against it, but the door held strong. He wished then that he was as tall and strong as his friend.

He cursed, then remembered the other door. He sprinted through it, swerved past the coffin, and threw open the door between the adjoining rooms. The scene inside the room stopped him cold.

Abe knelt on the couch over the reclining body of Elisabetta, his hands at her throat. Blood covered his fingers and had run down the front of Elisabetta's dress, staining it a bright red. She lay there insensate, her eyes closed and her limbs limp.

"Abe!" Quin said. "What have you done?"

"Nothing!" Abe said. "Come here and help me. I'm trying to save her life!"

Quin rushed to Abe's side and looked down at the woman. Her face had gone pale, but perhaps that was just in contrast with the blood that covered so much of her. "What happened?"

"She seemed fine when she came in," Abe said. "She had her hand at her throat, though, and when she removed it I could see a gash had been torn in it. She collapsed right here before I could catch her."

"What are you doing to her throat?" Quin couldn't quite wrap his head around everything he saw. Had the blood they'd seen on the couch originally been from Elisabetta?

"Trying to stop the bleeding the best I can," Abe said. "Can you find me a towel or a washcloth? Something I can use as a compress? My fingers aren't doing the best job."

Quin cast his gaze around the room. Those sorts of things would be in the bathroom, of course, but he hauled up short before he went after them. "This doesn't make any sense. If that's her blood all over the place, how did she disappear for so long? She didn't sound hurt when she was asking to be let in."

Abe glowered at Quin. "Are you going to stand there and quibble with me about silly details like that, or are you going to help me save this woman's life? I don't bloody care how it happened or how politely she asked to be let into her own stateroom. I'm not letting her die!"

Quin edged toward the bathroom, still clutching the splintered rod from the clothes hanger in his fist. "Have you forgotten about the coffin in the other room?"

"If you don't get me something to help stop the bleeding soon, we're going to have someone to put in the damned thing. Now move!"

Quin stayed rooted to the spot. "I fully expected to come in here and find her tearing your throat out, not the other way around."

"I didn't do this!" Abe spluttered in exasperation, unwilling to remove his hands from Elisabetta's throat. Quin was sure that if Abe could he would have placed them around his throat instead.

"I didn't say you did."

"Quincey! If you're not going to help me save this woman, then please go find someone who will! A doctor! Anyone!"

Quin hesitated as his friend glared at him. "No, Abe," he said. "Look at her. She's stopped breathing. It's already too late."

Abe looked back down at Elisabetta. Her chest didn't move. No breath escaped from her lips, and the flow of blood had slowed. It leaked from her wound now rather than flowed.

Abe removed his hands from the woman's body, and they shook with rage. "Dammit, Quin! We could have saved her." He launched himself off the couch and stood up to face his old chum. "You cold-hearted idiot! I've seen enough bloody death on this God forsaken trip!"

Quin put up his hands to give Abe pause, the broken rod still in his fist. "We couldn't have done a thing." He was upset too, but tried to keep his voice low and steady, hoping to bring Abe back down to earth before he became agitated enough to do something stupid. "She was dead before she walked into the room."

"So say you!"

Quin's mouth grew wide in horror as Elisabetta's eyelids fluttered, and she stared at him with furious eyes gone entirely black. "Abe!" He pointed at the woman as she sat up on the couch, the wicked smile on her face mirroring the shape of the bloody cut on her throat.

Without turning to see where Quin pointed, Abe replied, "You'd better go get the captain, Quin, right now, or so help me there will be another dead body in this room before anyone discovers this!"

Quin brought the broken wooden rod over his head with one hand and pointed at Elisabetta with the other as she rose to her feet, every bit the image of death. "Abe!"

"And now you're going to threaten me?" Abe gaped at him." What the hell's happened to you, Quin?"

"Turn around!" Quin grabbed Abe with his free hand and tried to spin him about.

Abe resisted Quin's attempt with a snarl. "Are you out of your–"

Before Abe could finish his sentence, Elisabetta rushed at him and leaped onto his back. She threw back her head, exposing inch-long fangs stabbing down from her upper teeth. As Abe hollered in protest, she brought her head down and sank those fangs straight into the corded muscles of his exposed neck.

Abe screamed in terror and pain. Quin cocked back his fist and then stabbed down with the rod, striking Elisabetta in the head with it. The point, such as it was, twisted against her skull, but it tore a gash in the side of her head, right over the temple. It did not bleed, leaking only some blackish tarry material instead.

Abe continued to scream and tried to buck Elisabetta off his back. She held on tight, her hands like claws set into his jacket's shoulders, and her teeth like a bear trap closed on his flesh.

Quin brought the rod back once more. If anything, the strike against Elisabetta's head had sharpened its splintered tip. He struck her with it again, and this time the rod stabbed straight into her left eye and stuck there.

This persuaded the woman to let go of Abe. She unleashed a scream that Quin thought might peel the paint from the ship's hull, and she shoved his friend away, clutching at her ruined face and the stick still caught in it. The same tarry fluid that had leaked from Quin's first blow dribbled from her eye socket and down her pale cheek.

"You animal!" she screeched at Quin. "Look what you've done!"

Elisabetta staggered back toward the couch, and Quin sprang to Abe's side to help his wounded friend to his feet. As they rose, they turned to gape at the woman as she plucked the rod from her face and stared at it with her one good eye. She cried thick black tears now, rolling past her cheekbones.

"No!" she said. "No!"

She drew in a deep breath and held it for an instant. Her skin turned from pale into an ash gray. She reached out for the two young men and screamed at the top of her lungs. As she did, she crumpled into a pile of dust – and was gone.

# CHAPTER THIRTY-SIX

Quin stared at the spot where Elisabetta had been and wondered what sorts of horrible things he had just learned about the true nature of the world. Nothing about this fit well with what he knew about how things were supposed to work, and it shocked him so much he had to remind himself to breathe. His gaze darted around the edges of the room as he hunted for any sign that he'd just experienced some sort of illusion, which would mean that the woman he'd just stabbed through the eye with a sharp stick might attack him again.

He jumped with a start the moment Abe groaned in pain, and he dropped to one knee to see how he could help his friend. Abe held a hand over the spot where Elisabetta had bitten him, and blood trickled between his fingers. He reached out toward it with a nervous hand, but Abe waved him off.

"How bad is it?" Abe asked.

"I can't tell with your hand over it."

"Should I take it off?"

"Hold on." Quin darted into the bathroom and grabbed a hand towel hanging on the railing inside. He returned an instant later and held it up before Abe.

"You wouldn't get that for me when I asked." Abe allowed

himself a gentle grin, which shifted to a pained grimace.

"I wouldn't get it for her." Quin held the towel up over Abe's wound. "For you, anything. Now move that hand."

Abe did as instructed, and blood gushed from the wound. Elisabetta had done more than just bite Abe's neck. After Quin had hurt her, she'd torn a good chunk of it away.

Quin pressed the towel down over the wound. "That has to do a better job than your hand."

"How is it?" Abe grabbed Quin's arm and would not let go.

"Not good," Quin said. "I need to go find a doctor."

"No worries about that," a voice said from down the hallway. It swept toward them on a thunderous tide of footsteps. "He's already on his way."

A sailor – Second Officer Crooker, Quin recalled – appeared in the doorway and surveyed the scene. "Good God!" he said, recoiling. "What happened in here?"

They would never believe the truth, Quin knew. He wouldn't have believed it if he hadn't seen it – hell, stabbed it – himself. But he couldn't come up with anything else to tell the man, so he chose to simply avoid it for now.

Quin stood up and hauled Abe to his feet. He rose, although on legs as shaky as those of a newborn fawn. "We need to get this man medical attention," Quin said, moving Abe forward. "Where's the doctor?"

"He was in the Smoke Room," Crooker said. "I sent word for him." He craned his neck to peer into the room, unwilling as of yet to step across its threshold. "What have you two chaps done here then?"

"We heard a scream," Abe said. "We came in here to help, and someone attacked me."

"And just where is this someone?" Crooker edged forward into the room, glancing about as if someone might step out and try to brain him at any moment. A number of other men crowded into the hallway where he had just been, each of them staring at the horrible scene through the open doorway.

"Disappeared," Quin said.

"Did you get a good look at him?"

Quin put a shoulder under Abe's arm, helping to keep him propped up. "No, but I think Elisabetta Ecsed did. If you find her, she should be able to identify the attacker."

"Isn't this her room?" a steward called in from the hallway.

"Of course it is," Quin said. "Who do you think we heard screaming? She was so terrified, she ran off. Find her, and you'll find the killer."

"Killer?" Crooker said. "Who's been killed? I don't see any body lying about."

"Attacker then," Abe said with a snarl. "Could you please quit quibbling about words and find me a physician?"

"Coming through," Doctor Griffiths shouted from somewhere down the hallway. "Gangway, my good people!"

Quin hauled Abe toward the voice and spotted the doctor coming for them. Lucy followed right behind the man, and she gave out a little scream when she saw the state that Abe was in. "She did this to him?"

"How do you mean 'she,' miss?" Crooker asked. "Do you have reason to believe you know what happened to this man?"

Lucy stared at Abe, her mouth open and her eyes wide. Crooker walked over to take her by the elbow and speak to her. As he did, the doctor rushed up to inspect Abe.

"What happened?" he said.

"Is that important?" Quin asked. "He's hurt. Help him!"

"It always helps if I know how he was hurt, young sir." The doctor peeled back Abe's fingers and the towel underneath them until blood squelched through them again. "It's bad. Very bad."

"He was bitten," Quin said in low confidence.

"I can see that," Doctor Griffiths said. "But by what? Or who?" He shook his head in frustration. "You're right. None of that's important now. We need to get this man down to the hospital right away. I may have to rig up a blood transfusion for him, or he might not make it through the night."

"You can tell that by just looking at him?"

The doctor jerked his head at the blood-splattered scene in the room beyond. "That gives me some indication as well. Come on now. Help me get him moving."

"You'll have to stay with me, miss," Crooker said to Lucy. "I have some questions I need you to answer."

"Not now!" she said, near hysterics. "You must go and find Elisabetta Ecsed. She's the key to all of this. I need to be with my friend. He's hurt."

Crooker hesitated, and the doctor called back over his shoulder to intervene on Lucy's behalf. "She can come with me, Mr Crooker," he said. "I'll keep an eye on her, and if her young friend here is as bad off as he looks we'll be a long time at it."

"Just make sure she doesn't wander off anywhere," Crooker said. He rubbed his chin as he relented. Quin could tell he was wondering just what to do about this awful mess.

"It's only one ship," Doctor Griffiths said. "How far could she get?"

# CHAPTER THIRTY-SEVEN

"Is he going to make it?" Quin asked as the doctor emerged from the curtained off area in which he'd been working on Abe.

Quin had spent the entire time sitting next to Lucy in the waiting room and holding her hand, calming her down, and explaining to her in rushed whispers what had happened in Elisabetta's cabin. She hadn't believed a word of it. Not at first.

"There's no such thing as vampires. I know what I saw but I refuse to believe it." Lucy set her jaw in the way that Quin knew meant she'd already made up her mind about the topic at hand. At another time in another place, he might have let her have her way. In most cases, no harm could have come from it.

"How do you explain what happened to Abe then?" Quin said. "Do you think I bit his throat?"

"You tell me, Quin." She glared at him with an intensity. "You were there. This time, just tell me the truth."

"What about the coffin?" Quin sat back in his chair. "You used to believe in vampires, Lucy. I still remember."

Lucy's cheeks turned a fierce pink. "I was just a little girl. You can't hold a childish imagination run amuck against me. My parents took it very seriously, at least."

"And what did they tell you?"

"That vampires don't exist. Of course."

Quin leaned forward. "But Lucy," he said, "what if they lied to you?"

"Why in the Lord's name would they do that?"

"Maybe they just wanted to let you finally have a good night's sleep. My parents used to tell me Jack the Ripper wasn't real either, and we both know the truth of that."

"But Quin." Lucy steeled herself, squelching down emotions that threatened to overwhelm her and drive her to give in to the tears welling up in her eyes. Quin knew better than to interrupt her at such a time. "Are you saying it's all true then? That you killed her?"

"It seems so." Quin shuddered as the image of Elisabetta crumbling to dust passed before his eyes. "I saw that myself – hell, I did it myself – and I can hardly believe it."

The doctor emerged from behind the curtains then, and Quin and Lucy stood to speak to him. Quin asked him about Abe's health. The man gave them a grave but determined look.

"He's about as bad off as anyone I've ever treated aboard this ship," he said. "But he's stabilized for now. We're only a couple days out of New York. As long as he holds out until we get there, and I can have him transported to a proper hospital, he should survive."

Lucy breathed a huge sigh of relief and clung to Quin's shoulder. He kept looking at the doctor though. Something about the man's statements had run hollow in his ears.

"'As long as?' Is there a reason why he shouldn't be able to do so?"

The doctor wrung his hands together. After a glance at the open doorway behind Quin and Lucy, he seemed to come to a decision and spoke.

"He's lost a lot of blood, Mr Harker," the doctor said. "A lot more than I would have thought possible from a wound like that."

"You saw the blood all around the cabin."

The doctor allowed himself a soft chuckle. "It would help if you came clean with me, my boy. We both know that not all of the blood spattered about that cabin came from Mr Holmwood's neck."

Quin looked at the floor for a moment, then at Lucy, who'd started to squeeze his arm in an iron grip. "I'm afraid I don't have a decent explanation for it, Doctor."

"Or at least one that you think I'd believe." The doctor gave up a wry grin and leaned his head toward the curtains that separated Abe from the rest of the room. "Those are fairly thin curtains, Mr Harker. There's not a lot that gets said in this room that I don't hear."

Quin swallowed hard and flushed red. "I'm afraid you've caught me taunting my friend here with a cruel joke. Please do forgive me for being so tasteless. My sense of decorum tends to leave me when I'm in such stressful situations as this one."

"Is it true that you killed Miss Ecsed?" He held up a hand. "Wait. Don't answer that. Instead, consider this: What's going to happen after the captain has the ship turned upside down looking for her? Will they find her? Or will they find a body with your fingerprints on it?"

Quin frowned. "I only struck her in self-defense."

"I knew it!" The doctor quivered in his shoes. "You did kill her, and she was a vampire!"

"What... what do you know about vampires?" Lucy asked.

Quin didn't understand what asking that kind of question could do to help him and Lucy, but he was grateful to her for distracting the doctor from his role in the affair as a possible murderer.

The doctor chuckled again. "My dear, you don't serve as a ship's doctor on a liner heading back and forth from Fiume without running into a vampire legend or three."

"So you only know about them from legends?" Quin asked. His disappointment sat in his stomach like a rock.

"I treated a woman here on the ship once. She had symptoms identical to that of your friend Mr Holmwood there."

"And what happened to her?" Lucy asked.

The doctor's face fell. "She died. I did everything I could to save her, but it wasn't enough. I even set her up with a number of transfusions, but it didn't work. No matter how much blood I pumped into her, she wound up sick and pale."

"Did you ever figure out what happened to her?"

"It's impossible to say," Doctor Cherryman said. "The autopsy listed traumatic blood loss as the cause of death. The kind that your friend Abe has back there."

"But you didn't believe it?"

"No. I monitored her day and night. The treatment should have worked. Something – perhaps someone – stopped it, and that killed her."

"And what or who do you think did it?"

The doctor shrugged. "I don't know, but I can tell you this. There was another passenger on that voyage who took a special interest in that young lady who died. Someone you know all too well."

"And that was?" Quin asked.

"None other than your supposed victim, Mr Harker. The one you have the crew tearing apart the ship to find right now: Elisabetta Ecsed."

# CHAPTER THIRTY-EIGHT

"Mr Dragomir?"

Dushko looked up from his overstuffed leather chair in the Smoke Room where he'd been sipping at a fine glass of port that tasted like vinegar in his mouth. A man had to keep up appearances, though, at least if he wanted to be able to make this trip above decks. He thought of being stuck down in the crowded hold with the others of his kind and repressed a shudder.

"Yes?"

He recognized the nervous man looming over him as second officer on the *Carpathia*, Mr Blum, his highest-ranking confidant on the ship. Dushko had taken great pains to cultivate the proper relationship with the man, and a good part of that meant that they rarely spoke to each other in public.

Most of the time Elisabetta had handled Mr Blum, but as a woman she wasn't allowed into the Smoke Room. That was the very reason that Dushko had chosen to hole up here, despite his actual distaste for food and drink. While he adored Elisabetta on many levels and they'd been companions for more years than he liked to count, he needed a bit of space from her each day. If they didn't spend some time apart, they started to bicker after a while, and he found such arguments tiresome. Better to find some means of separation rather than rub each other's nerves raw from too much togetherness.

"I have a matter of some importance that I need to discuss with you. Immediately."

Dushko made a show of rolling his eyes for the others in the room. "We're in the middle of the ocean," he said with a droll groan. "Can it really be that important?"

"I'm afraid so, sir." Blum gave Dushko a curt nod. "It involves Miss Ecsed."

Dushko loosed a derisive snort. "Of course it does." He stood, put his glass down on a nearby table, and gave a stiff bow to the men with whom he'd been pretending to have an interesting conversation. "Gentlemen, I must be off to attend to my lady's needs."

Amid a chorus of guffaws, Dushko took his leave and followed Blum out of the Smoke Room and onto the open section of the Boat Deck. With the *Titanic*'s lifeboats stacked up among the *Carpathia*'s, it felt a bit more cramped than normal, but it also meant that fewer people bothered strolling the deck. This gave Dushko and Blum as much privacy as if they'd locked themselves into Dushko's stateroom.

"What is it?" Dushko said to Blum. "What is so vital that Elisabetta needed to interrupt my evening away from her? I was going to clean those men out at cards later tonight. I might still if I can get back to them in time."

"There was an incident in Miss Ecsed's room," Blum said. "No one's seen her since, and the captain has us turning over the boat to look for her."

Dushko felt his irritation at Elisabetta wash away. "What happened?" he said. "Where is she?"

"I don't know," Blum said, his voice cracking with strain. "That's the thing. No one knows. We've been unable to find her."

"Did you check the hold?"

"Of course, sir."

Dushko gave Blum a hard look until the man squirmed under his gaze like a worm in the summer sun.

"I didn't actually go into the hold, of course, so it's possible that she's hidden down there, but the others told me that she hasn't been there since sundown."

Duskho ground his teeth. "What about Murtagh?" he said.

"No one's seen him either. Not that I know of, anyhow."

Dushko shook his head in frustration. "Find Brody and you'll find Elisabetta. I'd put money on it."

Blum stared at Dushko, his mouth hanging open. The man clearly had something else to say but couldn't bring himself to broach the subject.

"I've told you already," Dushko said. "I will not give permission for Elisabetta to bring you into our fold. Not now."

"But, sir." Pain marred Blum's normally stoic face. "You'd said that it would happen once we left America behind."

"Once we reached our destination, I said." Dushko spread his arms wide. "Does this look like Europe? We're on our way back to America. I can't have you disappearing into the hold for the rest of the trip. What would happen when we reached the docks in New York?"

The officer gave Dushko a reluctant nod to indicate he knew the man was right, even if he couldn't bring himself to like it. Dushko clapped a broad hand on the man's shoulder.

"Once we reach Fiume and disappear into the city," Dushko said. "Once we're all arrived and safe, I'll have Elisabetta fulfill her promise to you herself."

Blum's face erupted into a smile that faded away as fast as it had come. "That's the one thing I didn't mention yet, sir."

"About Elisabetta? What is it?"

"There was a fight in her room, sir. Blood everywhere."

Dushko ran his hands over his face. "Of course there is. It's Elisabetta. Damn it."

His mind raced over what he might have to say or do to help her explain this incident away. Had she gotten carried away during a feeding? It had been known to happen before. Either way, he would make it right. He always did.

"But that's not all, sir."

Dushko looked at the officer, surprised by how much he was cringing. "What is it, man? Out with it."

"I… I found a pile of dust in her room."

Blum said it as flat and plain as if he'd seen Elisabetta strolling out of the room himself. But Dushko knew what that meant, even if Blum didn't.

"She's dead?" Dushko said.

Blum swallowed hard and nodded. "No way to say for sure, of course, sir, but – it seems so."

Dushko allowed himself a soft snarl. "Perhaps," he said. "Perhaps. And should that prove true, then whoever might have stolen that lovely creature from my side after all these years will pay with far more than their miserable lives."

# CHAPTER THIRTY-NINE

"So you believe me?" Quin asked Doctor Cherryman. He glanced at Lucy. Maybe this would be what he needed to convince her that he was telling the truth about what happened to Abe. She knew that she didn't think he was lying. She just couldn't bring herself to admit that things like vampires might truly exist, especially aboard this ship.

The man bowed his head for a moment before speaking. "It runs against everything I've ever been taught or believed in. I'm a man of science, not superstition, but when evidence like this crops up, what am I to do? How do I explain it?"

"Just because you can't explain something doesn't mean it's not so," Lucy said. She reached out and put a hand on the man's arm, and that seemed to give him strength.

"Let's say it's true." Quin glanced at Lucy and saw her lips purse together as if she'd bitten something sour. "Just for the sake of argument. Call it a hypothesis, if you will."

"A hypothesis." Lucy nodded at the term.

"Let's formulate the hypothesis and test it. Just like we would for any science."

"Right." Doctor Cherryman's face lit up. Here was a way for him to grapple with the problem that the reality of vampires had presented him. "Let's say vampires exist. What does that mean?"

"That they're bloodsucking murderers here to kill us all?"

Lucy and the doctor gaped at Quin's bald-faced assessment.

"Tell me I'm wrong," Quin said.

"Let's avoid conjecture and stick to the facts as we know them," the doctor said. "They drink blood. They can mesmerize men."

"And women," Lucy said.

The doctor acknowledged this with a nod and continued on. "They can change shape: mist, bats, wolves, and so on. Have either of you read *Dracula*?"

Lucy and Quin shared a smile at this.

"What?" asked the doctor. "Did I say something humorous?"

"Our parents are old friends with Mr Stoker," Lucy said. "We used to call him Uncle Bram. I think Abe might have been named after him."

The doctor's jaw dropped. "Wait? Harker, Seward, and Holmwood? Are you serious?"

Quin waved off Doctor Cherryman's concerns. He'd had to explain this countless times throughout his childhood, and he'd become immune to the astonishment his family name sometimes produced in others. "He used their names for the heroes in the book. With their kind permission, of course."

"And you don't believe in vampires?"

Quin grimaced. "Not until today."

"It's a fiction," Lucy said. "I've read the book. Who hasn't? It's laughable to think it could be real."

"Did you never ask your parents?" The doctor's astonishment hadn't faded yet.

"Of course we did," said Quin. "They explained to us in no uncertain terms that such creatures did not exist. Emphatically. Several times."

Quin remembered the conversations all too well. He'd had nightmares about vampires from time to time over the years. Each time his parents had comforted him and told him that there was no such thing as vampires. Despite that, he'd believed in them so much that they'd taken steps to protect him, just to humor him. Or so they'd said.

Quin felt ill.

"What is it?" Lucy took his chin in her hand. He'd faded away from the conversation and not even realized it. "You're white as a ghost."

Quin stared into Lucy's concerned eyes and swallowed down the bile rising in his throat. "Did it ever strike you as odd that our parents always kept a large supply of garlic handy around the house?"

"They loved the smell of it cooking," Lucy said. "I remember coming home from school to find the house soaking in it. The scent always brings me right back to my childhood."

"That doesn't strike you as odd?" Doctor Cherryman said. "It's not exactly a traditional staple in English cooking."

"They grew it in our garden. We had heaps of it. My father told me that they'd brought it back with them from a fantastic trip to Italy in their youth, before any of us children were born. All our fathers had been along on it. Quin's mother too."

"We had an awful lot of crucifixes around our house," Quin said.

"I don't see that as unusual for members of the Anglican church," said Lucy.

"Over every door and window?"

"Dear God." Lucy's hand flew up to cover her mouth. "We are such fools."

Doctor Cherryman shook his head. "If you grew up surrounded by such things your whole life, it's easy to see why you wouldn't think them unusual. Let me assure you, though, that most homes in England are not suffused with garlic and crosses."

"What do we do?" Lucy said. "Even if you destroyed Miss Ecsed, that Mr Murtagh is still out there, trapped somewhere on this ship with us."

"Maybe he's not a vampire," the doctor said. "Maybe he's a servant, like Renfield in the book."

"A servant wouldn't throw himself overboard in the middle of the Atlantic," Quin said. "Not unless he thought he could – oh." He stared at the others. "He must have changed into a bat after he leaped off the railing."

"Then what do we do?" Lucy asked again, her voice creeping higher as she spoke. "I can't go to sleep tonight knowing there's a vampire creeping about the ship."

"According to *Dracula*–" The doctor put up a hand to head off Quin's interruption. "I don't care to reopen the argument about whether the book is fiction or not, but it serves as a fine hypothesis for how vampires function, does it not?"

Quin granted the man this point with a nod.

"The book lists vampires' weaknesses as well as their powers. They cannot enter a room without an invitation from the owner. They cannot abide garlic, crucifixes, and holy water. They dislike sunshine and mirrors, in which they cast no reflection."

"It's a novel," Lucy said. "Can we really rely on its prescriptions against vampires? Can we trust that with our lives?"

"Do you have a better resource?" the doctor asked. "The research about the reality of vampires seems a bit thin otherwise."

"We don't trust anything until it's been proven to work," Quin said. "Let's gather our prospective tools together, though, and test them as we go."

Lucy shuddered. "I can only pray that some of them work."

# CHAPTER FORTY

"Where is he?" Dushko shouted as he stormed into the *Carpathia*'s hold. He glanced around, his eyes eagle sharp, hunting for some sign of Brody Murtagh. Finding none, he slammed the steel hatch behind him and bellowed at the people inside the hold with a voice that rolled like thunder.

"Where is he? Don't any of you dare try to protect him. Don't you dare get between me and him, or so help me I'll pitch every damned one of you into the sea so you can watch the sun come up one last damned time!"

Piotr stood up and opened his mouth. Dushko flashed a savage grin at the man, exposing his fangs as he did. He could always count on Piotr to spill his guts before he tried spilling blood.

The man froze before he could utter a single word of what was on his mind, staring in horror at something in the distance. It took Dushko a moment to realize that Piotr had been captivated by the sight of something behind him, to his left. He spun about to see what it was, but he was already too late.

The blunt side of a large baling hook smashed into Dushko's face, catching him right under a cheekbone. The forceful blow snapped his head back and sent him sprawling on the floor of the hold.

"I don't need protection, boyo!" Brody stood shaking the heavy iron hook at Dushko, his face flushed and angry. "Not from the likes of you!"

Dushko shoved himself to his feet and squared off against his attacker. He felt his cheek. Had he still been breathing, it would have been shattered for sure. He wiped the injured area with the back of a meaty hand, and it came away stained with blood.

"What did you do to Elisabetta?" Dushko could barely contain his rage. He wanted to rip the man's head off right here and stomp his brains out of it, but he knew it would go better if the others heard Brody confess his crimes first.

"Not a damned thing," Brody said. "She invited me into her cabin, and a steward interrupted us while she fed on me."

The rest of the people in the hold gasped from the various corners in which they cowered. Dushko stifled a self-satisfied smile. If Brody had allowed them to be found out, no penalty would be stiff enough. Dushko could do to him whatever he wanted without fear of repercussions. Still, the man was responsible for even worse crimes, and Dushko wanted to expose him for those too.

"And where is she now?" Dushko knew the answer, of course, but he wanted to know if Brody did.

"Last I saw her, she'd killed the witness. I helped her hide the body. There was no harm done."

This was the first Dushko had heard of this little wrinkle. "Dumped the body over the railing just like you were seen doing earlier?" He let sarcasm drip from his lips with every word. "You have become too bold over the years, boy. You have become careless."

"Me?" Brody brandished the hook at Dushko again. Dushko had to force himself to stand strong and not back up a single step. "What the hell have you been up to for the entire trip?

The rest of us loll about down here in this hellhole while you parade about with the breathers upstairs, just daring them to find you out. And once they do that, what happens then? You think they'll be content?"

"No one has ever suspected me," Dushko said. "I have decades of experience in covering my tracks, in posing as a part of the still-living world. Elisabetta did too. She would still be alive if not for you!"

Brody dropped the hook in surprise. "Alive? What happened to her? What have you done, you bastard?"

Brody launched himself at Dushko again, but this time Dushko was ready for him. He braced himself for the impact and caught the smaller Irishman in midair, snagging him by the lapels of his jacket. Then he thrust his head forward and shouted into Brody's face.

"What did *I* do to her? It's you, you useless fool. You broke the rules. You were spotted. And it's Elisabetta that had to pay for it!"

Dushko hurled Brody away from him, sending the man tumbling head over heels toward the far wall of the hold. He landed there with a sickening, satisfying crash among a stack of crates. These toppled over on top of him, burying him beneath the wood.

Dushko wondered if he might somehow be so lucky for one of the crates to have splintered in just the right way. He imagined Brody lying there underneath the wooden boxes, a shattered plank spearing him through the heart. Despite his fury, he couldn't help but smile at that vicious image.

"Sir?" Piotr said, his voice trembling. "How can you be sure Lady Ecsed is dead?"

Dushko scowled at the spindly man and considered tearing him limb from limb as a demonstration to the others of just what he was capable of doing when in a state of rage like this.

The lack of any movement from the crates that had crashed down on Brody, though, gave him pause. Perhaps he'd already done enough.

"I cannot." Dushko shoved past Piotr as he stalked toward the fallen crates. "Not any more than I can be sure I just killed Brody." He lifted them up one by one, tossing them aside the way a child might root through a toy box, until he reached the bare deck beneath.

Brody wasn't there. He'd disappeared, either turned to mist or become a bat or slipped away some by some other means. The fact was he'd got away again, and that made Dushko madder than ever.

"And he's gone!" Dushko shouted. The others in the room scattered away, pressing themselves into the smallest, darkest, safest places they could find. They sensed what was coming next.

Dushko picked up one of the crates he'd just tossed aside. It stretched eight feet long, three feet wide and three feet high, just like all of the others he'd paid to have brought aboard the ship for this long-planned voyage. Each of them bore the words FRAGILE, HANDLE WITH CARE, and THIS SIDE UP on them, supposedly because they contained prized flower bulbs that he was transporting back to his native land to transplant and sell.

Dushko took the crate and smashed it against the nearest bulkhead. It splintered into countless pieces, and the earth inside of it burst out and spilled to the floor below. He set it aside and picked up another.

"You live in these boxes, you sleep in the dirt of your homeland, and you think because you stay silent and keep to yourself, that you are safe." He spoke not to Brody, not to himself, but to everyone else in the room. He smashed the next box to pieces and grabbed another, swinging them about as if they were as light and easy to handle as baseball bats.

"You think because you keep your head down, that no one will notice you."

He smashed the crate in his hands into one sitting skewed on the floor. Splintered wood and fresh-turned earth burst everywhere.

"You forget that the actions of those around you matter."

He grabbed another crate and hurled it against a tall stack of crates nearby. The entire tower toppled over, and people scrambled away from it in fear for their lives. Dushko knew they had little to worry about, outside of a freak accident. Like Brody and – damn them all – like Elisabetta, they were hard to kill.

Dushko set to the remaining crates with righteous fury, shouting out epithets at the others as he went. He chased them from their hiding holes. He flushed them into the open, and then he stood there and screamed at every one of them.

"You are dead already, you fools. You think that protects you, and you are right. But it also leaves you vulnerable – mostly to those of your own kind!"

He stopped and stared at the destruction he'd wrought upon the hold. He'd ruined more than just his own boxes. There would be hell to pay when the ship finally made it back to port, but he'd deal with that when it happened, just like he always did. Right now, he was making a point.

"All it takes is for one of us to make one mistake. Just one! And we are hauled out from the cover of darkness and thrust into the harshest sunlight!"

A few of the others hissed at this. Some of them had been careless about their exposure to the sun before and still bore the burn scars from it.

"This should not be me bringing down the hammer on that damned bastard Brody! It should be all of us. Every one of us!"

The others nodded along with Dushko now, the fear he had

put into them transforming into something darker, something hateful, directed not at him but at the target he'd placed before them.

"There is only one solution to this. We stick together! Against Brody and against the rest of the world. The next time that he comes crawling back here, you must do the right thing for all of us. You kill him on the spot, if you can!"

A rough cheer of approval went up among the others, and hope rose in Dushko's heart for the first time since he'd heard about Elisabetta and her fate. Maybe he couldn't bring her back, but he could use her death as a stick to beat his people back into line. Otherwise, they would all be doomed for sure.

"But what if he never comes back?" a woman said, speaking to Dushko for the first time in the entire trip. "What do we do then?"

Dushko nodded at her, recognizing her courage. He spoke in low, harsh tones now, his voice a whisper compared to the bellowing he'd given himself over to before. In the silence that followed his stormy rage, though, his words carried to every part of the hold.

"There are people out there looking for us now. Looking for Brody. If they cannot find him on their own, then I will feed the jackass to them."

# CHAPTER FORTY-ONE

"I don't have a good feeling about this," Lucy said.

Quin looked back at her, a rope of garlic strung over her shoulders like a necklace. With Doctor Cherryman's help, they'd raided the ship's kitchen for it, taking one for her and for Quin too. Then he'd given them his keys, a set that he claimed would open every door on the ship, shoved a flashlight into Quin's hand, and sent them on their way while he returned to the ship's hospital to look after Abe.

Before heading out to look for Murtagh, though, they'd stopped by their own quarters for supplies. Each of them had a crucifix in their luggage, something their parents had insisted they bring along on their journey with them. Thinking back, Quin had thought it an innocent enough request, and he'd been happy to humor his mother by complying with it. Now he wondered just how much they might have known.

Quin had also grabbed the Bowie knife his father had given him on his sixteenth birthday. Then he'd smashed apart a chair in his cabin and used the knife's oversized blade to trim two of the legs into wooden stakes that he hoped they would never have to use. He'd attached the knife's sheath to his belt, and they'd set off, each carrying a crucifix in one hand and a stake in the other.

He had to admit, they looked ridiculous. He was far beyond caring about that, though, and Lucy appeared to have given up any lingering sense of decorum too – other than her occasional comments.

"This is madness," Lucy said as she and Quin made their way deeper into the ship.

Quin did his best to ignore the sentiment, tempting as it was to share it. She was right, after all. What was madder than searching through the rooms of an ocean liner in the middle of the night, hoping that they might find a vampire they could slay?

"It's been a hell of a few days," Quin said.

Lucy snorted at this. "Are you sure we didn't die on the *Titanic*? That we didn't go down with all the rest of those poor souls on the ship?"

"What?" Quin shot her a curious look. "You think this is all some sort of purgatory that we've entered? That God's sent us here to rot rather than ushering us along?"

Lucy shook her head. "No. I'm afraid it's our own particular kind of hell."

Quin stopped and put his hands on Lucy's shoulders. She looked so beautiful – and terrified but ready for whatever might be thrown at them by this world or the next.

"I might believe that for myself, Luce," he said with every bit of earnestness he could summon. "But I could never imagine that for you."

"You're far too kind, Quin," she said. "I've done plenty of wrong things in my life."

"But never anything evil."

She peered into his eyes. "How can you be so sure?"

He smiled. "I know you, Luce, better than anyone. Maybe better than you know yourself. You're as good as they come."

"Really?" A guilty look crossed her face. "I don't think the feelings I've had for you are all that pure."

Quin blushed. He found himself unable to summon a reply.

"Oh, that's not what I meant!" Lucy blushed too then. "It's just that I should be with Abe, shouldn't I? He's my beau, the one I'm expected to marry someday. That's the way it is. The way it's been."

Quin reached out and took her hand. "It doesn't have to stay that way."

"But Abe's your best friend," she said. "You two have been inseparable since we were kids. I can't come between you."

"We've all been that way, Luce. All three of us."

"You say that, Quin, but that was when we were kids. When we went away to different schools, we did drift apart. Especially you and me."

Quin knew this to be true. Lucy was a few years younger than he, and when he'd gone away to study Law, she was still in secondary school. She'd blossomed into such a beautiful woman by the time he'd graduated, but she'd somehow wound up dating Abe in the meantime.

"I know," he said. "It was just timing, I suppose. And I guess that favored Abe."

"I thought you'd decided to ignore me."

Quin looked at Lucy and put his hand on her cheek. "Not that," he said. "Never that."

Quin found himself drawn to Lucy's lips with a hunger he'd rarely known. They moved closer to each other in a tender way, and he could feel the heat of her breath on him. He leaned in to kiss her, but she froze at the sound of a horrible thumping reverberating through the ship.

"What is that?" she said. "You don't think we've hit another iceberg, do you?"

For an instant, Quin wanted to laugh at the thought that the *Carpathia* might meet the same fate at the *Titanic*. It struck him though that there wasn't anything humorous about that notion at all.

Quin backed off from Lucy, the moment that had passed between them already evaporating so fast it seemed as insubstantial and yet beautiful as the Northern Lights. He cocked his ear and concentrated on listening for the sound that had interrupted them. He'd heard it too – or felt it in his shoes at least.

It came again, a tremor that reverberated through the floor. It came so soft that he was sure he would have missed it entirely had he not been listening for it. In fact, if he and Lucy had not stopped chatting at the right moment, he was sure they'd never have heard it.

"Where is that coming from?" Lucy asked, her face a porcelain mask of concentration.

"From the aft of the ship, I think. Maybe toward the bottom." Quin moved down the hall in that direction. The sound came again and seemed just a little bit stronger now. "Maybe it's just a fault in the engines. They lie in that direction."

Lucy curled a lip at that. "After everything we've been through tonight, do you really believe that?"

Quin shook his head. "Of course not. But a man can always hope."

# CHAPTER FORTY-TWO

Quin led Lucy deeper and deeper into the bowels of the ship. They passed through the empty halls that snaked through the steerage cabins, creeping along as silently as they could manage. It was late now, in the wee hours of the morning, and if anyone else were awake in this part of the ship, they didn't show themselves to prove it.

Soon they reached the end of the long hallway and met up with a door labeled Crew Only. Quin looked about in all directions, but the halls that led to the door still stood empty. He tried the handle, and the door was locked.

Quin pulled Doctor Cherryman's keys from his pocket and tried them. He had no idea which of the keys might work for this particular lock, but there weren't too many of them. In no time at all, he felt the lock turn, and with a twist of its knob the door opened wide.

Before he opened the door, Quin turned to Lucy. "You should go back to your cabin," he said. "I can handle this."

"Don't be a twit." Lucy screwed up her face at him. "We've known each other far too long for you to become chivalrous for me now. As a suffragette, I find it insulting."

"I know, Luce, and I'm sorry, but–"

"But what? What's there to 'but' about? I'm no wallflower you need to protect from the brutal realities of the real world. Now open that door, and let's get on with it."

Quin wanted to explain to her that he knew she was right but still couldn't stomach the idea of walking with her into danger. No matter how capable she might be, the thought that she might be hurt or killed rattled him to his core. Part of that came from his growing sense of how much he truly loved her. The rest came from just having watched their best friend Abe torn apart by a vampire that very night. He didn't think he could bear watching the same thing happen to Lucy.

He left all of this unvoiced though. He knew the exact arguments she would lay out for her side of the case, and he knew that she wouldn't allow him to get rid of her. In the end, he had to admit to himself that he wanted her there with him anyhow, and allowing himself just that small bit of selfishness was one of the hardest things he'd ever done.

"All right," he said to her. "If you want to come along, I won't try to stop you. I just want you to realize exactly how stupid an idea this is."

"If it's not too stupid for you to get involved, how can it be too stupid for me?"

Quin permitted himself a soft smile. "If that's your only criteria, then I'm afraid you're doomed. From what I can tell from my actions over the past week, there's very little that's too stupid for me to become involved with it."

# CHAPTER FORTY-THREE

Abe awakened with a horrible pain in his throat. At first, he flashed back to leaping off the *Titanic* and spending that long, terrifying night trying to balance atop an overturned lifeboat with Quin at his side, and he wondered if his memories of being rescued had been little more than a fevered dream. Then he tried to swallow, and the agony that caused reminded him of Elisabetta and pain and blood.

He opened his eyes to find himself reclining in a hospital bed curtained off from the rest of what he assumed was a larger room. Although he could see no portholes from his bed, he could feel the slow motion of the ocean liner rocking back and forth on the waves beneath him, and by this he knew he was on a ship. It had to be the *Carpathia*, he felt sure, although he had no means of confirming it at the moment.

"Ah, you're awake," a man in a doctor's white coat said as he pulled aside the curtain and strolled up to Abe's bed. Abe recognized the man as Doctor Cherryman, the one who'd helped Quin and him out after they'd been pulled from the freezing water and into the *Carpathia*'s warmth.

"What happened...?" Abe couldn't finish before his throat ran painfully dry, reducing him to a painful cough.

The doctor waited for the coughing fit to pass, then gave Abe a cup of water that had been sitting on the table by his bedside. Abe gulped at it like a man who'd been dragged in from the desert, then stopped when the pain started again. He switched to sipping tiny mouthfuls of water from it, and soon the awful tickle subsided.

"Don't you remember what happened to you, Mr Holmwood?" the doctor asked. "You've had one hell of a night."

Abe shook his head as he felt the patch of gauze that had been taped to the wound in his throat. He'd thought he'd been dead, that Quin would never have been able to find help before he bled to death. He thanked Fate, Fortune, and God that he'd been wrong.

"I remember." Abe spoke with a slow and distinct purpose now, endeavoring to avoid aggravating his injured throat. "I want to know what happened to Quin."

"Your friend?" Abe wouldn't have thought it possible, but the doctor's face grew even more serious. "He helped bring you here, and he sat with your young lady. Lucy, I think?"

"She's not mine," Abe said. "Lucy's her own girl."

The doctor grimaced and stared at Abe close-mouthed. He looked as if he had to tell Abe that everyone else on the ship had been killed in the most gruesome way conceivable.

"Out with it, sir," Abe finally said. "What is it?"

"Your two friends believe you were attacked by a vampire. While your friend Quin claims that the creature who injured you is dead. They went hunting for others."

Abe breathed through his nose and looked at the doctor for a long moment. "And what do you believe?"

The doctor glanced at his feet before he answered. "I helped set them up with supplies and gave them both my blessing and my keys."

Abe granted himself a smile for the first time since he'd awakened in this bed. "For this, you have my utmost thanks, sir." He gestured toward his injured throat. "As well as for the services you've performed for me tonight."

The doctor waved off Abe's gratitude. "Were I truly heroic, I'd have accompanied your friends on their hunt. Instead, I opted to play nursemaid for you."

"I find that extremely heroic," Abe said. He tried to sit up, but his head swam so hard he had to lie back down.

"You're stable," Doctor Cherryman said, "but you're far from well. You should remain in that bed until we return to New York."

Abe frowned at the thought of being stuck in this room for the rest of the journey. "And just how long might that be?"

The doctor checked his watch. "The sun will soon rise on Wednesday, April 17. The captain tells me that with luck we should reach port by tomorrow night. We might be forced to wait until the following morning to actually dock, but my guess is we'll be allowed to do so whenever we arrive, due to the circumstances. By which I mean the rescue of the *Titanic*'s survivors."

Abe nodded. He hadn't been out for more than a few hours, it seemed, and he could manage being holed up here for another couple days if need be. "All right," he said. Exhaustion overcame him then, and his head fell back against his pillow once more.

"Get as much rest as you can between now and then," the doctor said. "Once the press gets their hands on you, you'll need it. I'll check in on you from time to time to determine your condition."

Abe nodded again, his eyes drooping as he did. It seemed to him that he had only blinked, but when he opened his eyes, the doctor was gone. The curtain had been drawn once more, and he was alone.

Abe blinked once more, and this time when he opened his eyes, she was there, standing by the side of his bed: Elisabetta

Ecsed, the woman he'd seen crumble to dust. He opened his mouth to scream, but she placed a firm hand over it, cutting him off. Her palm was soft and delicate, but cold, as if she'd been the one who'd gone into the water with the *Titanic* and never quite managed to warm herself up again.

He goggled at her in terror and tried to pull her hand from his face, but he was too weak to manage it. He stared at the ruin of her eye, the one Quin had stabbed through. The eyelid drooped over the punctured globe that sagged loose in its socket, but she paid it no heed.

The woman put a finger to her lips and shushed Abe until what energy he still had left him. He sagged against the bed then and fought the urge to weep in frustration and shame. She clucked her tongue at him until he blinked the welling tears away.

She gazed deep into his eyes with her one good orb, an enchanting color he couldn't quite place. Even with her injury, her beauty took his breath away. She seemed younger and more vibrant than he'd ever seen her before.

As Abe's fear drained from him, he found a strange hunger for her flowing into its place. He knew then that she'd taken far more from him than his blood with her bite. She'd stolen his will to resist her as well.

"Can I trust you not to shout?" Elisabetta said.

He nodded, certain that she already knew the answer to her question before she'd asked it. She hadn't left it to chance. Whatever she wanted, he would give her. All she had to do was ask.

# CHAPTER FORTY-FOUR

"Where do you think you're going?"

Quin had dreaded hearing someone say those words since he'd led Lucy through that labeled door in steerage and into the engine room beyond. He'd managed to avoid using the flashlight, sure that would only draw attention to them. They'd had enough light so far to make their way by, but only just.

Dressed as Quin was, he knew it would be clear to anyone who spotted him that he didn't belong below decks on the *Carpathia*. At least he was a man striding about in a man's world and might be able to pass as an off-duty officer or steward, maybe one from the *Titanic*. No women worked in the underbelly of the ship, though, and Lucy stuck out there like a beacon in the night. It would only be a matter of time before someone became suspicious, he knew, and it had finally happened.

Quin turned to see a sweat-coated man dressed in coal-stained clothes walking toward them from between a pair of boilers to his right. He carried a battered shovel with him, but he held it as a tool not a weapon. He was curious about the stranger who'd entered his steamy realm in the middle of the night, but he did not fear them.

"Just passing through." Quin put his stake and crucifix behind his back as he tried to brush by the man. He felt Lucy take them from him, freeing up his hands. "Don't mind us."

The shovel shot out then and blocked the way forward. Quin hauled up short, and Lucy pressed up against his back for one surprised instant.

"There's nothing back there but the cargo holds," the man said, his blue eyes standing out against his soot-darkened skin like a lantern on a moonless night. "There's naught to see for good folk like you."

Lucy giggled then. Shocked by the lightness of the sound, Quin turned to gape at her, but she wasn't looking at him. She'd turned all her radiant attention on the stoker.

"Forgive us, sir," she said with a lusty smile. "We didn't mean to disturb you. My friend and I were just looking for a little bit of privacy. Away from my parents' cabin, if you know what I mean."

The man's face broke into a knowing grin. "Say no more," he said. "You're not the first young couple to wander past my post here." He winked at Quin, who hoped that the darkness of the engine room – which was lit only by the hellish fire from the boilers at this hour – might mask the furious blush that had rushed to his face.

"A word of advice," the man said. "On your way back, don't come through here. My shift changes soon, and the bloke who takes over from me isn't nearly so understanding."

"Right," Quin said, nodding his thanks as the man lowered his shovel to let them past. "Truly appreciated."

Moments later, Quin and Lucy found a door that permitted passage through the next bulkhead, and this stood unlocked. Passing through it, they emerged from the engine room and found themselves in a large, dimly lit chamber that stretched full across the ship from port to starboard – at least thirty yards,

Quin guessed – and roughly as far back along the ship's floor, where it terminated in another bulkhead. Every sound they made seemed to echo in the high-ceilinged chamber, especially the clacking of Lucy's shoes as they wound their way through the place, slipping around boxes and pallets filled with goods and luggage.

"There are two doors through the next bulkhead," Lucy said. "Should we take the one on the right or the left?"

"I don't suppose it much matters." Quin fingered the rope of garlic around his neck. The stoker hadn't seemed interested in it. Perhaps he thought they were stealing away down here to cook dinner. It seemed hot enough  that they might have been able to pull it off. He loosened his collar for some relief.

"The left it is then."

Lucy led the way now, despite Quin trying to step in front of her and cut her off. Her eyes shone with some strange mixture of curiosity and mounting fear, and he found he could not move fast enough to stay in front and offer her protection. He took his stake and crucifix back from her then and hefted the wooden weapon in his hand. If he couldn't stand between Lucy and danger, he'd have to keep himself ready to strike at any threat on an instant's notice instead.

Quin craned back his neck and stared up the steel stairwell that led toward the decks above from the center of the room's floor. It snaked back and forth until it disappeared through the ceiling and came out through the floor of the Main Deck. A pair of hatches framed it fore and aft, wide enough to lower a truck through and still have room to spin it about on the end of the crane.

As large as the room was, it didn't have much to fill it. Quin supposed that the *Carpathia* would be packed with emigrants – people like Lucy, Abe, and him, he reflected – on the way to the States, but would have far fewer passengers on its return trips. It was a shame that the ship didn't carry more in terms of American exports to sell in Europe, but he'd heard that the rumblings of troubles on the Continent had caused such trade to slow. No one wanted to ship material overseas if they thought that a war might disrupt their chances to get paid for it – at least not the kind of cargo you'd find on something other than a warship.

Beyond this hold, they found another just as badly lit as the first. This was smaller than the previous one, just as wide across but not nearly so long. A set of stairs rose out of the floor here too, but there was only room for one hatch near it, not two.

"Can you imagine being lowered all the way down through that shaft?" Lucy said. "It would feel like descending into a mine."

She spoke with a strong voice rather than a whisper, but Quin could barely hear her over the thrumming of the engines. The drive shaft that turned the ship's propellers had to run somewhere under their feet, Quin guessed, but he didn't see where or how they could get to it. Not from here.

The dull pounding they'd been following had long since stopped. It had grown in intensity for a minute and then ceased altogether. Faced with no better choices, they'd decided to keep moving back through the holds until they found something of interest or ran out of ship. He guessed they'd just about done exactly that, but he saw one more bulkhead loom before them, and Lucy pressed on toward it.

She reached the door before him and put her hand on it and pulled. It refused to give.

Lucy turned toward Quin and spoke straight into his ear, her breath warm against his skin. "It's locked," she said. "The first one that's been locked since we went below decks."

Quin gave her a grim nod. "Not a good sign," he said. "Get your things ready. I'll get the lock."

Quin stuffed his crucifix into one coat pocket and pulled the keys from another. As he tried a key in the door, Lucy brandished her crucifix before her like a weapon she planned to use to defend him.

The first key failed, as did the second. The third worked, and Quin gave Lucy a meaningful look before pocketing it. He reached out to open the door, and it gave with a stiff pull, gliding open on well-oiled hinges.

Blackness beckoned from beyond.

# CHAPTER FORTY-FIVE

Quin thumbed on the flashlight the doctor had given him but kept it aimed at the floor. He didn't want to alert anyone inside to where he was, although he guessed that it might already be too late. To anyone inside the hold beyond, he would be silhouetted in the doorway. He might as well have placed a target on his chest.

"Can vampires see in the dark?" he asked Lucy in hushed tones.

She shrugged at him as if to say, "How would I know?"

Quin sucked at his teeth, then brought the flashlight's beam up to see what lay before them. It cut through the inky blackness and illuminated along its length parts of a hold almost as large as the first one they'd entered. No stairwell ran through the center of this one though. All Quin could see were the remains of wooden crates someone had smashed open, letting their contents spill across the floor.

"What was in those?" Lucy whispered as she moved past him and entered the room beyond. Her soft footsteps echoed with a hollow metal sound.

Quin shrugged as he joined her, leaving the door open behind them. He shone the light into one of the broken crates. "Whatever it was, it was packed in dirt."

"No," Lucy said, her voice tightening with every word. "I don't think the dirt was the packing. It was the contents."

Quin froze as he realized what she meant. The crates they saw spilled open all around them – countless numbers of them crushed together so that he couldn't tell where one ended and another began – they weren't just crates.

They were coffins.

Lucy gasped. "God," she said. "How– how many of them are there?"

"I don't know." Quin swept the flashlight's beam around the room. Everywhere he turned it, he spotted more of the destroyed crates. "What did this?"

"Don't you mean who?" Lucy crept closer to Quin. He was sure she would have clutched at his arm if she hadn't still been holding her crucifix and stake.

"Do you think they were smashed open from the inside, or did someone else do this? And if so, who?"

"That's not what concerns me the most at the moment," Lucy said, her words barely louder than her breath.

"What's more important than that?"

"If there were vampires in those boxes," she said, trembling through her resolve, "then where are they now?"

Quin shuddered at the thought of so many of the violent, bloodsucking creatures infesting the ship. If they were loose, did the people aboard the *Carpathia* have even a ghost of a chance of survival? To think that the survivors of the *Titanic* had already endured so much, and had now to suffer through this, boggled Quin's mind. He found it hard to believe that a loving God would permit such things to happen.

Quin brought the flashlight up to see if there were any hatches that let into this hold. He knew there had to be – at least originally, according to the shipbuilders' intent – but he didn't see any sign of them at first. Then he spotted them both.

There were two of them set into the room's high ceiling, both painted black and closed up tight. Quin played the light's beam across them and between them, trying to find their edges. As he did, he spotted something hanging in the rafters that held up the deck above the hold.

"What is that?" Lucy asked as Quin held the beam on one of the dangling things. It seemed like someone had tied a sack of something long and heavy to one of the rafters and left it to hang there like a drying side of beef.

Quin peered at it, moving closer as he focused on it. It took him a long time to realize just what it and the others hanging all around it in other parts of the rafters were, because it was upside down. Then he realized that the thing was a person.

"Lucy." Quin reached back with his arm to guide her toward the still-open door. "We need to leave here. Now."

"What is it?" she said, still not understanding. "What are those things?"

"They're people, Luce."

She choked back a gasp. "Are they vampires – or victims?"

Quin shone the light back up into the rafters again. He couldn't tell for sure. Maybe they were both.

"What time is it?" Lucy asked. "Has the sun come up yet?"

It was Quin's turn to shrug helplessly. His watch had been damaged the night the *Titanic* sank. He'd hoped to replace it in New York – assuming he managed to survive that long.

"It's possible, I suppose," he said. "Do you think they're just sleeping?"

"If they are, then they're vampires. If not, they're dead instead." She groaned. "I'm not sure which would frighten me more."

Quin turned the light straight up, and it fell upon a man wrapped in a weathered coat, hanging from the rafters by his ankles. As the beam struck him, the man winced, much in the way of someone cringing when the lights were turned on in a bedroom so early that the sky was still dark outside. The man craned back his neck and opened his eyes to stare down at the light.

Quin had never in his life felt as much like prey as he did at that moment. The man stared down at him, temporarily confused, but with awareness growing in his soulless, dark eyes.

"Now." Quin turned and ushered Lucy toward the doorway. "Now, now, now."

Lucy moved fast, her heels clacking against the steel floor as she went. Quin wanted to gather her up in his arms and run, but that would mean dropping the flashlight and the stake in his hands. He didn't want to leave them so defenseless.

When they were mere feet away from the door, Quin heard something large and light rustle above him, and the man he'd seen on the ceiling flipped down to land in front of them, standing directly between them and the open doorway. The man hissed at them like an angry snake and drew back his lips to expose long fangs sprouting from his mouth.

"Where do you think you're going, little dogies?" the man said. He stood tall and broad, with a square chin and long, lanky hair, and he spoke in a Yankee accent that Quin couldn't quite place. "Didn't anyone ever tell you it's rude to enter someone else's bunkhouse without an invitation?"

# CHAPTER FORTY-SIX

Lucy thrust out her crucifix before her, and the vampire standing between her and Quin and the door flinched. "Get back, you filthy beast!"

The man put up his hands as if Lucy were holding a gun on him. "Now, just relax there, little lady. There's no need to pull those kinds of tricks around here. We're all harmless enough – once you get to know us."

Quin slashed out with his stake and caught the man on the side of the head with it. He went down as if Quin had struck him with a club, collapsing to the floor in pain. Quin pushed Lucy toward the open doorway, a rectangle of light caught on the edge of the hold's pitch-blackness.

He followed straight behind her, but as he stepped past the vampire who had accosted them, the man's hand snaked out and caught Quin around the ankle as fast and as hard as a whip.

"You think it's that easy to beat me?" The man stood up and hauled Quin's feet out from underneath him as he went.

Quin hit the steel deck hard, landing on his shoulder and rattling his bones. The stake fell from his hand, but he managed to keep a grip on the flashlight. He wondered if that meant that he'd at least be able to get a good look at the face of the man who was about to kill him.

"Damn, you folks reek," the vampire said, screwing his face tight as he yanked Quin upside down into the air and held him there, dangling from one ankle. "And the living say the dead smell bad."

It was the garlic around his neck, Quin knew. Hanging around his neck, it must have been far enough away that the vampire hadn't minded it when he was laid out on the floor, but now that the tables had turned, the rope of the pungent spice disgusted the creature.

Quin kicked out with his free foot and caught the vampire in the chin with his heel. That only served to enrage the man, who squeezed Quin's ankle tight enough to make him holler out in pain. "Run, Luce!" he shouted straight after that.

Quin couldn't say he wasn't afraid of dying, but having brushed so close with death during the sinking of the *Titanic*, he'd become accustomed to the idea that it didn't bother him as much as he once thought it would. At that moment, his greatest fear wasn't that some man-sized tick would feed on his blood but that the same thing might happen to Lucy. As terrified as he was for himself, he felt far more fear for her.

Quin wanted nothing more than to see the door that led out of the room slammed shut and locked tight. If that meant that Lucy would get away clean, he could stomach having his only avenue of escape cut off. It would have been a small price to pay. Instead, he heard Lucy rush toward them, her heels clacking out a furious beat.

"No!" Quin said. "Leave me! Run!"

Lucy stabbed at the vampire with her stake, but he batted it aside with his free hand. As he indulged in a rough chuckle at Lucy's efforts, he gave Quin a good shake that rattled his eyes in their sockets.

He stopped laughing when Lucy smacked him across the cheek with her crucifix.

The vampire dropped Quin and clutched his hands to his face, screaming in pain and staggering away from her. Quin snatched up the flashlight and his own stake and scrambled to his feet. He grabbed Lucy by the hand and darted for the door, but rather than joining him, she held fast, her feet rooted to the floor.

"Lucy!" Quin pulled at her arm again, but she stood there aghast at the man she'd attacked. Quin had not looked back at the vampire after he'd dropped him. He brought his flashlight up to see what had fixed her attention so.

The vampire had collapsed to his knees on the unforgiving floor and had taken to keening in a low voice that cracked as it rose and fell. Blood dripped through the man's fingers, which he held clutched over the side of his face where Lucy had struck him. He looked far older, his muscles frail now and his hair growing white. He glared at them both with baleful eyes gone pale with pain and hate.

A rustling sound had started in the rafters overhead. It began as a whisper and grew steadily from there into a full-throated roar. Quin pointed the flashlight upward and saw the other creatures who'd been hanging upside down moving about now, rousing themselves from their slumber.

"We need to leave here, Luce." Quin grabbed her by the shoulders and spoke straight into her face. "Now!"

Luce stared at him in blank horror until something fluttered through the air overhead. This startled her and brought her back to herself. Without a word, she charged straight for the open doorway, and Quin had to sprint to catch up with her.

As they reached the doorway, Quin paused to let Lucy go through first. As he did, he heard something hiss behind him and felt a clawed hand slash down. The sharp talons sliced open the shoulder of his jacket but did not penetrate his skin.

He ducked down lower and dove through the door. Lucy slammed it shut behind him, then turned the key that was still in its lock and threw the deadbolt that would keep it sealed.

Something strong or heavy – maybe both – slammed into the steel door from the other side. Despite the violence with which it had been struck, Quin hoped that the door would hold. It was made of steel as thick as the bulkhead that separated the hold from the rest of the ship, designed to hold back thousands of pounds of water pressure in case the chamber beyond flooded.

Of course, Quin reflected, he'd thought the bulkheads in the *Titanic* would have held and kept the ship from sinking too, and he'd clearly been wrong about that. Something slammed into the door again, and he grabbed Lucy's arm and took several steps back.

Quin took the rope of garlic from around his neck and tore it into two separate lengths. He hung the first over the lintel of the door before him, then raced over to the other door in the bulkhead and did the same.

"Why did you use all of yours?" Lucy said. "We could each have hung a rope over a door."

"Which would have left us with none at all for ourselves," Quin said. She tried to offer him her garlic, but he waved her off. "Keep it. Yours served you better than mine did."

The doors shook as something hit each of them, shaking the entire bulkhead. Quin couldn't imagine the vampires would be able to knock them down, but he feared to think what might happen if they got free. Eventually they'd find a way out, and the entire ship would be in danger if they did.

Quin took Lucy's hand again and headed for the stairwell that led straight up out of the hold they were in. "We can't do this," he said. "We need to find help."

"What if they break free while we're gone?" Lucy asked.

"I don't know," said Quin, "but I'm sure of one thing. We'd be better off not being here when it happens."

# CHAPTER FORTY-SEVEN

"This is complete and utter madness," Captain Rostron said to Quin and Lucy.

"Captain, sir," Lucy said, "I know how crazed it sounds, but you must believe us."

Quin leaped in to back her up. "You have an infestation of vampires in your aftmost hold, and if you don't do something about it soon, they're bound to get free and slaughter every man, woman, and child on the entire ship."

The captain nodded along as Quin spoke. Then he gestured toward Quin and Lucy and looked to Mr Crooker. "Get these people off my deck."

Crooker hesitated. "Are you sure, sir?"

Rostron's face fell. "Dear God, not you too. First Doctor Cherryman comes to me with some cockamamie story straight out of a dime novel, and now you don't have the sense to question the outlandish tale these young fools have brought me? I had thought of you as a professional, man."

Crooker stiffened his upper lip. "I know it's insane, sir, but their story makes some weird kind of sense."

"Can you hear yourself? You're saying that the existence of real-life vampires makes sense. In what world might that be?"

"Well, it would serve to answer a great deal of the questions for which you yourself charged me to find answers. I can't think of anything less strange that could manage it."

Rostron closed his eyes and bent his head as he pinched the bridge of his nose between a forefinger and thumb. When he lowered his hand and reopened his eyes, he spoke in clear and gentle words.

"We've all been under a great deal of stress here, I know." He looked at Quin and Lucy. "I'm sure that surviving the sinking of *Titanic* would have tried the sanity of all the saints, but I'm begging you to calm down and listen to reason before you make it worse."

"I'm afraid it's already worse than we know, sir," Lucy said. "The only way you could make it even worse than that would be by refusing to listen to us until it's too late."

Quin stared out of the windows that lined the front of the bridge. The sky to the west was still dark blue, although dawn had already broken behind the ship as it steamed toward New York. He couldn't see the sunrise from here, but it comforted Quin to know that it had come and that the day would only get brighter from here. After the horrors of the night he'd had, he clung to that thought like a lifeline.

"The horrors we've witnessed on this ship are far darker than anything we witnessed on the *Titanic*, sir," Quin said. "The sunrise may have given us a respite, but if we fail to act before the sun sets again, we'll have sealed our doom and will have no one to blame but ourselves."

The captain mused over this for a long moment, leaving Quin to wonder if he would grant their request for help or have them locked in their rooms for the safety of the rest of the ship. If that happened, Quin would have to figure out a way to get himself and Lucy off the *Carpathia* before night fell. Floating adrift in the middle of the ocean seemed to offer much better prospects than waiting for the vampires in the hold to wake up and devour every soul on board one by one.

The captain tugged at his chin for a moment, then stood ramrod straight to announce his decision. Everyone in the room mirrored his motion and paid him their full attention. He cleared his throat and spoke.

"Mr Crooker. Assemble a team of men and go with these young people to open the hatch above the aft hold."

Lucy gasped in glee and clapped her hands together. A broad smile grew on Quin's face. Even Mr Crooker seemed relieved.

"If there's nothing to be found, I expect our guests here to make a full apology and to refrain from making such wild accusations for the remainder of the trip. I'll be generous enough to attribute their lunacy to the stress that they've undergone on their voyage, but that will be the end of it."

Lucy wrinkled her brow at the captain. "But if you don't believe us, sir, then what has possessed you to humor us in this way?"

A thin smile flickered across the captain's lips. "As the man in charge of this ship, I am in a position in which I can afford to grant my guests such leeway. I don't believe you'll find anything so horrific in her hold as you claim, but I don't think that a little sunshine is likely to damage the kind of cargo the *Carpathia* carries either."

Quin vigorously shook the captain's hand. "Thank you so much, sir!" he said.

Captain Rostron arched an eyebrow at Quin. "It's rare for me to see someone so grateful for not having won my trust."

"And it's just as rare for me to be pleased about such a thing," Quin said. "I'm just happy to be given a chance to prove the truth of what we say."

The captain gave Quin a sage nod. "If what you say is true, though, I would think you'd have been happier to have been proved wrong."

# CHAPTER FORTY-EIGHT

Lucy squeezed Quin's hand as they stood on the Upper Deck and watched the sailors prepare to open the *Carpathia's* aftmost hatch. It was early still, but the sun had already risen over the eastern horizon. A small set of rooms that included the ship's laundry, among other things, sat aft of the hatch and cast long shadows across that part of the ship. Where Quin and Lucy stood, though, the sun's rays had already begun to work the night's chill from their weary bones.

"Step lively there," Mr Crooker said to the sailors who had surrounded the hatch. They worked to remove the battens from the edges while the crane operator lowered his hook into place so that one of the other sailors could attach it to the set of ropes that ran from a central point over the hatch to each of its edges. The men moved with the surety of people who had spent years on the seas and knew their jobs well.

Once the crane was in place and attached, the other sailors stepped back from the hatch, and the crane operator set to work. Crooker came over to stand next to Quin and Lucy. "Take care of the hatch once it comes free," he said. "We're running on smooth seas right now, but we normally don't use the cranes except when we're in port. There's rarely a need."

"You have our undying thanks for making an exception for us, sir," Lucy said. She shivered despite the warming sun, and Quin offered her his coat.

She declined. "It's not the temperature that's bothering me," she said. "You're very kind, but I don't think stealing your coat would help either one of us."

Despite that, she took Quin's hand in hers and held it tight. He couldn't help the smile that came to his face.

Crooker gave the crane operator the signal. "Bring her up!"

The crane whined into action, taking up the slack in the line until it pulled taut against the ropes attached to the hatch. It hesitated there for a moment, and Quin held his breath. Then the hatch came free from the hole it covered.

The hatch gave a metallic creak, and a rush of foul air came from below. The sailors nearby recoiled from it, cupping hands over faces and grunting in disgust. "Smells like a butcher's," one man said.

Nothing came flying out of the hatch as Quin had feared might happen. Still, he hesitated to move toward the now-open hole and gaze down into the hold below. Crooker and the other sailors held back as well, and it wasn't until Lucy took the first step forward that Quin moved too.

Crooker joined them both at the edge of the hole and peered down into it with them. Blackness beckoned.

Crooker glanced at Quin and Lucy. "Is this what you were expecting to find?"

"The sun's not quite high enough yet," Quin said as he pulled his borrowed flashlight out of his jacket pocket. He thumbed it on and pointed it down into the hold.

The light's beam barely reached to the hold's distant floor. If Quin hadn't known about the smashed boxes and spilled dirt down there, he might not have been able to recognize them. Still, he'd been hoping for more.

"Blimey!" Crooker said. "Someone's destroyed the cargo. It's like a herd of elephants got loose down there."

Quin didn't say a word. He and Lucy knew what had done it. Now they just needed to show everyone else.

Lucy grabbed Quin's arm with one hand and stabbed a finger down into the darkness with the other. "There," she said.

Quin brought the flashlight in line with the direction in which Lucy was pointing. He spotted one of the vampires hanging upside down from the rafters that bordered the hold. He was barefoot and grasped onto the steel beam above him with clawlike toes. He had his arms crossed in front of him in the manner of a corpse on display, and leathery wings that sprang from the undersides of his arms wrapped around him like a blanket. He swung there with the rhythm of the ship as it rocked on the waves. He seemed thin and frail, as if his bones were hollow, and he slept there undisturbed by the light filtering down toward him.

"God Almighty," Crooker said, his voice but a whisper. "I'd been hoping you two were bughouse insane."

"So were we," Lucy said. "So were we."

Quin brought the flashlight's beam around the edge of the hole and caught several more of the creatures in its light. They included both men and women of a variety of ages, all of them hanging upside-down from their deformed feet. A few of them squirmed as the flashlight's beam touched them, and Quin moved it away fast lest he bring them fully awake.

Some of the other sailors came forward now. They spotted the vampires as well and pointed and whispered about them in horrified tones. Many of them crossed themselves, and not a few blanched in fear.

"So what do we do now?" Crooker said. "Can't we just seal the hatch and leave them there until we reach New York?"

"I don't think that's an option," Quin said. "Even if we

sealed them in with garlic or a line of crucifixes, they might find a way to get out. Vampires are supposed to be able to turn to mist. If that's so, we'll never keep them contained in there."

"Then what hope do we have of being able to kill them?" Crooker said. "If they can just evaporate when we come at them, we don't have a chance."

Lucy shook her head. "They can only manage that at night-time, when their powers are at their peak. Right now, they're stuck as they are. They're still dangerous, but they can be attacked. They can be beaten."

"How?" Crooker asked, his voice full of disbelief.

Quin looked up and noticed everyone on this end of the deck staring at him, hanging on his every word. He looked to Lucy and nodded. "Show them."

Lucy reached into her pocket and produced a small compact she'd borrowed from the ship's store. She opened it and turned it over, letting the makeup powder fall out of it. It caught in the wind, which swirled it away.

Lucy held the compact high, shoving its mirrored side into the sun. Then she angled the mirror to reflect the sunlight straight down into the hold below. As Quin watched, she aimed it at the first vampire they'd spotted.

The sunbeam hit the vampire square in the exposed part of his legs, and the skin there burst into flames. He let go of the steel beam from which he hung and spread his wings wide, but it was too late. Once set ablaze by the sun, he couldn't put out the fire. It snaked along his flesh until it engulfed him to the waist and kept climbing.

Howling in terror and agony, the vampire flapped around the hold, trying to escape his own blazing skin. The light he cast illuminated new parts of the hold and revealed many more vampires hiding down there, each of them cringing at the creature's distress but none of them moving to help. Some of them even stayed asleep, apparently undisturbed by the dying vampire's horrible screeching.

The vampire let out an ear-piercing howl and came flapping straight up for the open hatch. Quin pulled Lucy back just as the thing zipped past them, striving for some means of escape. He felt the heat from its flames scorch his face.

The sailors all fell back in horror as the vampire climbed higher. As it rose above the level of the hatch, it came fully out into the sunlight, and its entire body burst into an incinerating fire. The heat caused everyone on the deck to recoil.

The vampire let out one last gut-wrenching scream before the blaze consumed it from head to toe, leaving nothing behind but a thin column of ash. The westerly winds caught this in midair and swept it away off the back of the ship, where Quin could only imagine it would settle into the ocean and be churned into the waters by the *Carpathia*'s wake.

The vampire gone, Crooker stared at the compact in Lucy's hand with a mixture of horror and respect. He swallowed hard and spoke. "I think we're going to need a lot more mirrors."

# CHAPTER FORTY-NINE

At Crooker's orders, the sailors gathered every spare mirror they could find and brought them back to the open hatch. By the time they returned, a number of the passengers had been awakened by the commotion and had crept out onto any section of open deck with a view of the open hatch to see what was happening. Crooker had ordered the deck around the hatch to be roped off, and a number of people from steerage had gathered in growing ranks behind it, trying to rubberneck for a better view.

Captain Rostron had come back from the bridge to join Crooker, Lucy, and Quin. He stood there next to them and stared at the hatch, shaking his head. "It appears I owe you good people a sincere apology." He spoke as if he couldn't believe the words were forming in his mouth.

Quin shook off the man's request for forgiveness. "No need at all, captain," he said. "I would have felt the same way as you in such circumstances. Until I was confronted with proof myself, in fact, I did."

"Thank you for being open minded enough to allow Mr Crooker to verify our claims, sir," Lucy said. "It would have been far too easy for you to ignore our pleas."

"Yes, well." The captain cleared his throat. "It's to all our fortune that I didn't, and that goes down to your persistence. We owe you all a great debt."

"We're not out of this yet, captain." Quin shuddered to think about how hard it would be to root the vampires out of the ship. "Have you seen Mr Dragomir this morning?"

The sailors with their mirrors gathered around the edges of the hatch. The sun had risen higher in the time it had taken them to collect their supplies, which Quin knew would make their task that much easier. He wished the day would hurry up to noon so that the sun could stand directly overhead and offer them the best of its protection, but he knew that he'd then want time to stop so it could stay there forever – or at least until they reached New York.

The captain frowned. "I'm afraid he's not turned up. I sent some men down to his cabin to rouse him, but they reported back that it was empty."

"Perhaps he's down in the hold with the others," said Lucy.

The captain looked shocked. "Do you have evidence that Mr Dragomir is one of these vampires of yours?"

"Not as such," Quin said, "but he is – was – Elisabetta Ecsed's companion. I would find it hard to believe that he wasn't at least aware of her true nature, even if he did not share it."

The captain grunted. "Mr Dragomir is a powerful and wealthy man. He's been a passenger on this ship more times than I care to count. He's dined at my table often."

"Do you count him as a friend?" Lucy asked. Quin heard the note of sympathy in her voice, and it reminded him once again of how much he loved her.

The captain shrugged. "Perhaps not as such, but I am concerned for him. He's either a victim in all of this or a perpetrator. Either way, I'd like to find him."

The sailors lifted their mirrors to the cloudless sky then, and on Crooker's command they used them to reflect the sunlight down into the farthest reaches of the hold below.

From the first moment, a horrible choir of screeches arose from the exposed bowels of the ship. The stench of death and burning joined it soon after. Within moments, one of the vampires attempted to escape into the open sky and met the same demise as the one who'd tempted fate that way earlier in the day, when the sun was still low in the horizon.

The passengers and crew who stood in the open air, protected by the daylight that enveloped them, gasped in horror as the first creature incinerated in the unadulterated sunlight. Many men cried out in surprise, and more than a few women screamed, joined by the children who clutched at their skirts. A few of them were overcome and vomited over the nearest railings, into the sea below.

The next vampire to attempt a desperate but doomed escape was a woman. From what Quin saw of her before the flames took her, she'd been young and beautiful, although perhaps that had been some function of her state as a vampire, an illusion brought about by her habit of feeding on the innocent. Still, a pang of sympathy stabbed through him as he wondered who the woman had been before she'd been changed into a vampire.

She'd probably had family and perhaps even friends before-hand, Quin thought. She might have screamed out in pain and terror when she'd died. What would it have been like to return from that, to become one of the undead? To discover a hunger in her that could only be sated by consuming the blood of other beings?

As more and more vampires climbed into the open sky to disappear, to be consumed in a puff of fire and ash, Quin felt his sympathy for them wane. They might have all once been human, but no matter who happened to be at fault they'd been transformed into deadly monsters. He had no doubt that they would not have shown a moment's hesitation to kill every living person on board the ship should their positions have been reversed.

Lucy turned to him and buried her face in his shoulder. "I can't bear it any longer," she said, her voice thick with grief. "Not for another moment. All those people."

Quin held her to him and stroked her hair as the tears rolled down her cheeks. "It's all right," he said. "You know it's for the best."

Lucy pulled back to look up at Quin with her glittering eyes. "Yes, of course, but must we murder them like this?"

"They're not human, Luce. Not any more."

"But they're not animals either. What about Brody Murtagh? I pulled him from the waters. I spoke with him. He wanted to live as much as anyone."

Quin nodded and brought Lucy closer to him again, comforting her with his embrace. "We didn't kill them. That happened a long time ago."

He looked up to see another vampire vanish in a puff of hot ash.

"We're just helping them along to their eternal reward."

# CHAPTER FIFTY

"Ladies and gentlemen." Captain Rostron stood and raised his glass of Chianti. "I would like you to join me in a toast."

Quin glanced at Abe, who sat to the captain's left side, and Lucy, who sat to Quin's right. Lucy squirmed in her seat, uncomfortable with all the attention. Quin had seen her stand up and give rousing speeches in favor of the suffragette movement, so he knew that she didn't fear crowds, even those who had been far more hostile toward her than the people assembled in the *Carpathia*'s first class dining room tonight. To her, it was the idea that they would be praised for having instigated such wholesale destruction that rankled.

Abe, on the other hand, showed no emotion at all. He'd smiled a bit when Quin and Lucy had recounted for him how they'd found the vampires and trapped them in the hold so the *Carpathia*'s crew could get rid of them, but he'd been otherwise listless throughout the day. He'd insisted on joining them for dinner, though, and Doctor Cherryman had cleared him to do so, as long as he returned to the hospital straight away afterward. Quin hadn't had the heart to object, especially when he'd seen the relief that washed over Lucy's face.

After watching the destruction of the vampires, Quin and

Lucy had checked in on Abe to find him still sleeping, and they'd decided they should do the same. Lucy had worried about closing her eyes while there might still be vampires aboard the ship, but the doctor had insisted that the crew could handle the matter now that Captain Rostron had seen the light. They weren't needed as part of the hunt, but they'd been up so long that he ordered them to bed for some much-needed rest.

Quin had escorted Lucy back to her cabin, but she'd shaken so much when he went to leave that he agreed to accompany her inside. Once there, they'd lain down next to each other on her bed and he promised to hold her until she fell asleep. She'd kissed him once then, with more tenderness than he had ever known, and within moments she'd nodded off.

Quin had told himself that he would only watch her for a few minutes to make sure she was all right before he headed back to his own cabin. During that time, he closed his eyes, though, and exhaustion overcame him. They'd awakened hours later, rested but embarrassed, to a steward's knock at the door.

Quin had gone to his cabin to dress for dinner, and he'd returned to escort Lucy to the captain's table, where they'd found Abe already waiting for them. And now the captain was offering a toast to them for their bravery, and Quin found that rather than basking in the gratitude of the rest of the people on the ship, he only wanted it all to be over. He didn't feel like a hero – just like a survivor once more.

"To this trio of young people – these heroes – whose curiosities and actions helped save the *Carpathia* and every soul aboard it. To have survived one horrible disaster this week only to stand ready to put a stop to another is a testament to both their fortitude and their bravery, and each and every one of us owe them a tremendous debt."

The captain raised his glass higher, and everyone else in the room stood. Quin and Lucy joined them, but Abe remained seated, a pained look on his face.

"To Mr Harker, Mr Holmwood, and Miss Seward," the captain said. "Despite the fact that they've proved capable of rising to meet any task, may they know the joy of far less eventful lives in their future. They certainly deserve it."

The other diners rose to their feet and let loose with a thunderous round of applause for the three friends. As this went on, Lucy elbowed Quin in the ribs. "Say something," she said.

"Why don't you?"

She shook her head. "I'm just not feeling all that triumphant today."

Quin squeezed her hand and gave her an understanding nod. The applause seemed like it might never end, so he raised his hands to indicate that he would like to speak. The crowd quieted down, and he cleared his throat before he began to talk.

"Thank you, but we're no heroes." The crowd tried to deny him his point, but Quin kept talking. "Really, we're not. We're just people who found themselves in a tight situation and refused to give up until we managed to wiggle out of it."

He looked around the room and saw every face staring at him. For an instant, his throat threatened to close up on him, but he glanced toward Lucy and saw the pride she had for him in her eyes. That gave him the courage he needed to go on.

"I look around this room, and I see many heroes. I see our fellow passengers from the *Titanic*, and I count every one of them as brave as we three could aspire to be. I see the determined souls who began this strange journey aboard the *Carpathia*, who came to our rescue when we needed it most – people who not only pulled us up out of that freezing water but took care of us like we were family from the moment we set foot on this ship."

He gazed out of the window for a moment to collect his thoughts. The sky had turned a blazing red as the *Carpathia* raced toward where the sun had set in the west, and the beauty of the moment struck him like a fist.

"I've had a few moments over the past week when I thought death had come for me. I was all but sure that I would never see the sunrise again, but I never gave up. Neither did any of you."

Quin raised his own glass to offer a toast. "Here's to every one of you, proof positive that our world is filled with heroes, and that any of us can be one if we refuse to give up."

The diners erupted in another round of applause, this one even louder than the first. Lucy squeezed Quin's hand tight and even leaned in close to give him a spontaneous peck on the cheek. He smiled at her with all his might, so hard it almost hurt. He couldn't ever remember having been so happy in all his life.

And then Dushko Dragomir strolled up to the entrance to the dining room and said, "Good evening, my good people. Do you mind if I join you?"

# CHAPTER FIFTY-ONE

Dushko stood at the threshold to the dining room and waited there with his arms wide open, as if the crowd there might rush forward and greet him like a long-lost son. Colonel Gracie got up from his table and seemed about to invite the man in. Startled into action, Quin shouted out, "No! Don't do it. He's waiting to be invited in. A vampire can't enter a place without being invited first!"

The colonel clapped his mouth shut and flushed a bright red at what he had almost done. No one in the room said a single word, as if they feared that any sentence they might utter could be somehow twisted around in a way that would allow the beast within their midst. Dushko gave them a pained look as he stood framed in the doorway.

"Really," he said. "Is this any way to treat a fellow guest aboard the *Carpathia*? I had thought the Cunard Line to be above engaging in such superstitious nonsense."

"If you are a man and not one of the undead, then you should be able to enter the room of your own accord," Quin said. "Do so, and we will give you the welcome you deserve."

Lucy grasped Quin's arm and shook her head. She knew something was wrong with what Quin had proposed.

Dushko smiled at him. "I will take you at your word as a gentleman." With no further bit of ceremony, he crossed over the threshold and stood fully in the room. He clicked his heels together as if he had just performed a magnificent feat worthy of the center ring in the finest circus.

The people in the room gasped at this and turned toward the captain's table to see what response the people there might have. Captain Rostron looked to Quin, who gazed at the man in confusion. "You were with Elisabetta, a known vampire. How did you escape her spell?"

Dushko sauntered forward. "Perhaps I didn't," he said. "Perhaps I am a vampire. I've dined in this room on many occasions. Someone must have invited me in at one point, correct?"

Lucy squeezed Quin's arm. "Exactly what I had thought," she said. "A steward could have invited him in once, giving him free run of the place."

Dushko wagged a finger at her. "You are one smart young lady," he said. "That's exactly what happened. The Cunard Line's stewards are trained to be the friendliest on the seas, and you can believe that I took advantage of that if you like."

He gestured toward the windows on either side of the dining room. "However, I don't know if they'd be so accommodating for all my friends."

As he spoke, Quin realized that a fog had sprung up after sunset, obscuring the view of the nighttime sea outside the dining room's windows. It seemed to cling to the windows, climbing up them as if it hungered for the meals being served beyond them. Then the mist began to separate out into distinct shapes, columns of wispy clouds that coalesced into human shapes, becoming darker and more solid as they assumed their original forms.

"Vampires," Lucy said, her voice little more than a whisper. "We're surrounded by vampires."

"Now see here," Captain Rostron said in a cross voice. "You can't just come in here and threaten all these good people. I won't have it."

Dushko chuckled at this. "My good captain, what makes you think you have a choice? You and your men here slaughtered dozens of us. Fine people who had done you not a lick of harm. You incinerated them while they were defenseless."

He strode forward as he spoke until he stood opposite the captain, across from his dining table at the head of the room. "Do you know how painful it is to be burned to death? To have a life you thought of as immortal stripped from you in seconds? What moral grounds do you think you have to stand on here?"

Quin glanced at Abe, who still sat there next to the captain. If possible, his friend had grown even whiter upon Dushko's entrance. Looking like a hollow ghost of the man he'd once been, Abe stared up at Dushko and shivered so hard he seemed like he might fall to pieces at any instant.

"You started this," Lucy said. Her voice rang with vehemence. "Brody Murtagh killed a man aboard this ship. We saw him dump the body overboard, and that wasn't the only one of us to share that fate. And your Elisabetta tried to rip out Abe's throat."

"You judged our actions by a rogue member of our family," Dushko said. He pointed at Quin. "You killed Elisabetta. By the same criteria, I should bathe in the blood of every last one of you."

Quin felt every eye in the room turn on him. The people who had just been singing his praises as their hero stood ready to turn against him now, to condemn him for exposing them to this horrible threat. "Isn't that what you plan to do anyhow?" he asked.

Dushko flashed a broad, even smile. "Why of course it is."

"But you can't invite those creatures into here," Quin said. "Only someone who legitimately lives on the ship – who belongs here – can do that."

"Exactly right," Dushko said, but the smile never left his lips. "And exactly wrong. You're right that only someone who belongs on the ship can invite a vampire into its rooms. Fortunately, I'm not just a passenger on the Cunard Line. I'm also its largest stockholder."

Quin felt his heart skip a beat.

Dushko took advantage of the shock running through the diners to turn toward the windows and speak to the vampires standing beyond them, glaring with vicious hatred at the men and women inside the well-lit dining room, just beyond their reach. "Come in, my friends! Enter and be welcome! You may treat this ship as your own!"

As one, the vampires leaped into the air and smashed into the windows before them. Glass panes shattered all around as the creatures cascaded into the room, emerging unharmed and exposing their angry fangs at the screaming passengers they stalked.

The vampires halted there, though, just steps inside the windows. The passengers cowered before them, unsure as to what they could do from that point forward to save themselves. A woman near the edge of the room fainted, and her husband failed to catch her before she toppled into the chair behind her.

"You don't have to do this," Captain Rostron said.

"Wrong again!" Dushko said. "As long as our existence could have been kept a secret, I might have agreed with you, but how many of you saw our friends being slaughtered today? How many people will they tell if they are allowed to leave this ship?"

He grabbed the edge of the captain's table and tossed it aside as if it were little more than a child's toy.

"I bought this shipping line to avoid this trouble. I was going to bring my people back to my homeland on this voyage, to remove them from the temptations and the dangers of the New World. We had no intention of harming anyone on this trip."

Dushko stalked up to the captain and stood there, glaring into the man's face. He was so close that Quin could smell the rotten air of the breath escaping from his undead lungs.

"We would have slipped away in the night and never bothered you again. But now you've forced my hand. Because of what you have done, every living person on this ship must die."

# CHAPTER FIFTY-TWO

Quin reached into his pocket and drew out the crucifix he still had hidden there. The moment he did so, Lucy did the same. They both thrust them at Dushko, who flinched at the sight of them.

"You two and your damned trinkets," he said, glowering at Quin and Lucy as he backed away, keeping them at a safe distance. "I'll make sure you're buried with them."

Quin glanced around at the other passengers. Some of them had their own crosses or crucifixes or rosaries with them, he saw, and they were fishing them out of their pockets or from the chains around their necks as well. "We might not be such easy prey as you think."

The vampires lining the outside of the room looked to Dushko for instruction, but the man stood there, frozen for the moment. Perhaps he'd hoped that the passengers had given up all religion after destroying the vampires trapped in the hold. Either way, he seemed utterly unprepared for the appearance of these things, and Quin wondered how such a man would have made such a terrible oversight.

Then he realized that Dushko wasn't glaring at him any longer. He was staring at something behind him.

Quin snapped his neck around to see Brody Murtagh standing along the room's fore wall, grinning at him. He spoke one word in a soft and easy voice. "Boo."

Lucy let out a little scream she couldn't manage to entirely stifle. Quin reached out and held her hand, and she clutched it hard enough that he feared for his fingers. "Quin," she said as she gaped at the man. "He has a gun."

Quin's gaze fell to Murtagh's hands, and he spotted the pistol stuffed in the man's fist. It was a hunk of black metal, polished and deadly, and it was pointed straight at his heart.

"Just like an Englishman," Murtagh said with a sneer. "bringing a crucifix to a gunfight. You're always fighting your last war, and you never realize when the game has changed."

Quin stepped in front of Lucy, putting himself between her and Murtagh. The man laughed.

"You should worry about yourself more than your lass there, boyo. I won't harm a hair on her head. She saved my life, didn't she?" Murtagh winked at Lucy. "Or at least you tried to. Too bad I didn't have a life to save."

Lucy scowled at the man as she stepped in front of Quin. "You leave him alone," she said, holding her crucifix before her.

Murtagh winced at the sight of the crucifix and readjusted his grip on his pistol. "Now don't go getting any fancy ideas in that head of yours, fair Lucy. I'd much rather not shoot you." He licked his lips, running his tongue past his exposed fangs, long and white. "I've much more entertaining plans for you."

Quin stepped up next to Lucy, his crucifix held before him, forming a wall past which Murtagh could not pass.

The man rolled his eyes at them both. "Yes, yes, very cute, but you misunderstand my intentions here, folks. I'm not here for you." He pointed the gun over Quin's shoulder. "I'm here to kill him."

Quin glanced back to see Dushko standing in Murtagh's

sights and glaring at him with utter indignity and defiance. The vampire spat on the floor between them, the spittle a thick red, and said. "So it's like that now, is it, Brody? Do your worst."

Murtagh spoke to everyone in the room then. "You people here in the room – you breathers. This man proposed killing every last one of you. If you help me kill him instead, I'll let you live."

"You're a damned liar!" Dushko said. "You'll keep them as cattle and feed on them at will."

Murtagh winked at Dushko. "And what's so wrong with giving their lives a purpose?"

"Death would be a finer mercy."

Quin couldn't believe the two vampires were arguing over which of them offered a better deal: death or domination? He started to edge away from the line between the two of them and pulled Lucy along with him. He tried to catch Abe's eye, but his friend wouldn't take his attention off of Murtagh.

"This is an abomination!" Captain Rostron said. "I order the two of you off my ship immediately. None of us have any intention of complying with either one of you, and we will fight you for both our freedom and our lives to our very last breaths."

"How excellent," Murtagh said with a wild gleam in his eye. "And here I was thinking you weren't going to be any fun at all."

Dushko spoke to the other vampires. "It's time for us to put an end to this."

Murtagh appealed to them as well. "Damn right it is. Stick with me, boyos, and we'll end all this nonsense about going back to the old country and burying ourselves deep. Once we take the ship, I'm going to drive it straight into New York harbor – and then we start to feed. The entire city will be ours!"

Dushko's jaw dropped open. "You can't be serious. You would jeopardize us all for the sake of sating your appetite?"

"It's not us I'm planning to jeopardize, friend. It's time for the vampires to step from the shadows. We're at the top of the food chain, and it's time the human race found out."

Dushko threw back his head, and his fangs jutted out from his mouth like those of a howling wolf. His hands formed into horrible claws, and his eyes filled up with a crimson red. "No. It's time to put you down like the rabid beast you are!"

With that, Dushko launched himself at Murtagh. Quin pushed Lucy out of the way, and the older vampire hurtled past them, straight at his prey. Murtagh had time to squeeze off a single shot with his pistol before Dushko was on him.

# CHAPTER FIFTY-THREE

The first class dining room erupted into a riot. As Murtagh and Dushko crashed into each other, the other vampires began attacking everything in the room that moved. Some of them seemed to have chosen to back either one of their leaders or the other, and these found foes on the opposite side and brawled amongst themselves. Others took advantage of the chaos to attack the nearest humans, tearing into them and feeding with horrifying abandon.

Screams of terror rang throughout the room. Men and women fought for their lives and for those of their loved ones. Children scrambled under tables or joined the few adults able to flee, screeching and crying as they went. Blood flew everywhere and spattered everything.

"Grab the captain," Quin said to Lucy. She did just that, reaching for the man and holding her crucifix before her to ward off the vampires who dared to venture in their direction.

Most of the vampires seemed to give the fight between Murtagh and Dushko a wide berth. While they might be willing to pick a side in the battle, they didn't wish to get involved in the actual fight, perhaps for fear that they'd be ripped apart in the melee. From the vicious way in which the two leaders clashed, Quin could sympathize.

Quin darted past Lucy and the captain and grabbed Abe by the arm. His friend had sat there, watching the fight with interest but showing no concern for his own safety. Quin hauled him to his feet and dragged him after Lucy and the captain, who were racing for the smashed-open windows on the dining room's starboard side. As he went, he held the crucifix before him like a shield, and the few vampires who veered in his direction moved off in search of easier prey.

The captain climbed through the busted window first and then helped Lucy out after him. Quin pushed Abe out after her and then joined them on the Boat Deck. Sounds of mayhem trailed behind them as they charged forward up the open deck, weaving their way past the lifeboats from the *Titanic* that lay scattered there.

"We need to get to the bridge," Captain Rostron said.

"Why?" Lucy said. "What good will that do us? They can find us there as easily as anywhere."

"True enough, Miss Seward," he said, "but it's not our own lives I'm worried about any longer. As far as I'm concerned, every man, woman, and child aboard this ship is already doomed."

Quin sprinted forward and grabbed the officer by his shoulder, hauling him to a halt as they reached the bottom of the stairs that led down to the Bridge Deck. "I don't like to hear that kind of talk, sir," he said. "As long as any one of us is still breathing, there's hope. If surviving the *Titanic* taught me anything, it's that."

Rostron shrugged off Quin's hand. "Yes, well, I suppose that's very comforting to all the people who went down with her, isn't it?"

"They're not here to argue with you, captain," Lucy said. "So we'll just have to stand in their place."

The captain put up his hands. "We are no longer on a passenger ship. These vampires have declared war on the human race, and there's only one way for us to win it."

"What?" Quin felt a horrible chill shoot through him. A new round of screams erupted from the dining room they'd left behind. He gave the captain a hard look. "What do you have planned, sir?"

Captain Rostron grimaced. "I thought we'd finished them all," he said. "You witnessed how many of them we ripped out of the Number Nine Hold and destroyed. But they seem to have infested the entire ship like rats."

"But how, sir?" Lucy asked. "Where else could so many of them hide, even on a ship this large. They have to have slept through the day somewhere."

The captain shook his head. "That's not the point now. It's clear that it's impossible for us to ferret out every last one of them. Even if we somehow manage to survive to the morning, they'll just crawl out of the woodwork the very next night. There aren't many solutions to a problem like this. Not many damn options at all."

Quin and Lucy gaped at the man. Abe stared at him without a hint of expression on his face.

Captain Rostron straightened his jacket and stared back at them with his chin stuck out. "I know my duty. I will do what must be done."

Abe spoke then for the first time since the troubles had begun. Until now, he'd seemed to be sleepwalking through the disaster, a mere observer at the most horrible point of his life. "You're going to scuttle this ship." He seemed to be surprised to hear the words leaving his lips, as if he hadn't thought of them until he spoke them. "You're going to kill us all."

The captain stiffened at this. "You heard those creatures in there. No matter which one of them wins, we're already dead. The best we can hope for is to take them down with us."

"You can't do that," Lucy said. "We– we can't die like that."

"You can't stop me," the captain said. Lines of weariness appeared on his face, and he loosed a deep sigh. "Yes, you two young men might be able to wrestle me to the ground and hold on to me until the vampires come to kill us all. What good will that do any of us?"

"How do you plan to do it?" Quin asked.

"I'll order the boilers blown." The captain spoke in a grim, clipped tone, as if reporting the fact that the deed had already been done. "It will take some time for the steam to build up until it creates enough pressure to explode, but when they go, the boilers will blast holes in the bottom of the ship. She'll founder soon after that."

Lucy blanched, and Quin felt a shiver go through him. They'd just managed to survive another shipwreck days ago. He couldn't imagine having to undergo that again.

"How long do we have?" Abe said in his absent voice.

"It's hard to say. The boilers are designed to prevent just such a thing, of course."

"What do we have at the least?" Lucy said. "An hour."

"At least," said the captain. "Perhaps much more. There are many variables to consider, and my men will have to work hard and fast to make it happen."

Quin felt sick. "How will you persuade them to do that? Isn't that tantamount to suicide?"

The captain nodded. "They're sailors, and it's a dangerous world out there. We hear rumblings of war all across Europe, all the time. They knew when they signed on that it might come to this. They'll do their duty, or they'll die trying."

Quin shook his head. "Seems to me they'll die either way."

# CHAPTER FIFTY-FOUR

When Dushko leapt for Brody, he knew the man would make him pay for it. The gun went off long before he could reach the Irishman, and the slug tore through his right shoulder, taking a good chunk of his flesh along with it. It didn't hurt much, but then there were few things that could make Dushko feel anything. A tiny bit of lead wasn't going to do it.

Dushko had healed from worse wounds in his long years as a vampire. It seemed like someone always wanted a piece of him. As a brother to the wolf, he understood that the pack would often have a young pup in it that wanted the alpha's post and was willing to make a grab for it as soon as he thought he was ready. He had spent far too much of his time squelching such efforts before they got rolling, but Brody had proved to be an especially determined aspirant. Dushko had already decided that he would have to kill the man before this. It would only be a matter of time.

Perhaps sensing this, Brody had stepped up to challenge him for the pack's leadership again, taking one last desperate shot at it. This time, one of them wouldn't be knocked down to lick his wounds and regroup for another attempt later. This time, one of them was going to die. Dushko was determined to make sure that it would be Brody who was destroyed, not him.

Despite being shot, he still landed square on Brody's chest and knocked the smaller man to the ground. He pinned the bastard down with his legs and started laying into him.

Dushko slashed out with a savage claw to knock the pistol from his foe's hand. He didn't know what kind of damage the weapon might do to him if a bullet found his heart or his brain. He might survive it. He might not. But he decided he didn't want to find out.

"Smart boy, bringing a gun into the fight," Dushko said with a snarl as he slashed at Brody again and again, tearing chilled blood from the man's cold flesh. "You needed it. But now it is gone, and where does that leave you?"

Brody disappeared then, transforming into a mist, and Dushko found himself kneeling on the deck rather than his foe. "Nicely done," he said, "for a coward. Bring your body back here, so I can tear it apart for you."

Dushko got to his feet and saw that the captain and the others who'd orchestrated the destruction of so many of his people had departed. He scanned the room and spotted them – Rostron, Harker, Seward, and also Holmwood – climbing out through one of the starboard windows his vampires had smashed in. Deciding to ignore Brody for the moment, he started after those four, sure that they would be up to some sort of deadly mischief designed to finish the extermination they'd started earlier in the day.

That turned out to be a mistake, because he didn't see Brody materialize behind him. By the time he heard the man it was too late.

Brody had grabbed the captain's wooden chair and slammed it down over Dushko's back. The boy had gotten smarter since the last time he'd thrown down a challenge over the pack's leadership. He'd remembered that wood hurt a vampire a lot more than metal.

The chair splintered across Dushko's spine, breaking into several large pieces. The impact sent the older man sprawling across the floor, his head spinning.

"You've been in charge of our little family for far too long." Brody picked up one of the chair's legs and flipped it around in his hand to use it as a club. He brought it down against Dushko's skull as the other tried to push himself to his feet.

Dushko felt fire explode in his head, and stars swam before his eyes. He groaned in pain and struggled to come up with the will to turn himself into mist, to escape in the same way that Brody had. It might be a cowardly thing to do, but turnabout was fair play. Besides which, he could not let this bastard win.

Before he could manage it, though, Brody cracked him across the base of his skull again. He struggled to press himself up on his arms, but he failed and fell face first against the wooden floor.

Brody grabbed Dushko by one shoulder with his free hand and flipped him over. Then he smashed him across the jaw with his makeshift club. "Not looking so good now, are you?"

Brody sneered down at Dushko and smacked him with the club in the side of his head. This time, the chair leg broke apart from the impact. It took a while for Dushko's vision to clear, but he consoled himself with the thought that at least Brody would have to find something new to beat him with.

When Dushko's eyes started working again, he saw that Brody had a long, meaty splinter of the chair leg in his hand, the end of which looked as sharp as a nail. The Irishman held it over his head with both hands wrapped around the top of it, and he brought it down hard and fast, right toward Dushko's chest.

Dushko put up his arms to fend off the blow, but he didn't have enough strength or time to manage it. Brody's makeshift stake came straight down through his ribcage and pierced his heart. It went straight through him and blunted itself on the floor below.

Dushko reached out to pull at the stake, but he found that his strength had left him. He'd spent so many decades stronger than anyone around him, and now he felt weaker than an infant. With the stake twisted as it was behind him, it would have taken a superhuman effort to dislodge it, and he no longer had such power in him.

Brody stumbled away from Dushko and returned a moment later with his gun back in his hand. He pointed it down at Dushko's, aiming it right between the man's eyes.

Dushko wanted to scream out for help, to beg for mercy, but he couldn't draw the air into his dead lungs. The stake had taken every bit of power from him, leaving him with nothing to negotiate his freedom or even his life.

He glared at Brody with every bit of hatred he could muster, hoping that this simple act might give the man pause. Perhaps it would delay him until one of the vampires loyal to him could step in and save him. Maybe even one of the humans might do it.

Brody pulled the trigger, and the bullet went right through Dushko's skull, splashing his brains out onto the deck beneath him. He emptied the rest of the revolver's rounds straight after it, leaving Dushko's head nothing but a bloody mash of red and white and gray.

# CHAPTER FIFTY-FIVE

As the captain raced to the bridge, Quin stood there on the Bridge Deck with Lucy and Abe and wondered what they could do. "We still have time," Quin said. "This isn't over yet."

"True," Lucy said. "We need to alert every living person on the ship and have them head for the lifeboats."

"Right," Quin said, already striding toward the davit located on the starboard side of the bridge. It suspended a single, canvas-covered white lifeboat in the air above. "Abe and I can handle that, just as soon as you're safely away."

Lucy dug her heels in and stopped cold. "Quincey Harker!" she said. "Have you lost your mind?"

"It's women and children first," Quin said, taking her by the hand. "It's a maritime tradition. I can't help that."

"It's chauvinism, pure and simple," she said. "I should never have let you talk me into taking advantage of it back on the *Titanic*, and I'm not about to repeat that mistake."

"But Luce–" Quin said.

"No, Quin." She reached out and took his hand. "There's nothing you can say to make me leave here without you."

Quin gazed deep into her eyes and knew that she was right. As terrifying as it might be, he didn't want to ever be away from her again, not even in a situation like this. He didn't feel right about leaving the ship behind, though, with so many people still on board, but at the same time he couldn't conceive of keeping her there with him.

"Look, you two." Abe spoke in a voice low and weary. "This is not an orderly evacuation of a ship. It's an attack, an invasion. The people on the lower decks likely don't even know anything is wrong yet. The first indication they'll have may be right before the vampires tear out their throats."

"What are you suggesting?" Quin gaped at his friend. "That we should abandon everyone here along with the ship?"

Abe stabbed a finger at the lifeboat hanging over their heads. "I'm saying you should get into one of these things, put it in the water, and get as far away from here as you can."

"But, Abe," Lucy stepped toward him, furrowing her brow, "what about you?"

Abe offered up a wan smile. "It's too late for me, I'm afraid." He pointed at his neck. "I'm already done for."

"Don't be silly." Quin reached out to put an arm around Abe's shoulders. The man looked far more piqued than Quin had ever seen him before. "We're not leaving without you."

"Someone has to operate the davit to lower you two into the water."

"I'll do it," said Quin. "I'll lower the two of you down and then dive in after." He looked to Lucy now. "I promise."

"We don't have a lot of time to argue about this," Abe said. He pointed back toward the first class dining room. "One side or the other will win out soon, and once that happens, they'll start cutting through the people here, either killing or capturing them. We cannot be here when that happens."

"Fine," Quin said, "but we're all going. Together."

He and Lucy worked the davit to get the lifeboat over their heads swung out over the water, and then they lowered it until its gunwale was even with the railing next to them. Abe sat down on the deck while the two of them worked the ropes, offering bits of advice and encouragement as they went. Quin and Lucy exchanged dark looks.

They both knew that Abe wasn't doing well. He'd pushed himself too hard, and the appearance of the vampires was sure to have overstressed him at the moment he could least afford it. Quin cursed himself for not insisting that Abe stay in the hospital under Doctor Cherryman's care, but Abe had appeared to be rallying at that point. He was paying the price for that foolhardiness now, and Quin worried that in the end it might cost him his life.

"Hold her steady," Abe said. "Right up against the railing."

"We have it." Lucy started to work the straps that kept the lifeboat's canvas cover stretched over its top. Quin leaped in to lend her a hand.

"I'm going to miss you two when I'm gone," Abe said.

"I think that's the other way around," Quin said. "The dead don't miss anyone."

"And you're not dying today," Lucy said. "So quit being so maudlin."

A thin smile crept across Abe's lips. "Ah," he said. "Well, there's always tomorrow."

Quin tried to stifle a laugh as he helped Lucy strip off the lifeboat's cover. He failed, though, and Lucy caught the edge of it and started to giggle too. A moment later, all three of them were laughing in a way that Quin couldn't remember them managing in far too long.

It lasted until the cover came off the lifeboat and Lucy peered inside. What she saw there made her scream.

"What?" Abe said. "What is it?"

Lucy recoiled from the lifeboat and went to shudder against the wall opposite the railing. "Oh, God," she said. "Oh, God."

Quin reached into the boat and pulled out a handful of dirt from the yards of if that lined the boat's floor. It crumbled between his fingers: good, rich soil, fresh and soft.

"This is where they were," Quin said. "The vampires weren't just sleeping in that hold. They made a makeshift cabin out of this lifeboat too."

"They were probably in all of the lifeboats," Lucy said. Her voice shook as she spoke. "Every damned one of them that says *Carpathia* on the side, at least."

"That's how the crew missed them. Captain Rostron asked them to go over the place with a fine-toothed comb, but they never thought to look inside the lifeboats."

"I don't think that's important right now," Abe said. Quin looked up from the boat and saw his friends pushing himself to his feet by shoving his back against the wall behind him.

"Why's that?" asked Lucy.

Abe jerked a thumb toward the aft part of the ship. Quin and Lucy followed it back to spot Brody Murtagh striding towards the rail, his face a mask of death.

# CHAPTER FIFTY-SIX

Murtagh stood on the section of the Boat Deck on which the first class dining room perched, staring down at Quin, Lucy, and Abe from the foremost railing. He carried a body over his shoulder. Quin thought he recognized Dushko's suit on it, but its head was such a mess that he couldn't be sure if it was in fact that man.

Murtagh heaved the body up over his head and hurled it overboard. It arced out into the darkness and disappeared into the Atlantic with a splash. Unlike when he'd disposed of the body when Lucy and Quin had spotted him at the ship's stern, he did not skulk about. Instead, he raised his hands over his head and shouted into the starlit sky in triumph.

Looking out past where the body landed, Quin spied points of light floating on the horizon. They might not reach New York City until sometime tomorrow, but they were closer to land than they'd been since they'd left Queenstown on Ireland's southern coast, the last stop on the *Titanic*'s maiden voyage. If that realization caused Quin's heart to leap with hope, what he saw next sank it to the bottom of the sea.

Murtagh leaped up onto the foremost railing, then jumped down to the Bridge Deck to land mere feet away from Lucy,

Abe, and Quin. Spatters of blood covered his face, and it had soaked through parts of his jacket on the side where he'd been carrying the body. He smiled at them with an insane gleam in his eyes. To Quin, he seemed like a blood-mad wolf who'd already killed and eaten his fill but couldn't stop from gorging himself again.

Quin and Lucy held up their crucifixes before them. It seemed ridiculous to trust the small and fragile icons as a defense against such a powerful creature, but they had nothing else at hand. Quin's gaze darted about and fell upon the wooden oars resting inside the lifeboat. They were too long and unwieldy to be of any use there on the promenade on which they stood, but it comforted him to have something nearby that he might be able to break into a stake.

Murtagh came to a halt a respectful distance from the crucifixes. He wiped his crimson-covered chin on the sleeve of his jacket and favored Lucy, Abe, and Quin with a lopsided grin. It seemed to acknowledge that they were safe for now, but that wouldn't last long.

"I owe you three a debt of gratitude." Murtagh spoke with a slur, like he was drunk on the blood that trickled from his fang-filled mouth. "If you hadn't meddled about in Dushko's business, I'd probably be dead by now."

"How's that?" Quin said. He tried to step between the vampire and Lucy, but she would have none of it. She clasped his hand instead and held him to her side. Abe joined them, standing on Lucy's other side.

"Sure, you set him on me in the first place, spotting me tossing that bloke's body overboard, but that was my fault, wasn't it? I was being sloppy. And Dushko wanted to kill me for it."

Murtagh leaned in, and Quin could smell the blood on the man's breath. "But then you got his attention, didn't you? Went and killed so many of his pack. He couldn't ignore it anymore. Couldn't pretend to be hiding any longer. You forced his hand."

A new round of screams rang out from the exposed forward section of the Shelter Deck, behind Quin. If he turned around, he could have seen down there from where he stood on the Bridge Deck, but he didn't dare take his eyes off Murtagh. Abe had no such compunctions, though, and he twisted about to gaze down over the railing that separated them from the deck below.

Abe didn't gasp in horror or sympathy. He just stared down at the tableau on the Shelter Deck and frowned so deep that Quin wondered if the lines on his face might be made permanent. "They must have finished up in our dining room," Abe said, his voice flat and emotionless. "They've moved on to the second class now."

Quin recalled that the second class dining room sat directly below them. He'd passed through it before while searching for Lucy, and he could imagine the vampires bursting in and continuing their blood-drenched rampage. It would only be a matter of time before they completed their grisly work and turned their attention to the masses of people in steerage. And when they were done with them, they'd come for anyone else still living.

"You might as well toss your little trinkets there into the deep blue sea," Murtagh said. "Why delay things? Make it easy on me, and return the favor."

"You have no power over these so-called trinkets," Lucy said defiantly, "just as you have no power over us. We'll not hand that over to you willingly. Not ever."

"What's more," Abe added, "all we have to do is wait you out. Once the captain scuttles the ship, you'll be as doomed as us."

Quin and Lucy goggled at Abe. Murtagh glowered at him with the full hatred of a man who can see his dream being plucked from his grasp. Abe looked back at them both with a blank stare.

"How?" Murtagh said. "Where?"

"You don't care about who, when, or why?" A hint of a smile curled Abe's lips. "I suppose you think you've figured all that out on your own."

Murtagh pounced at Abe, his hands out like a wolf's slashing claws. Quin stabbed his crucifix between them, and slapped the vampire on the hand with it. He didn't have time to think about what he was doing or why. He only knew he had to keep Murtagh away from his friend.

Murtagh snatched his hand away and leaped back out of Quin's reach, howling in pain the entire time. He stared down at his hand to see where the crucifix had touched it, and he saw the skin there begin to boil away.

"How is he going to do it?" Murtagh screeched. "Tell me, damn you, or I'll kill everyone aboard this ship!"

"You were already going to do that," Abe said. "At least this way, we're taking you with us."

Still cradling his burning hand, Murtagh bellowed his frustration at them, then turned and dove overboard. Lucy, Quin, and Abe rushed to the railing to watch him fall. He hit the waves with a rough splash and was gone.

# CHAPTER FIFTY-SEVEN

Brody dove deep beneath the ocean's surface, trying to put an end to the horrible burning on his skin. At first he had feared that the bubbling destruction of his hand might work its way up his arm until it reached his body and put an end to him, but it seemed to stop as soon as he got far enough away from the damned crucifix that had caused it. Perhaps the waters of the North Atlantic had quenched the destruction instead. Either way, it still hurt like he had stuffed his fist into a blazing bed of hot coals.

Once he was sure he would survive, Brody swam back to the surface as fast as he could. The moment he broke through the waves from beneath, he transformed into a bat and flapped his way back up toward the ship. It seemed to be slowing down now, which made it easier to catch it, but only served to confirm Brody's suspicions that those fools on the Bridge Deck hadn't been lying to him.

A part of him had hoped that Lucy and her friends had only been trying to bluff him into heading off on a desperate hunt through the ship, trying to figure out how the captain planned to sink it. Now it seemed he would have to do just that. He would have to act fast. If he failed to stop the crew from scuttling the ship, it might mean the end of them all.

The breathers could survive the end of the *Carpathia*. All they had to do was find their way into a lifeboat and wait for help to arrive. The vampires didn't have that luxury.

If they couldn't make it to land in time, the chances that they would find some sort of shelter from the sunlight when it rose the next day was small. Most of them would wind up roasting with the coming of the new day. Failing that, they might sink to the bottom of the sea. While vampires didn't need to breathe, Brody knew of the horrible pressures at such depths, and even one of the undead might be crushed permanently under such incredible circumstances.

Brody flew up and landed on the rear railing of the Shelter Deck, right where he'd leaped from after Lucy and her damned friend Quin had spotted him dumping that body over it the night before. Unlike that night, the deck did not stand empty. Scores of people filled it now, having been herded there by a force of hungry vampires blood-drunk on their earlier kills and heads swimming with the thought that the time for hiding in the shadows of humanity had finally come to an end.

As he watched, a man stepped up to protect some of the others. Brody recognized him as Doctor Cherryman, and he saw that he held a rosary in his hand and swung it before him like a lantern against the vampires' darkness. He had gathered a group of people behind them, and they huddled together, pressing against his back for protection.

Furious about the injury that Quin had done him, Brody let loose a ferocious growl that froze everyone on the open deck in their tracks. Both vampires and humans stopped to stare up at him, some in shock and terror, others in anticipation of what he might say next. Brody leaped from the railing and landed before the doctor, just out of reach of his rosary.

The vampires who had been standing there cleared out of the way for him before his feet hit the ground. Cherryman's charges gasped in horror, but the doctor himself thrust his rosary forward. "Stay back, you beasts! You've had enough blood for tonight!"

Brody sneered at the man. "You think because you keep bits of heaven about you that they can protect you from hell? So educated, and yet so naïve."

"The power of God protects us!" The doctor stepped forward, using the rosary as a shield. "I command you and your kind to leave this ship!"

Brody arched his eyebrows at the man and then started to laugh. "You're a precious one, aren't you?"

The doctor's eyes went to Brody's injured hand. "You've already witnessed the power of God," he said. "Do not dare to tempt His wrath again!"

"His wrath?" Brody couldn't believe what the man had said to him. "*His* wrath? Seems to me you ought to be a lot more terrified of mine!"

Brody reached back into the crowd of people behind him and grabbed a steward by his white jacket. The man had been cowering among a group of his fellows, hoping that someone wouldn't notice him, and Brody relished the horror awakening in the man as he realized his impending doom. He lifted the man up off his feet and presented him to the doctor so that he could hear the steward whimper.

"That rosary might be a shield against me," Brody said, "but I'm hardly the only dangerous thing aboard this ship."

With that, Brody whirled the man in a circle around him and hurled him at Doctor Cherryman as fast as he could. The steward slammed into the man, and the impact sent both of them sprawling back into the small crowd of hopefuls who'd taken shelter behind the doctor. The rosary flew out of the doctor's grasp and skittered along the deck until it came to a rest near the railing.

Brody lunged forward and grabbed the doctor by the lapels of his jacket. He hauled him out of the pile of people and snarled into his face. "Where's your God now, doctor?"

Before the doctor could muster an answer, Brody's head darted forward, and he sank his fangs into the man's exposed neck. Rather than bite and drink, though, he savaged the man's throat and tore it apart.

As Doctor Cherryman's blood flooded from his body and onto the screaming people he'd tried to save, Brody howled in triumph. Then he brought the doctor back with one hand and used his body to sweep the rosary right off the deck and into the sea.

A roar of approval went up from the vampires, drowning out the whimpers and cries of the humans forced to bear witness to this awful display of deadly power. Brody turned to them and said, "You are now my people, and this ship is ours! But the people here are scheming to take it from us. They want to kill us all!"

Every voice but Brody's fell silent at his words. "The damned captain is trying to scuttle this ship. We need to stop him. Leave these cattle be, and help me save the *Carpathia*!"

# CHAPTER FIFTY-EIGHT

"We need to leave," Quin said to Lucy and Abe. "There's nothing we can do to stop Brody and his vampires. We have to trust to the captain and his men to succeed."

Lucy nodded in agreement. "We can't do anything else here. Our only chance to survive is to get off this ship as soon as possible."

Abe gave his friends a weak smile. His face was deathly pale. "I'm in total agreement with the two of you. I only wish I could come with you."

Quin stared at Abe. "What are you talking about? There's nothing keeping you here. Get in the boat with Lucy. I'll lower it down and then jump in after you."

"I was the one who made that offer to you, Quin," Abe said. "Did you believe me when I said it?"

"Why wouldn't I?" Quin didn't like the turn this conversation had just taken.

Abe grimaced and glanced at his friends. "I lied, to both of you. I have no intention of leaving this ship. At least not yet. I can't."

"You're ill," said Lucy. "You don't know what you're talking about."

"Right and wrong. I am ill, worse than I have ever been, so much so that death holds out the attractive possibility of an easy release. But I'm afraid I know exactly what I'm talking about. I can't leave here without her."

"Without who?"

"Without me."

Quin whipped about, startled, and found Elisabetta Ecsed standing there next to them. He hadn't heard her walking toward them, not a single step or breath. She looked much like she had before Abe and he had struggled with her in her cabin – all except for the black patch she wore over her eye, the one that he'd stabbed through with a pencil.

"I saw you... turn to dust." Quin's voice sounded hollow, even to his own ears.

"I got better." Elisabetta smiled at him without a hint of warmth, exposing the fangs jutting from her gums. She waved off Quin's disbelief. "It was after dark. I had just fed. I was in the full of my powers. What makes you think you could kill me with a pencil to the eye?"

Quin stared at her. "It seemed to have done just that."

"What do you want?" Lucy stepped forward, her crucifix held to her chest in what Quin could only interpret as a gesture of respect. She hadn't fought with the woman in her cabin, hadn't seen her bite into Abe's throat. In her gut, she didn't understand what Elisabetta could do.

"What I already have," Elisabetta said. "Your friend here is mine. I would like to leave with him."

"You can't come with us," Quin said.

Elisabetta laughed, an honest laugh of surprise and delight. "Oh, darling, I have no plans to put myself in a boat with the two of you. Not under the worst of circumstances. But my Abraham here can row away with me and keep me safe until we find a suitable haven."

"You can't go with her," Quin said to Abe. His friend only gave him a reluctant shrug, as if he'd signed a bad contract with the woman and now no longer could imagine any means of getting out of it.

Elisabetta reached out and slashed one of the ropes holding the lifeboat in its davit. The ship pitched over, hanging only from the rope attached to its prow. Dirt and supplies spilled out of it and into the still ocean below. Moving fast enough that Quin found her actions hard to follow, Elisabetta slashed at the other rope holding up the lifeboat, and the whole thing splashed down into the water.

"That's our lifeboat!" Quin stepped between Abe and Elisabetta, keeping his crucifix facing her. "You can't have it."

"There are plenty of other lifeboats on this ship," she said. "And not nearly enough living souls to occupy them. Go find a different one." She turned to Abe then. "Can you swim?"

Abe nodded. "I wouldn't have survived the *Titanic* otherwise."

"Then get yourself ready. I can find my own way into the lifeboat, and you'll have to do the same."

"Yes, Elisabetta."

Quin couldn't believe the way that Abe was acting. He knew the vampire was behind it. With her bite – which he had barely survived and from which he might still die – she'd established some kind of hold over him. Quin had to find some way to break it.

He reached out and slapped him across the cheek, hard. "Snap out of it!" he said.

Lucy had a more direct approach in mind. She lunged for Elisabetta with her crucifix. The vampire let out a little scream and disappeared in a puff of white mist.

Abe reached out and grabbed Lucy by the wrist. She tried to pull free, but he would not let her go. It surprised Quin to see his weakened friend display such a strong grip.

"Don't do that again," Abe said.

"You're hurting me."

"I consider any attack against Elisabetta to be an attack on me. I beg you to respect that and her."

Quin grabbed Abe's hand and pried his fingers from Lucy's wrist. They left white marks on her skin where they had been.

"Consider the same true of Lucy with regards to me," Quin said to his friend, his voice filled with ice and steel. "If you cause her harm, I won't care how little you can control your actions."

Abe gave Quin a curt nod to indicate his understanding. "I expect nothing less," he said in all seriousness. "And I thank you," he added in a whisper.

The two friends shook hands. Quin knew then that it might be the last chance he ever had to do so with Abe. If he and Lucy didn't figure out some way to destroy Elisabetta, Abe would be hers forever.

# CHAPTER FIFTY-NINE

Elisabetta appeared again on the roof of the bridge, looking down at the three friends below. "How delightful," she said in mock sincerity. "Now, if you two have finished trying to pry my Abraham out of my grasp, I'd like to offer you a deal."

Quin gaped at the woman's audacity, but Lucy snapped right back at her. "What makes you think we'd ever wish to make a bargain with a devil like you?"

"Because you have the best interests of Abraham at heart, darling, while I – let's be honest now – do not. I, however, would very much like to survive this little war that Brody has launched. If you can help me do that, I'll consider releasing my hold on Abraham."

Abe let out a soft whimper at these words. Lucy clapped a hand over her mouth to stifle a further outburst, but Quin could tell from the way her eyes glittered that she was near to tears. She just refused to let Elisabetta see them.

"Why would we help you for just the chance to have his release considered?" Quin said. "Doesn't sound terribly promising."

"I could lie to you and tell you I'll release him." Elisabetta gave him the kind of haughty look that nobles reserved for peasants. "I thought you'd prefer an honest deal."

Quin glanced at Lucy, who nodded at him with wordless vigor.

"All right," he said. "If you give us your word you will not harm us and will consider releasing Abe, then we will help you as best we can."

"Thank you," Elisabetta said. "I think you'll soon see it's in all our best interests."

A flock of bats appeared overhead then, fluttering down from the starry sky. Quin recognized them instantly for what they must be, and he thrust his crucifix before him. Lucy did the same, and the two stood flanking Abe, keeping him sandwiched and protected between them.

"Look out!" Abe shouted up at Elisabetta.

She turned in time to see the flying creatures transform into their human forms and alight on the roof of the bridge, forming a semicircle around her. She spun about, trying to evaluate the threat to her, but overwhelmed by the number of vampires she faced. It wasn't until Murtagh stepped forward and grabbed her by the arm that she put a smile back on her face.

"Oh, Brody!" she said, reaching for him. "I'm so glad to see you're all right."

He blocked her embrace and set her back a step. "I wish I could say the same to you, you traitorous bitch."

Elisabetta gaped at the man in shock. "How dare you talk to me like that? After all I've done for you over the years. Why, the number of times I intervened with Dushko on your behalf–"

"I won't be needing your help on that score any longer now, will I?"

"I must help her," Abe said flatly. He raced around the back side of the structure that contained the bridge. Quin and Lucy gave chase and found that he had discovered a ladder that ran up the structure's back wall. He was already starting up it.

Elisabetta batted her eyes at Murtagh. "Is that the only value I hold for you?"

Murtagh backhanded her across her flawless cheek. "I'm not nearly the idiot you take me for. You played both of us against each other. The only person you were ever concerned about was yourself."

Elisabetta straightened up and wiped blood from her lips. Quin saw that she had some spilling from the rims of her eyes as well. She addressed Murtagh with as much indignity as she could muster. "How can you possibly think that? After all the times I stood up for you? I was the one who made you a vampire in the first place!"

"So you could pit me against Dushko. You hoped we'd destroy each other so you could have a free reign among our kind, and it damn well might have worked – if I hadn't thrown out all your arcane rules about the proper things to do and destroyed him myself."

Abe reached the top of the ladder now and hauled himself up and over onto the roof of the bridge. Quin came right after him, and Lucy brought up the rear. Quin put an arm on Abe's shoulder to hold him back, even though the circle of vampires that stood between them and Elisabetta were enough to keep Abe away from her.

"And now what do you propose to do?" Elisabetta said. "If you get to the old country, you'll find a cold welcome there without either Dushko or me by your side. And if you propose to return to your old life in New York, you can forget it. We burned all those bridges when we set out on this voyage."

Murtagh's boot lashed out and caught Elisabetta square in the stomach. She cried out in pain, and Abe rushed forward to help her. A pair of vampires caught him by the arms and held him tight.

Quin came up behind Abe with his crucifix out, and the vampires holding him hissed and moved away. Rather than releasing Abe, though, they carried him with them, ignoring his protests and struggles.

Murtagh grabbed Elisabetta by the head and wrapped one of his arms around it. With his other, he picked up her body and wrenched it around, fast and hard.

Quin heard a sickening crack as Elisabetta's spine gave way and her head came free from her body.

Her head cut off from access to her heart, Elisabetta opened her mouth to scream, but as her lungs weren't connected either, no sound came out.

"I hope it takes you a long time to die, you witch," Murtagh said. With that, he grabbed Elisabetta's wide-awake head by her long hair and swung it around his own in a wide circle, going faster and faster with every instant. When her head seemed like a blur at the end of a hair rope, Murtagh released his hold and flung it as far out into the ocean as he could manage. It arced away so far out into the night that Quin never heard it splash down.

"You bastard!" Abe hollered as he struggled against his captors. "I'll kill you!"

# CHAPTER SIXTY

Quin had to admit, he had hesitated to step forward while Murtagh and Elisabetta were arguing. If that meant leaving Abe in the hands of a couple of vampires for a few moments, then so be it. Quin wanted Elisabetta dead so that Abe would be released from her spell, and he had no means of making that happen. The best he could have hoped for would be for Murtagh to take care of that niggling detail for him.

The Irishman had performed that job perfectly.

Now, though, Quin had to figure out how to rescue Abe and get both him and Lucy off the boat as soon as possible – but preferably not in the same manner in which Elisabetta had left. He wanted all three of them to live. Murtagh, he was sure, had other ideas.

"Now," Quin said to Lucy, and the two of them rushed forward at the vampires holding Abe, their crucifixes held out before them like battering rams. The vampires parted before them as if they were toxic, giving them a clear path to where Abe still stood trapped.

As they rushed forward, though, Murtagh leaped up on the lifeboat still hanging from the davit that suspended it over the other side of the bridge. He slashed open the canvas cover and reached down to snatch one of the long oars out of the craft.

"Hold it!" Murtagh said as he swung the oar over his head. "Get any closer, and your friend is dead!"

Quin wanted to keep charging the vampires holding Abe, but Lucy reached out and held him back. The oar zipped down into his path and smashed right into the spot where he would have been had Lucy not managed to slow him down. One side of the oar's blade splintered off from the impact.

Quin stopped where he was and glared up at Murtagh. He could see the man was wielding the oar with one hand, still favoring the one that Quin had burned with his crucifix. He ached to get close enough to the man to finish the job, but he suspected Murtagh was too canny to ever let that happen. Having been burned like that once, he would have developed an all-too-healthy respect for the crucifix and any who wielded it.

"What do you want?" Lucy said.

"What does anyone want?" said Murtagh. "I want to live."

"Not if I can help it!" said Abe. He strained against his captors' grip so hard that his face turned red, and the tendons in his neck stuck out. They seemed not to notice much.

Quin glared at Abe, trying to get his attention and signal for his friend to shut his mouth. He wondered about Abe's rage. He'd hoped that once Elisabetta had been killed, her hold over him would be released instantly.

That didn't seem to have happened. The only explanation Quin could think of was that Elisabetta hadn't yet died. He couldn't imagine how much longer she could survive. Without any limbs or body for support, her head had to be sinking to the bottom of the ocean. Quin had no idea how deep the sea was here, but he wouldn't have wanted to wish that fate on anyone. He'd wanted Elisabetta dead, but to think of even a person such as her enduring such horrifying torture turned his stomach. He only hoped she could finish dying soon, both for her sake and for Abe's.

Murtagh turned to Quin and Lucy. "I need to know how our blessed captain plans to scuttle this ship. Now."

"Why don't you just ask him yourself?" Quin said.

Murtagh frowned. "He sealed the bridge with crucifixes and garlic. I could get through to him if I had to. I could tear into the place through the ceiling or floor. But it would be danger-ous, and I don't know if I have the time for that." He snarled. "But you two can do it for me."

"Don't tell him anything!" Abe said. "If we have to die to kill them all, then so be it!"

"Quiet, Abe," Lucy said. "You're not in your right head."

"You're nothing but gutter scum, Brody Murtagh!" Abe said, a wild light dancing in his eyes.

Murtagh leaped down from the lifeboat to face Abe square on. The angry snarl on his face seemed to be the only thing holding his temper back.

"That's right," Abe said. "I know all about you. She told me how she found you, cold, starving, and nearly drunk to death in a Bowery alley."

"That's enough out of you now, I think." Murtagh's voice carried a threat as menacing as it was calm.

"She took pity on you that night, and you wept in her arms like an infant, didn't you?" Quin could tell from the way his tone rose as he spoke that Abe was just getting started. He'd seen him like this before, on rare occasion, usually when he was well in his cups, and there was no stopping him – at least not with words.

Murtagh strode toward Abe and glared down at him with silent, murderous intent, like a lion sizing up a lamb for its next meal. "You might want to watch that tongue of yours, boyo."

Abe ignored the man. "Despite everything she did for you,

despite the way she groomed you to replace Dushko, you killed her the first chance you got. You took the one person who'd done you a single kindness in your bitter, miserable excuse of a life, and you murdered her without shedding a single goddamn tear. You're an utter bastard, you are, Brody Murtagh, and I hope you burn in hell when the Devil comes to get you!"

To cap off his rant, Abe bit his tongue hard and spit a mouthful of blood square into Murtagh's face.

Murtagh stood there impassively for a moment, the bloody spittle running down his face. When it reached his lips, he reached out with the tip of his tongue to taste it. Then he wiped his face clean and replaced Abe's spit with a grim smile.

"I don't need three living people to do what I want," Murtagh said. "Just one. I can make examples out of the rest."

Abe froze. "You wouldn't dare," he said. "I– I worried that you'd be jealous of me, that you'd toss me in the ocean when you found out I was with her, just like you did with all the other people you killed. Just like you did with her." He shivered so hard Quin could see it from where he stood. "She said you wouldn't have the guts."

"Just one more thing she was wrong about." Murtagh reached out and grabbed Abe by the lapels of his coat.

Quin leaped forward, his crucifix before him. He could see where this was going, and he knew he'd only have one chance to stop it. "Leave him alone!" he shouted at Murtagh.

Quin heard Lucy following him into the fray. He could only hope that she'd keep the vampires off his back long enough for him to stop Murtagh from killing Abe. If she failed – if she fell – there would be nothing he could do about it, not if he wanted to have a shot at saving their friend.

Murtagh leaped into the air with Abe still in his grasp. They landed back on top of the still-stowed lifeboat, and it rocked beneath their feet on its davit. With a twist of his arms, Murtagh lifted Abe up over his head as if he weighed nothing more than a toddler.

"Put me down!" Abe screamed. "Don't throw me back in that water! I can't take it!"

With a mighty heave, Murtagh flung Abe into the night. Quin hollered in protest, and Lucy screamed as their friend spiraled high into the air and then arced down into the black and icy sea below. He disappeared with a splash.

Murtagh spit out over the *Carpathia*'s rail after Abe. "Looks like you were wrong about that too, boyo."

# CHAPTER SIXTY-ONE

Abe couldn't help but smile as he hit the water. His plan had worked perfectly. All he'd had to do was prod Brody about his past in front of others, and the man's temper had taken over and done the rest.

Abe only hoped it had all happened fast enough. He'd known that once Elisabetta's head had separated from her shoulders, she hadn't been killed. If she had, he'd have been freed from her influence once and for all. The fact that he could still feel her pull on his heart and mind meant something of her had survived her decapitation, if only for a little while.

That meant that Abe had one last trick in his pocket that he could pull to try to save Lucy and Quin and everyone else on the ship. He could become a vampire. All he had to do was die.

When Elisabetta had come to him in the hospital, she'd already tasted his blood and left him to survive. She could have killed him then and there to finish the job. Instead, she chose to expose her throat to him, open a pulsing vein in her ivory neck, and force him to drink.

It had been the most horrible thing that had ever happened to Abe, but he'd found himself unable to refuse. He'd swallowed every bit of her chilly blood as if it were mother's milk and licked his lips when she finally pulled away. Then she'd looked down at him with some twisted thing she might have thought resembled love in her eyes, and she'd explained to him what she'd done.

"When I drank your blood, you became mine. That is why you could not scream for help when I entered the room. You didn't want to. When you drank my blood, I became yours."

"You don't seem like mine," Abe had said.

She'd smiled then, with the most warmth he'd ever seen on her face. "Not yet, darling. You're mine until you die, and when that happens, my powers become yours. No, you don't steal them from me. You become like me."

"A vampire?"

She'd nodded, and he'd not had the will to shudder with the horror he'd felt.

The force of hitting the water meant nothing to Abe. The cold knocked the breath from him, but he wanted that too. He needed to get about the business of dying as fast as he could, and Murtagh had given him a flying start.

He flashed back to the moment he'd been swept from the *Titanic*. The icy water had battered him against the ship and then dragged him under so hard and so fast that he'd been sure he would never see the surface again. Only a fierce determination to live, to survive against all odds, and force his limbs to keep moving, to keep swimming, to keep hauling him back to the surface, to emerge into the freezing air filled with the desperate screams of the drowning and the damned.

He used that same determination now to swim in the opposite direction, down toward the bottom of the sea. He forced every last bit of air from his lungs as he went, which helped him lose buoyancy and made him sink farther and faster.

He couldn't see a thing in front of him. The ocean by night was featureless and black. He thought his vision might be growing dark, forming into a tunnel closing in around him, but he couldn't separate the darkness without from the darkness within.

At that point, Abe's natural instincts for self-preservation kicked in. His arms and legs tried to turn him around to move upward rather than down. His brain started to panic over the fact it didn't have any oxygen left to it. His lungs ached to breathe in any kind of air.

He used that last detail to his advantage. He opened his mouth and tried to suck as much of the ocean into his lungs as he could. He choked on the icy fluid flowing into him, but that only made his body try harder to respire, and he sucked more salt water in.

Soon everything turned black, and he began to sink farther beneath the waves. As he did, he hoped two things.

First, he hoped that Elisabetta hadn't been killed quite yet. If she was destroyed before he died, then he'd be freed from her curse. At this point, that would be fatal, and he would have no chance to return.

Second, he hoped that if he was about to become a vampire that the transportation would take place fast. There was no guarantee it would happen right away. If it took a long while, he might be too late to save Lucy and Quin. And if it took much longer than that, he might share in Elisabetta's ultimate fate.

But then it was too late to do anything else but hope.

# CHAPTER SIXTY-TWO

Quin threw himself at the lifeboat atop which Murtagh stood perched. He didn't know how, but he knew he was going to avenge Abe's death one way or another, and nothing was going to stop him. He just needed to get close enough to give Murtagh a fatal smack with his crucifix.

The other vampires parted before him and gave him a clear shot at Murtagh. Lucy did a wonderful job of covering his back, but Murtagh didn't just stand there and wait for Quin to take him down. As Quin leaped up to grab the edge of the lifeboat's gunwale with one hand while still holding onto his crucifix, the vampire snatched up one of the lifeboat's oars again and swung it down hard.

The oar caught Quin in the side of the head and sent him sprawling. Despite every bit of his being telling him to hold on to the crucifix, it went flying out of his hand, skipped off the roof of the bridge once, and disappeared over the edge. Quin gasped in pain and despair. He fully expected to be torn to pieces in seconds.

Lucy appeared above him, though, holding her crucifix before her like a shield. The vampires who'd leaped at the now-vulnerable Quin backed off as fast as they had come at him, hissing like angry snakes.

287

"Quin?" Lucy reached down for Quin's hand without looking at him, never daring to take her eyes off the vampires moving to surround them. "Can you stand?"

Quin put a hand to his head and felt something wet and sticky. His fingers came away covered in blood. Despite that, he pushed himself to his feet and wobbled there for a moment as if the *Carpathia* had been caught in a violent storm.

Quin opened his mouth to answer Lucy but then had to dodge an incoming oar blade again. It missed him and smashed into the roof near his feet, the entire blade breaking into long fragments. Quin scooped one of these up instantly, pleased to see it made for a passable stake.

He turned and brandished his stake at the vampires closing in on him. Lucy stood back to back with him, keeping the vampires away as best she could by swinging her crucifix all around in front of her and to her sides. She couldn't possibly cover every angle at once, and Quin felt the loss of his own crucifix sharply.

He should never have rushed at Murtagh. He had known it had been impossible to reach the man before he tossed Abe overboard, but he'd tried to stop him anyhow. He would have been smarter to have held back and stayed with Lucy, but he just didn't think he could bear watching his friend be killed without trying to do something. Now he would pay the price.

Quin saw the oar coming at him again, and he readied himself to dodge another wide swing. It came straight at him like a spear instead, and the jagged end of it caught him right through the leg.

Quin screamed in pain and clutched at his leg with his free hand as he fell down. The battered oar splintered in his flesh and then snapped off as he twisted away from it, leaving a length of wood stabbed into his outer thigh. Blood flowed from the wound, and the vampires surged closer, like sharks smelling their next meal in the water.

Lucy stood over him, swinging her crucifix in a wide circle around her, doing her best to keep the encroaching bloodsuckers at bay. As she turned, the ones who wound up behind her lurched toward her, forcing her to keep moving to cover every possible angle in time. It would only be a matter of time before her luck or her strength gave out and one of the creatures managed to get close enough to knock her flying.

Quin tried to get to his feet, but his injured leg wouldn't hold his weight, and he collapsed on the roof again. As he did, he saw Murtagh raise his broken oar, cocking his arm back to stab down at Lucy this time. Desperate to save her, Quin lunged between Murtagh and Lucy, prepared to take the spear through his chest if need be.

As the oar jabbed down at him, Quin caught the shaft of it in his hands and managed to twist it just far enough so that the blow missed his chest and passed under his arm. He held onto it then with all his strength, hoping to deprive Murtagh of his weapon.

Murtagh laughed and reversed his grip on the other end of the oar. Leveraging the shaft between his hands, he lifted the far end high up into the air – and Quin along with it. Quin hung on for his life, panic refusing to let him think of anything else he might do.

With Quin dangling high in the air over the bridge, Murtagh shouted down at Lucy. "Drop that crucifix, Miss Seward, or I'll shake your friend here loose and make a meal out of him!"

Quin winced in pain as he dangled from the end of the oar. Murtagh had swung him out over the Bridge Deck, which – when he glanced down at it – seemed dozens of feet below. He considered letting himself fall to the deck below, but the agony he felt in his leg with every movement forced him to hesitate.

Quin looked back at the roof of the bridge to see Lucy standing there, staring back up at him. Tears streamed from her eyes as the vampires encircling her crept closer, their fangs exposed and ready to sink into her tender flesh. She held the crucifix before her still, but her arms had sagged. Her strength had begun to leave them even if her will to live still flared bright.

"Don't do it, Luce!" Quin said. "Don't you dare!"

"I love you, Quin," she said, her voice hoarse and raw. "I can't let you die." Her shoulders slumped, and she began to lower her arms.

"No, Luce! No!"

Quin couldn't bear the thought of the vampires tearing into her, but he didn't know what to do. If he let go, the fall might kill him, and even if he survived he wouldn't be in any shape to help anyone, much less himself. His grip on the oar slipped just a bit in the cool night air, and he realized then that he should quit fighting that and go with it.

Murtagh let out a horrible laugh. "Make your decision, Miss Seward! What's it going to be?"

# CHAPTER SIXTY-THREE

Quin loosened his grip just a bit and slid right down the high-angled shaft of the oar, the wood running under his armpit. He picked up speed as he went, and he put everything he had into a vicious kick from his uninjured leg. His aim was true, and he caught Murtagh right in the chin with his shoe.

The vampire dropped the oar with a howl and staggered back along the interior of the lifeboat. He tripped on one of the rows of seats and went over backward into the boat.

Quin leaped at the vampire and was on him in a heartbeat. He beat at Murtagh with his fists, smashing them into his face again and again until his knuckles were bruised and bleeding. The entire time, Lucy screamed for him from below, calling his name over and over.

The fact that she could still scream spurred Quin on. If she still lived, then there was hope. He hammered at Murtagh, giving the man a murderous thrashing until his arms felt like lead and his strength was spent. He paused to take a breath as he looked down at his aching hands and felt the terrible pain still lancing through his injured leg.

That's when Murtagh looked up at him, a vicious smile exposing his elongated fangs. "Are you quite finished?"

With a single push, Murtagh flung Quin off of him. Quin sailed through the air and landed on the opposite end of the lifeboat. The impact jarred the wood still stabbing into his leg and knocked the air from his lungs. He tried to scream out in pain, but he had no air to manage it.

Murtagh stalked over to him and glowered down. Without taking his eyes off Quin, Murtagh hollered down at Lucy. "Last chance, Miss Seward. You throw that bloody crucifix overboard, or I'll tear out Harker's heart and make you eat it."

"Don't!" Lucy said in a voice cracked and raw. "I'll do it."

Quin tried to sit up to protest, to shout at her to never surrender, but Murtagh stopped him by stamping his boot square into Quin's chest. Quin grasped the man's ankle and put every last bit of strength he had into twisting Murtagh off of his body, but he couldn't get the fiend to budge. He just cackled down at Quin instead, the laugh of a winner whose cruel fun had just begun.

That's when Quin noticed something flapping about, just over Murtagh's shoulder. It was a bat, of course, and Quin's heart fell. He couldn't do a damned thing against Murtagh alone. What hope did he have against two of the creatures?

The bat transformed into human form then, a still-soggy man with a familiar face, but for the lengthened canines that now sprouted from his furious face. Quin whispered his name with the little bit of breath he still had in his chest.

"Abe."

Murtagh's eyes flung wide in surprise as he heard Abe's form land in the lifeboat, behind him. Quin renewed his grip on the man's ankle, trying to make sure that Murtagh couldn't escape. He wasn't sure if it would do any good, but if he had any means of making what was left of Murtagh's existence short and brutal, he meant to take advantage of it.

Abe lunged at Murtagh and hit him so hard that the entire lifeboat capsized from the impact. It toppled over in its davit, dumping the three men out of it to land on the roof of the *Carpathia*'s bridge.

Quin landed on top of Murtagh, which cushioned the fall, but only a little. The pain in his leg flared in protest, and he would have cried out in agony had the sensation not come so close to making him pass out. His hand went to the fragment of wood still spearing through his leg, and he found it soaked with his own warm blood.

The first thing Quin saw as the black blotches vanished from his vision was Lucy still standing there with the crucifix in her hand. She'd somehow managed to keep the other vampires at bay until now, and she returned to that purpose again with renewed vigor. The fact that she not only still lived but continued to fight on gave Quin new hope. If she refused to give up on them, how could he?

Abe had landed a few feet away from Murtagh and rolled toward the other vampires. They surged toward him now, sensing perhaps that he would be easy prey. Lucy leaped between Abe and them and slapped one overeager bloodsucker with the front of her crucifix.

The skin on the vampire's face began to boil away immediately, curling away from the bones beneath like newspaper in a raging fire. He howled in horror and leaped into the air as his flesh continued to fall away from his frame. He disappeared into the night, his pitiful screams cut off only with the merciful sound of a splash.

The other vampires hauled back then. They'd been getting braver about approaching Lucy, knowing that she couldn't hold out against all of them, not forever. The vivid display of her crucifix's power against them put caution back into their cold, still hearts.

Murtagh shoved Quin off and scrambled to his feet, snarling like a rabid wolf and ready to meet Abe face to face. Abe leaped up, his arms spread wide and his fingers flexing out into claws. Lucy wavered between joining Abe in his scrap with Murtagh and keeping the other vampires off his back. Quin pushed himself to his knees and groaned in pain as he pulled at the length of wood still caught in his leg.

A deafening explosion rang out in the night, and the entire ship shook.

# CHAPTER SIXTY-FOUR

A fireball erupted near the middle of the *Carpathia*, spouting from the starboard side. The ship rocked to the port from the force of it, knocking everyone on top of the bridge's roof from their feet. A few of the vampires panicked and transformed into bats as they fell, then fluttered away into the night.

The roar of the explosion echoed like thunder across the water. As it faded, the ship rocked back toward starboard, already heavier from the untold gallons of seawater that Quin knew must be flowing into the gaping hole the explosion had produced in the steel-sided ship. He hoped that the men who'd overtaxed the boilers to the point that they could produce such a blast had managed to escape the engine room before their fevered labors had borne fruit.

Murtagh stood on the listing roof and gaped at Quin, Abe, and Lucy in naked outrage. "What have you done?"

Abe helped Quin to his feet with a clawed hand that Quin didn't hesitate to accept. He could put a little weight on his injured leg without it giving way beneath him, but only just.

"It was the captain," Quin said. Despite the chilly air, the pain from his leg sent sweat running down his face. "He blew the boilers, just as he threatened. The *Carpathia* is doomed."

"You bloody, damned fools!" Murtagh raged at them, his fists formed into white-knuckled balls. "Going down with one ship wasn't enough for you? You've killed us all!"

The other vampires on the roof – as well as others throughout the ship – threw back their heads and howled in dismay. The sun would be up in a few hours, Quin knew, and they would have no protection from it at all. They did the only thing they could in such circumstances.

They fled.

One by one at first, and then in larger groups, the vampires ran for the edge of the roof and hurled themselves off of it and into the frigid night. Quin listened for the splashes, but not one of them hit the water as they went. Instead, they changed themselves into bats and flapped away into the starry sky.

"Come back!" Murtagh shouted after them. "You think there's a place out there for you to hide on the water? We have to make our stand here! We have to make it now!"

Lucy crowed in triumph, and Abe slapped Quin on the back. Quin couldn't help but grin at the captain's success, but he never once took his eyes off Murtagh, whose fury grew with every second.

Elsewhere on the ship, people screamed, cried, and bellowed for help. The sounds reminded Quin so much of that fateful night aboard the *Titanic* that they caused him to shiver.

Even if the ship went down faster than the *Titanic* – and by the way it was already listing so hard, Quin suspected that it would – at least the *Carpathia* was sure to have enough lifeboats for the people aboard. She not only had all of her own, but many of the ones taken from the *Titanic* as well. Even if the captain hadn't had the Marconi operator radio for help, they were in a busy shipping lane off close to the coast of the United States. The people fortunate enough to become stuck on a lifeboat wouldn't be trapped there for long.

"You did this," Murtagh said, turning on Lucy, Abe, and Quin with a nasty snarl. "The three of you spiteful little human cattle."

"We were defending ourselves, and everyone else aboard this ship too," said Quin. His voice sounded shakier than he would have liked, but the words rang true.

"And we'd do it again," Lucy said, her chin stuck out in defiance, the crucifix still in her hand.

With the departure of the vampires, she'd regained much of her composure, far more than Quin, he had to admit. And in the middle of it all, she'd told him she loved him. The memory of that brought a smile to his lips as he gazed at her. He took her free hand in his, and she smiled back.

Abe nodded. "I gave my life to stop you." He let go of Quin and looked down at his hands. "I allowed myself to be turned into this abomination." He looked up into Murtagh's eyes. "It was worth it."

"If you don't like this shadowy life of ours, boyo, then allow me to relieve you of it!"

When Abe had released Quin, he'd moved just far enough away from Lucy to be out of reach of her crucifix. Having seen what it could do to a vampire, Quin didn't blame him for being uncomfortable around it. Staying well away from it, though, gave any other vampire a clean shot at Abe too.

Murtagh charged at Abe like an enraged bull and bowled them both clean over the edge of the roof. Quin tried to reach out for his friend, but he was gone and past him before he had a real chance. Lucy shouted out Abe's name, but that did as little as Quin's effort to keep the two vampires from tumbling away. They landed on the open section of the Shelter Deck fore of the bridge with a sickening thud.

# CHAPTER SIXTY-FIVE

Quin glanced around for the fastest way to drop the two levels to where the vampires wrestled with each other. He didn't know how he could be of any help to Abe, but he was determined to try. He spotted a rope hanging down from one of the cranes on the forward deck that hung attached to the edge of the bridge's roof, and he went to unhook it from its mooring.

"What are you doing?" Lucy asked as she knelt to help him with the hook.

"I have to get down there." Quin freed the hook and pulled on the rope. It had a little give to it, but not much. He hoped that once it took his weight it wouldn't just play out freely and let him fall.

Down below them, Murtagh had sprung to his feet. He'd picked up a deck chair and hurled it at Abe, knocking him flat. That having succeeded, he threw everything else he could find at Abe: tables, lifebuoys, and more. He finished up with a cover he tore off a hatch and flung it at Abe, spinning it like a buzz-saw blade.

Abe withered under the assault. He'd never been much for brawling outside of an occasional bout in the ring, and even during those rare matches he'd fought like a gentleman.

Murtagh, on the other hand, scrapped like a back-alley stray. There was no blow too low for him to strike, and he was happy to try them all.

Quin hefted the heavy steel hook in his hand and stepped up to the edge of the bridge's roof. As he did, the ship tilted at an even sharper angle. The *Titanic* had taken hours to sink, but she'd only been holed near her prow. She was supposed to be unsinkable too.

While a good ship, the *Carpathia* had never had that term applied to it, and the hole blown in its side meant that the entire ship could fill up with water that much faster. Quin also suspected the captain had purposefully left the bulkheads unsealed. If so, that would leave the ship with little in the way of defenses against the incoming sea.

All that meant to Quin was he had less time than ever. He took a deep breath to steel himself and then leaped out into the open to swing out over the Shelter Deck.

Lucy sprinted up and leaped onto Quin just as his feet left the bridge's roof. "You're not leaving without me!" she said.

Delighted as he might have been to hear that under other circumstances, Quin hollered out in pain and dismay as Lucy grabbed onto him. He felt like his arms might give out at any second, but he knew that if he let go too early he would drop them from too high up and risk killing them both, so he held on not only for his own life but for Lucy's as well.

Abe gritted his teeth and held on until they reached the low point of their swing. This put them only a few feet above the deck but did nothing to affect their momentum. Quin let go, and they fell the last little bit to the deck and went tumbling along it.

The wood in Quin's leg stabbed even farther into his flesh, and he howled out in pain. As Lucy extricated herself from the jumble of limbs they'd created, she looked down at his wound and let fly an unladylike curse.

"You're not going anywhere with that leg of yours," she said. She pulled her crucifix from where she'd stuffed it inside the collar of her dress before she'd hopped on board him for the ride down to the Shelter Deck. As she did, she knelt down and kissed him on the lips. "I have to help Abe. I'll be back as soon as I can."

Quin put a hand to his mouth and stared after her for an instant as she turned and left. Of all the things that had happened to him today, the kiss might have been the most shocking. He knew, though, that he couldn't let her join the fight against Murtagh without him. She and Abe would need all the help they could get.

He tried to get to his feet, but the wood lodged in his leg made it impossible. It just hurt too much every time he moved. He had to remove the gigantic splinter from his flesh as soon as possible.

Gritting his teeth, Quin reached down and grabbed the splinter of wood with both hands and pulled with all his might. It slid out of his flesh far more easily than he had hoped, but he still screamed through every inch of its withdrawal. It hurt like hell, but removing the wood also gave him an odd kind of relief.

It also allowed him to move again. He shoved himself to his feet, the splinter – which was as long as his forearm – still grasped in his fist. At first he thought that he'd taken a concussion and that it had thrown off his balance, but then he realized it had to do with how badly the ship was listing instead. Waves lapped at the starboard rail, showing how hungry the sea was for the entire ship.

Quin staggered across the canted deck on unsteady feet and spotted Lucy standing between Murtagh and an injured Abe near the ship's prow. The edge of the fragment of the hatch that Murtagh had hurled at Abe had caught him in the chest and tore through his jacket and flesh. It seemed to have stopped shy of his heart, but Quin could see even from here that such a blow would have killed any still-living man.

"You stay away from him!" Lucy said to Murtagh. "It's over, Brody! You lost!"

"True," Murtagh said, "but that doesn't mean you can't lose too."

Murtagh had a length of railing in his hand that he had torn from somewhere, and he cocked back his arm to hurl it straight at Lucy. Knowing he had run out of time, Quin lunged at the man, screaming from the pain he felt with every movement of his injured leg. He held the splinter he'd yanked from his leg up above his head in a two-handed grip, ready to drive it down into Murtagh's heart.

# CHAPTER SIXTY-SIX

Murtagh heard Quin lumbering up behind him and turned to meet his charge. Too late for him to stop, Quin kept moving forward and brought the splinter down toward Murtagh with every bit of strength he had left. He only had one last chance left to save Abe and Lucy, and no matter how slim it might seem, he meant to take it.

Murtagh swung out with the pipe in his hand and caught the splinter with it, knocking it clear out of Quin's grasp. It tumbled out over the starboard railing and landed in the Atlantic with a splash.

"You idiots. How dare you?" Murtagh spoke with such menace in his voice that it made Quin want to curl up into a ball and cover his ears to escape it. "You've ruined everything. And for what? Your short, pathetic lives?"

Quin tried to scramble away, but his leg betrayed him, buckling underneath. He might have still managed to stay on his feet, but Murtagh backhanded him to the deck. Blood flowed from his mouth, and the vampire loomed over him as he stared up in horror with water-filled eyes.

"You're mortals, and you spend your time fearing gods before destroying them." Murtagh tossed the pipe to one side and bared his fangs, preparing to feed. "Well, it's time for the gods to fight back."

Murtagh fell on Quin and grabbed him by the head, forcing him to bare his throat. Quin struggled against him as hard as he could, but the vampire's grasp was like a steel vice from which he could not break free. Quin punched at Murtagh until his knuckles bled, but the vampire ignored every blow as he darted in for the kill with his ferocious teeth.

Before those fangs punctured Quin's skin, though, Lucy leaped on Murtagh's back and stabbed her crucifix down into the nape of the vampire's neck.

"You're no god," she said. "Only a devil!"

Murtagh arched his spine in agony and howled in unforgivable anguish, flinging Lucy off his back as if she were a murderous child. He pushed himself off of Quin and reached back to where his skin was already bubbling away at the point the crucifix had entered his flesh. He plucked the wooden icon from his dissolving muscles and held it out before him, gaping at it in immortal horror.

Quin saw the bones from Murtagh's fingers already showing through his hand as the meat there dripped away to land in sizzling puddles on the deck. The destruction spread fast from there, lancing up Murtagh's arm to consume it whole and stretching forward from the base of his neck to expose his naked skull.

The man flopped over like a marionette with severed strings and collapsed in an awkward heap of snapping tendons and vanishing flesh. Soon, there was nothing left of him but a naked skeleton, its bones already bleached white by the last bubbling bits of its skin.

Quin shoved himself to his feet and fell into Lucy's welcoming arms. He held her tight as she shuddered against him.

"Are you all right?" she said.

He nodded against her. "Yes."

"Thank God," she said. She looked up at him, smiling through tears, weeping in relief.

"No, Luce." Quin kissed her lips, soft and warm and full of life. "Thank you."

Abe staggered up to them then, the wound in his side already knitting back together, as Quin could see through his tattered clothes. He gave Murtagh's remains a wide berth. "Is it over?" he said.

Quin and Lucy each reached out an arm and brought Abe into their embrace. They held each other there for a long moment, one that Quin hoped would never come to and end. Once they let each other go, they'd have to deal with the aftermath of what had just happened, of everything they'd done, and he didn't know how he could manage that.

The ship's deck pitched even harder to starboard then, and Abe had to hold Lucy and Quin tight to make sure they didn't go sliding down the polished wood, topple over the railing, and tumble into the silent sea. In the distance, Quin could hear people screaming in fear and shouting orders. He glanced back down the length of the ship and saw lifeboats being rowed away from the ship, filled with women, children, and even many men.

"We need to go too," Quin said. "We can't stay here."

Lucy nodded as she wiped the tears from her cheeks. "I can't believe it," she said. "To think that this nightmare is finally over."

"I'm afraid that's not quite true yet." Abe grimaced and gestured to himself. "We still have one vampire left."

# CHAPTER SIXTY-SEVEN

Getting to the lifeboat that Elisabetta had cut loose had been difficult, but the three of them managed it. They wanted to make sure they had their own boat, so they were willing to leap into the icy waters and make the long swim to where it had floated away. Quin was grateful that Lucy had suggested they take the time to bind up his leg before they set out. Otherwise, he was sure he would have passed out from lack of blood.

Once they reached the lifeboat, Abe had lifted them in and found blankets in the storage compartments that had been buried beneath the graveyard dirt. He wrapped Lucy and Quin in them and had set to the oars himself, working tirelessly to bring them toward the distant shore that Quin had spotted before. As soon as Quin had stopped shivering, he'd insisted on lending a hand, but Abe had refused.

"Save your strength," Abe had said. "You'll need it come dawn."

They had yet to reach the shore when the first rays of the imminent sunrise broke over the eastern horizon. They spotted a few bats flying high overhead, ones that they guessed had become disoriented in the night and not known which way to fly. Now that they had wandered close enough to the shore to see it, they made a beeline for it.

Quin could tell, though, that they would never reach land in time. A couple of them that were higher up in the air burst into flames as they flapped along, falling into the sea like shooting stars that screamed. Others hung closer to the waves, avoiding direct exposure to the oncoming sunlight for now, although Quin was sure that they would run out of time soon.

After the first bat fell burning from the sky like a little Icarus, they took the remaining blankets out and wrapped Abe in them. Then they folded the remnants of the lifeboat's canvas cover over that in as many layers as they could manage. Then Quin and Lucy shoved Abe as tight as they could under a seat and covered any exposed bits as best they could with their legs.

"How do we know if that will be enough?" Lucy said.

"We don't." Quin eyed the sun as the top of it broke over the horizon. "But we'll find out soon enough."

The two of them sat there in the boat and held hands as the sun rose higher into the sky. After a little while, its rays reached over the top of the lifeboat's gunwale and spilled down into the boat. They kept a close eye on the bundle beneath them as sunlight coated more and more of the interior. When the rays fell square on one end of the bundle they'd been unable to completely cover, they held their breath and waited for some sort of reaction from the friend they'd buried beneath so many things.

Quin and Lucy had seen the vampires burst into flames as they emerged from the *Carpathia*'s hold. They knew what would happen if even the slightest bit of sunlight managed to penetrate the materials with which they'd covered Abe. They'd only have seconds to leap clear of him themselves before the conflagration scorched them too, and there was a real chance that the blaze would destroy their lifeboat and leave them floating in the sea, still a long way from land.

Nothing happened.

Lucy and Quin exhaled then and held each other and allowed themselves to enjoy a single sweet and tender kiss. Then they set to the oars and rowed for the still-distant shore.

"It bothers me to think of Abe under all those things," Lucy said as they neared land. "I know he can't breathe beneath all that."

"He doesn't need to breathe, Luce. Not any more."

"I know," she said. "That's what bothers me."

About midday, they reached a barren patch of shoreline and beached the boat. After a short rest, they worked together, using the oars as levers, to flip the boat over with Abe still inside. After checking to make sure he was still all right, they took shelter in the shade the boat provided and fell asleep.

They awoke as the sun set over the land on which they sat, and Quin thought that he had perhaps never seen such a lovely thing in his life. They were parched and hungry, so Quin crawled under the overturned boat and found some bottles of water and crackers in one of its storage compartments. He and Lucy had just finished making a light meal of his findings when they heard something under the boat start rustling around.

Quin and Lucy reached under the boat and hauled the bundle of blankets in which Abe lay wrapped out into the open air. They carefully unwrapped the first few layers around him and then cried out in surprise when the blankets collapsed into an empty pile of cloth. A white mist leaked out of the fabric and soon reformed in front of them as their undead friend.

"Thank you," Abe said. "That may have been the longest day of my life."

"Last night was certainly the longest of mine," Quin said.

"Worse than when the *Titanic* sank?" asked Lucy.

Quin weighed the two torturous nights back and forth in his hands. "Close enough," he finally said.

They laughed together at that, and Quin reveled in delight at the sound, holding onto it for as long as he could. The three of them stood there in silence then, watching the last bits of the sunset fade across the sky from crimson red to black. None of them wanted to speak, for they knew the questions that must be asked, and they feared the answers.

In the end, Lucy could take it no more. "What do we do from here?" she said.

Quin and Abe glanced at her and then traded uncomfortable looks. "I suppose my plan's the same as ever," said Quin. "I'm heading to New York to look for work."

Lucy nodded. "And I have university starting in the fall. It's a long time until then though."

They both remained quiet then, waiting for Abe to speak.

"I want to live," he said.

"Even like this?" Lucy said.

He raised his eyes to peer at her, but his gaze was so intense that she had to look away. He nodded and looked down at his hands, which Quin thought seemed as human as ever, if a bit pale.

"I'm a monster," he said. "I know. But that doesn't mean I have to live like one."

"How can you say that?" Lucy shuddered. "Don't you have to feed on human blood?"

"We don't know that," Quin said. "We don't know anything other than what Uncle Bram wrote in that blasted book, and who can say how much of that was true."

"Some of it, certainly," Abe said, "but maybe not all."

Lucy's head bobbed up and down as she considered this. "And what happens if it turns out that it is?" She looked up then to see the look of dismay on Quin and Abe's faces. "I don't mean to– I just killed a vampire last night. I don't know if I can handle doing that again."

"Would you kill me, Lucy?" Quin had to strain his ears to make out Abe's whisper. "I don't mean that as an accusation. I'm being serious. Would you do it if I asked you to?"

Lucy lowered her face into her hands, and her shoulders began to shake. "You can't ask that of me, Abe," she said. "You can't. Not ever."

Abe sighed. "I don't plan to Lucy, but if the monster inside me turns out to be something I cannot control…"

Lucy turned toward Quin then and buried her face in his shoulder. Her tears soon soaked through his shirt.

Abe looked to Quin and gave him a helpless shrug. Quin gave him a grim nod. "Should it prove necessary, I would be honored."

Abe's shoulders relaxed at this. He stuck out his hand for Quin, who shook it, ignoring just how cold his old friend's skin had become. "Take care of her," Abe said.

"You know I will."

Lucy released Quin then and flung herself into Abe's arms. "Stay with us," she said. "Don't leave."

Abe put his hands on her shoulders and pushed her back far enough that he could look down into her eyes. "I would like nothing more," he said. "But not now. Not yet. Not until I know I can trust myself."

"I was wrong before," she said, sniffling away her tears. "I know you're a good man. We can trust you."

Abe shook his head. "You never were a very good liar, Lucy. That's how I always knew you never loved me."

"I did too!" she said, indignantly. "I still do."

A wan smile crossed Abe's face. "Not the way you love Quin."

Lucy opened her mouth to reply but found she had nothing to say. She clung to Abe again, holding him closer and tighter. "I don't care," she said. "I'm never going to let you go."

"But you can't hold me, darling, no matter how hard you

try. No one can." He leaned over and kissed her on the top of the head. The next moment, he was gone, nothing left of him but a white mist on a wind blowing west.

Lucy stood there alone for a moment, then turned and walked to Quin, who had been waiting for her with his arms open wide. She tilted her lips up toward his, and they met in a long and lingering kiss.

She opened her eyes and looked up at him. "Would you consider looking for a job in Boston instead?"

Quin smiled down at her and nodded. "I won't leave you, Luce," he said. "I promise."

# ABOUT THE AUTHOR

Matt Forbeck has worked full-time on fiction and games since 1989. Frankly, he is a creative machine, and thus utterly perfect for Angry Robot. His many publishers include Adams Media, AEG, Atari, Boom! Studios, Atlas Games, Del Rey, Games Workshop, Green Ronin, High Voltage Studios, Human Head Studios, IDW, Image Comics, Mattel, Pinnacle Entertainment Group, Playmates Toys, Simon & Schuster, Ubisoft, Wizards of the Coast, and WizKids. He has written novels, comic books, short stories, non-fiction (including the acclaimed *Marvel Encyclopedia*), magazine articles and computer game scripts. He has designed collectible card games, roleplaying games, miniatures and board games. His work has been published in at least a dozen different languages.

Matt is a proud member of the Alliterates writers group, the International Association of Media Tie-In Writers, and the International Game Developers Association. He lives in Beloit, Wisconsin, USA, with his wife Ann and their children: Marty, and the quadruplets: Pat, Nick, Ken and Helen. (And there's a whole other story.)

*forbeck.com*

# ACKNOWLEDGMENTS

Many thanks to my understanding and kind editors and the rest of the team at Angry Robot. Special gratitude to Lee Harris for catching my mistakes and to Marc Gascoigne, our Robot Overlord, for his continuing inspiration.

In memory of the more than 1,500 souls who lost their lives when the *Titanic* went down on that fateful night in April of 1912. You may have been gone one hundred years, but no matter how much time passes, we shall never forget.

# REMIXING THE ROBOT

Before I set down to write *Carpathia*, I had the honor of working with songsmith John Anealio on the song "Angry Robot," which you might recall is the name of the publisher of this book. John had created a short version of the song as the theme song for the Angry Robot podcast hosted by Mur Lafferty, but he wanted to add some verses to make it complete.

John and I had met at the World Fantasy Convention in 2010, and we'd hit it off. Since I was an Angry Robot author, he contacted me to see if I'd be interested in helping him out with the lyric. I grabbed that chance by the throat and throttled it good before John had a chance to change his mind, and in short order we had made a great little song even better.

Then Marc Gascoigne, our esteemed publisher, had the idea of offering up the separated tracks of the song for a remix contest. The prize would be a role in *Carpathia* as a character to meet a grisly death.

The entries were so good we had a hard time choosing a winner, but in the end we settled on Dale Chase's excellent rap-laden entry. Denis Cherryman took second place, and David Ritter claimed third.

While we'd only promised prizes for the top three winners, we were so taken with the many of the other entries that we decided to toss their creators' names into the book too. They included Justin Achilli, Raleigh Blum, Mike Crooker, David Griffiths, Trevor McPherson, and Chooch Shubert.

For fun, you might want to go back through the book and figure out their individual fates.

If you'd like to hear the songs entered in the contest, John assembled them all into an album you can download for free.

*http://bit.ly/iMroft*

And you can get the original on his site too.

*http://johnanealio.com/track/angry-robot*

## A Note About Our Winner

I had the hardest time working our first-place winner into the book for one reason. Dale is African-American, and according to history there weren't any African-Americans on the *Titanic*. There was a single Haitian family on which I could have modeled Dale's character in the book, but I decided I wanted to be truer to him than that.

*Carpathia* is fiction, sure, but it's historical fiction. The horrific elements in the book work that much better because they're grounded in the historical reality. So I decided to come up with a plausible story for how an African-American musician could have wound up on the ship.

In my research, I stumbled across a popular song from the African-American toast tradition, called "Shine and the *Titanic*." It's about an African-American stoker who tries to warn the captain about the disaster and then swims all the way back to New York to save himself from the sinking ship.

Of course, things don't work out well for the fictional Dale Chase in *Carpathia*, but I'd promised the real man a momentous death for his character. I hope he enjoys the terrifying end I delivered.

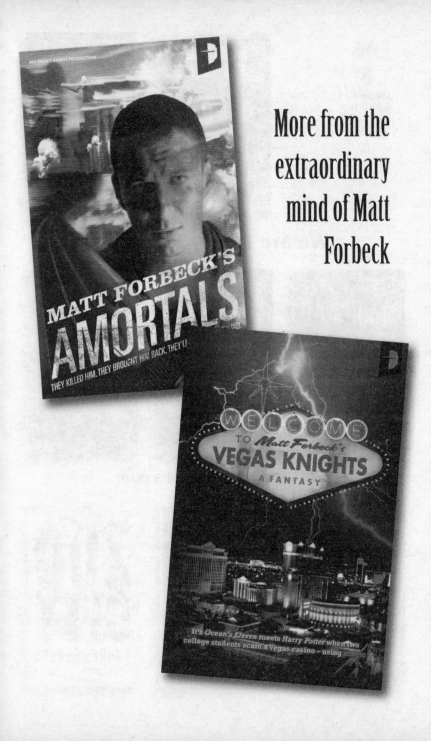

More from the extraordinary mind of Matt Forbeck

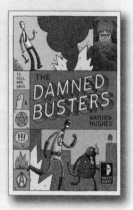

# SELL YOUR SOUL TO GET THEM ALL
## Snag the complete Angry Robot catalog

**DAN ABNETT**
- [ ] Embedded
- [ ] Triumff: Her Majesty's Hero

**GUY ADAMS**
- [ ] The World House
- [ ] Restoration

**JO ANDERTON**
- [ ] Debris

**LAUREN BEUKES**
- [ ] Moxyland
- [ ] Zoo City

**THOMAS BLACKTHORNE
(aka John Meaney)**
- [ ] Edge
- [ ] Point

**MAURICE BROADDUS**
- [ ] King Maker
- [ ] King's Justice
- [ ] King's War

**ADAM CHRISTOPHER**
- [ ] Empire State

**PETER CROWTHER**
- [ ] Darkness Falling

**ALIETTE DE BODARD**
- [ ] Servant of the Underworld
- [ ] Harbinger of the Storm
- [ ] Master of the House of Darts

**MATT FORBECK**
- [ ] Amortals
- [ ] Vegas Knights

**JUSTIN GUSTAINIS**
- [ ] Hard Spell

**GUY HALEY**
- [ ] Reality 36

**COLIN HARVEY**
- [ ] Damage Time
- [ ] Winter Song

**MATTHEW HUGHES**
- [ ] The Damned Busters

**TRENT JAMIESON**
- [ ] Roil

**K W JETER**
- [ ] Infernal Devices
- [ ] Morlock Night

**J ROBERT KING**
- [ ] Angel of Death
- [ ] Death's Disciples

**GARY McMAHON**
- [ ] Pretty Little Dead Things
- [ ] Dead Bad Things

**ANDY REMIC**
- [ ] Kell's Legend
- [ ] Soul Stealers
- [ ] Vampire Warlords

**CHRIS ROBERSON**
- [ ] Book of Secrets

**MIKE SHEVDON**
- [ ] Sixty-One Nails
- [ ] The Road to Bedlam

**DAVID TALLERMAN**
- [ ] Giant Thief

**GAV THORPE**
- [ ] The Crown of the Blood
- [ ] The Crown of the Conqueror

**LAVIE TIDHAR**
- [ ] The Bookman
- [ ] Camera Obscura

**TIM WAGGONER**
- [ ] Nekropolis
- [ ] Dead Streets
- [ ] Dark War

**KAARON WARREN**
- [ ] Mistification
- [ ] Slights
- [ ] Walking the Tree

**IAN WHATES**
- [ ] City of Dreams & Nightmare
- [ ] City of Hope & Despair
- [ ] City of Light & Shadow